T0253203

Praise for

GOSHEN ROAD

by Bonnie Proudfoot

"*Goshen Road* is rich with life and characters who command our attention. These beautiful intertwined stories introduce a wise and wonderful voice."

— Gail Galloway Adams, author of *The Purchase of Order*

"*Goshen Road* is a rich, multigenerational tale exploring women's expanding roles in a rural environment. The women are afforded few opportunities here, and they often settle for much less than they deserve, but they are resourceful and ultimately as resilient and reliable as the untamable land."

— Marie Manilla, author of *The Patron Saint of Ugly*

"Bonnie Proudfoot writes the kind of book that means something, a book that carries weight in a way that only serious fiction can. Her words delight and move, but they do much more than that. She interrogates the truth of the people and place of Appalachia. Her debut should be savored by those who admire timeless fiction."

— Charles Dodd White, author of *In The House of Wilderness*

"It takes no more than the opening sentence of *Goshen Road* to bring vividly to life the ruggedly forested mountains of West Virginia and the resolute people who make their lives among them. Told alternately through the voices of a family, Proudfoot does not merely allow readers to witness her characters' lives, but brings us among them as visitors. Her characters are not the 'other,' an archetype that is the bane of Appalachian Literature; they are not the meth addicts or oxycontin dealers that pollute so much of what is written about our region today. The community of *Goshen Road* is economically depressed, but it is not damned by impoverishment; its citizens do not suffer from 'learned helplessness.' They care for family and community and in their lives evoke the heroics of everyday struggle."

— Chris Holbrook, author of *Upheaval: Stories*

"*Goshen Road* is like a detailed and lovely landscape painting, with much to draw—and keep—us in. With a fine attunement to the ironies of human behavior, Proudfoot treats her characters with dignity, honors their complexity, and renders them with poetry."

— Mark Brazaitis, author of *The Incurables*

"Bonnie Proudfoot's novel-in-stories unerringly drills down to the bedrock of human relationships. How do we love? How do we make a living? Proudfoot never bewails her characters' choices, but rather acknowledges their failures while admiring their dreams and creative, intelligent loyalty to each other and their West Virginia home."

— Meredith Sue Willis, author of *Their Houses* and *Out of the Mountains*

GOSHEN ROAD

GOSHEN
ROAD

A NOVEL

Bonnie Proudfoot

SWALLOW PRESS / OHIO UNIVERSITY PRESS / ATHENS, OHIO

Swallow Press

An imprint of Ohio University Press, Athens, Ohio 45701

ohioswallow.com

To obtain permission to quote, reprint, or otherwise reproduce or distribute material from Swallow Press / Ohio University Press publications, please contact our rights and permissions department at (740) 593-1154 or (740) 593-4536 (fax).

Printed in the United States of America

Swallow Press / Ohio University Press books are printed on acid-free paper ⊗ ™

30 29 28 27 26 25 24 23 22 21 20   5 4 3 2 1

Library of Congress Cataloging-in-Publication Data

Names: Proudfoot, Bonnie, 1954- author.

Title: Goshen Road : a novel / Bonnie Proudfoot.

Description: Athens, Ohio : Swallow Press/Ohio University Press, [2020]

Identifiers: LCCN 2019041147 | ISBN 9780804012225 (hardcover ; acid-free paper) | ISBN 9780804012232 (paperback ; acid-free paper) | ISBN 9780804041072 (pdf)

Subjects: LCSH: Working class families--West Virginia--Fiction. | Appalachian Region--Fiction

Classification: LCC PS3616.R68 G67 2020 | DDC 813/.6--dc23

LC record available at https://lccn.loc.gov/2019041147

To my mother,

my aunt,

my grandmothers,

my children

And thou shalt dwell in the land of Goshen and thou
shall be near unto me, thou and thy children's children,
and thy flocks and thy herds and all that thou hast.

—Gen. 45:10

CONTENTS

ACKNOWLEDGMENTS

Many thanks to the West Virginia Department of Culture and History for their support of this project, and to Gail Adams, Susan Sailor, Ethel Morgan Smith, Cathy Hankla, Jeanne Larsen, and others whose guidance, vision, and enthusiasm never failed to propel this forward. Thanks, too, to Sharon Hatfield, Deni Naffziger, Reneé Williams, and especially Daniel Canterbury, generous readers, and to Samara Rafert and Rick Huard and the editors and staff at Swallow Press. Earlier forms of "Canning Peaches" and "Gun Season" appeared in *Kestrel*. This is a work of fiction. Any resemblance to people, events, or places is purely coincidental and not intended to be taken as accurate historical depiction.

ONE

SNAGGED (1967)

THOUGH HE WAS ONLY SEVENTEEN, LUX CRANFIELD knew some things about how to get along in life. He knew how to file and clean a horse's hoof, so he could ride his dappled gray mare for hours on gas pipeline roads and ridgetop trails without needing to call a blacksmith to have her shod. He knew how to scan the fields to judge where deer bedded down for the night, how to note dimples in the soft dark earth for fresh tracks, how to search saplings for ragged marks where bucks scraped the bark with their antlers, and how to crouch down behind a giant chestnut stump, remain perfectly still, and wait for dawn, so he could take a silent shot with his compound bow, then track it, bleed it out, gut it, and get it home before the local game warden left his driveway to go to work.

Some things came naturally to Lux and some he had to work at. He'd worked hard to learn how to throw a fastball to catch the inside corner of the strike zone, sinking as it sailed by the knees of a batter. He'd practiced this, just as he'd practiced downshifting his Jeep into second gear with his left hand while letting go of the steering wheel, resting his right hand on the knee of a girl next to him, not lugging the engine or spilling an open can of Iron City. He'd learned how to drop a towering red oak by sawing a deep wedge across its base at the correct height and angle, then how to slice down into the wedge, so that the weight of the tree shifted gradually and gravity took over, trunk and crown falling where he wanted it to, downhill toward the skidder.

Lux knew he had a knack for some things and he had good aim, and that these skills had gotten him the job of his dreams, cutting timber for A-1 Lumber, but if that didn't work out, he could beat the draft by enlisting in the U.S. Army or the West Virginia National Guard and take a couple of years to figure out his next steps. This decision would be his to make in August, his eighteenth birthday, and he was keeping it to himself. But on an early spring morning in April 1967, after his left eye was cut open by a locust snag, Lux began to think his backup plan was no longer an option, and that he had to give serious thought to the course his life should take.

It couldn't have been a better morning to be out cutting timber. Dense, cool fog kept away the glare of the rising sun. On the forest floor, ferns and wildflowers had begun to leaf out. On the steep hillside, the ground was firm enough for good footing under his steel-toe boots, not slick or soggy like during the March thaw. Lux was out by daybreak as part of a five-man crew, clearing scrub timber that lay between County Road 57 and a stand of second-growth red oak on the steep side of North Fork, when a dead locust limb high above his head dropped out of a tangle of vines, bounced off his hard hat, and slammed into the left-hand side of his face, knocking him off his feet and pinning him on the ground. He came to hearing the scream of saws above his ears and the shouts of men working to get him out from under that mess.

On the hour-long drive to the Fairchance ER, with the left side of his face wrapped in his blood-soaked shirt, after realizing that this was not just a bad dream or something happening to some other guy, and after moving each joint and swelling finger to reassure himself that no bones were broken, Lux realized that some might call him screwed and some might call him lucky, but more likely what his mother had told him for the whole of her short life was correct, the Lord was keeping an eye on him. He'd been called to account, and he did not want to come up wanting. He had to quit running wild and staying out half the night, get more of a grip on his life, and settle down with someone calm and steady, the right girl who would keep him on the right track.

In the last straightaway before town, Lux knew who that girl should be. He sat up for a moment to catch his breath and clear his throbbing head in the passenger seat of Alan Ray's speeding Bronco. He wiped his brow with the back of his sleeve, brushed dirt and saw-dust from around his good eye, and in the fierce, slanting light of the morning sun he saw Dessie Price leaning forward beside her golden retriever while she waited for the school bus at the end of her drive-way. "Will you look at that?" Alan Ray called out, waving his A-1 cap at Dessie from the driver's seat, and Lux turned and squinted as Dessie waved back. He could swear she was smiling right at him. For two days in the hospital, through a haze of painkillers, as the doc-tors worked to try to save his eye, Lux held on to the memory like a secret keepsake: Dessie's sudden smile, her long blond hair, and her red sweater flashing by like a bright spark against the long pale green shimmer of her father's hayfield.

ON A warm spring afternoon a couple of weeks after the accident, when most of the swelling was gone from his face, Lux stopped by the high school. Below his rolled shirtsleeves his forearms were scarred and scraped, and purple traces of bruises could be seen along his left cheek and under the brim of his A-1 cap. He wore new black Levi's, a new pair of black cowboy boots, a plaid flannel shirt, and over his left eye a black eyepatch partially concealed a wad of gauze bandages. Thick black hair curled out from around his ears and below the rim of his cap. After the last bell, Dessie Price and a few school friends gathered around him for the details.

"How'd it happen, Lux?" asked Billie Price, Dessie's ninth-grade sister. Her dark hair hung around her neck, and she shook her bangs out of her dark eyes as she looked up at him.

"Well, I can't say exactly, but I'll tell you what I think happened," Lux said, scratching the back of his neck, which had begun to sweat. "It felt like the woods was waiting, like it was set up like a damn trap, and I was the one who sprung it," he said without a trace of a smile. This would be repeated around the schoolyard and beyond, he knew. He pulled back his shoulders, cleared his throat, stretched his long fingers out, cracking each of his knuckles.

It was right before sunrise when he'd gotten to work, he said, and as the dawn broke he finished sharpening the chain on his saw. The crew spread out in the woods to start cutting. He was downhill, clearing a path for the skidder through an overgrown patch of woods and vines that had been clear-cut years earlier. "It was a nasty setup from the get-go," he said. "I wanted to take down this one elm first off, so I could see what I was getting into. Set down the lunch pail, took a few steps uphill, and ripped into the tree." He shook his head slowly, pulled down the brim of his cap. "Something didn't feel right, the tree was half dead, but I didn't pay it any mind. 'Bout halfway through the first cut, the damn elm started to shift and fall, way too soon, and that limb slammed down from above, dragging greenbrier, grapevine, Virginia creeper, you name it. Never heard it coming, with the saw so loud."

He cleared his throat. As he spoke, the small group of students gazed at him, scanning the bruises on his face and arms, the eyepatch. Lux was six feet tall, and the boots made him feel like he was a head taller than the others. Usually height had given him an edge, but today it made him feel distant, more like an outsider, and suddenly the intensity caught him off guard. Talking about it made it more real.

"Damn snag," Lux said, brushing his forearm over the eyepatch. "A locust branch, maybe twenty feet off the ground, twenty, thirty feet long. It must have hung up there for years." He took off his cap and rubbed at a shaved spot on his scalp, above his left temple. "It knocked me flat on my ass, jabbed into my eye and done my face up pretty bad. A stroke of luck I had that hard hat on. That thing is in pieces, and Doc won't say nothin' yet about my eye."

He took a breath, turned his head toward his blind side, and noticed Tim Sutton, the varsity shortstop, a former teammate and a steady guy.

"Who found you? Did Alan Ray know you were down?" asked Tim.

"Alan Ray? Alan Ray was halfway up the hill already," Lux said, nodding slowly. "One minute I was sawing, the next I was pinned on my back, my saw ten foot down the hill. I can't rightly say who got to me first. Took them boys a half hour, more maybe, to cut me out, and that's when Alan Ray got busy on the bleeding. I owe all of them guys." His face turned in the direction of Dessie Price.

Dessie's blue eyes were the level of his chin, focused intently on his good eye. He wondered whether she knew that he was in the red Bronco as it sped past her that morning. He wondered if he'd dreamed her smile, her return wave. She seemed to be visualizing each moment as he related it. "That's what Dad says," Dessie said. Then she blinked at few times and brightened up a bit. "So, what happened to your pa's shell box from the war? Isn't that what you carry for your lunch pail?" she asked with a bit of a grin.

His good eye settled on a small dimple in her chin. How many other times had he noticed that dimple over the last few years? Now, though, she was taller, her neck slimmer and longer, her hair curled around her collarbones. The school bus behind her, as yellow as if it had just rolled out of a crayon box, revved up its engine and pumped clouds of diesel exhaust into the air. Lux scratched at a scab on his forearm, set his A-1 cap back onto his head. "Oh, shoot. That damn shell box," Lux said, smiling back at her. "I been meaning to go back for that. I'll bring it around the house if I can find it," he said.

"I CAME by to show this to y'uns," Lux told Bertram Price early that evening. Bertram was on the front porch of the white clapboard two-story farmhouse, sitting back in a sagging plaid recliner and listening to the Pirates game through the crackle of a transistor radio. He completely filled the La-Z-Boy. His legs had worn grooves into the raised footrest, and his thick fingers dwarfed a beer can. Cigarette smoke curled out from a dark green glass ashtray on a milk crate beside him.

Lux stood on the bottom step, eye-level to Bertram's heavy scuffed work boots, the soles caked with clumps of reddish clay from walking the pipelines for Pennzoil. Lux had always liked the look of Bertram, his sonic boom of a voice, the odd bump in his nose where he'd broken it in the service, and he liked the way the tall man carried himself, the way people took him at his word. Bertram spoke his mind, whether or not you wanted to hear what he had to say. He'd been a play-by-the-rules kind of coach, a leader, and a no-nonsense competitor. He'd earned Lux's trust by standing up for fair play and for the players on his team. Back when Lux was brought on as a pitcher, he knew how to hurl the ball fast and in the strike zone, and he'd thought that was all he'd need. But Bertram had taken him under his wing, teaching him how to size up a batter, drilling him on curveballs, change-ups, sinking fastballs. "Don't throw your arm out the first inning," Bertram advised. "Let 'em chase your bad ones. Keep your best pitch in your pocket, Ace, and play that card later in the game, when they ain't expecting it." These tips took Lux and the Harriers to the state semifinals, only the second time in the history of Fairchance High.

Lux knew that showing up at a man's house was not the same as showing up for practice. He also knew that coaches, parents, teachers, all elders, needed to be handled just right. He'd have to get a feel for things. Sooner or later too, he'd have to deal with his pa, who'd mixed it up with Bertram one night three years earlier at the AmVets about a gas well right-of-way. Lux hoped there were no bad feelings toward the Cranfield family remaining on Bertram's side. His pa, on the other hand, still swore a blue streak whenever anyone mentioned Pennzoil, Bertram Price, or even the AmVets.

Lux shifted around. His good eye squinted at Bertram's round face. He held out what was left of the green World War 2 army-issued shell box. The handle was ripped clear off one of the steel hinges, the square metal top was crushed down into the bottom like a ten-ton coal car had driven over it.

"Bring that up here, Lux, let's take a gander. Look at that thing! Made it all the way to Europe and back, and it gets done-in half a mile from home," Bertram said, shaking his head and looking Lux over. "I can still see the letters. U.S. Army. Must be infantry. Them poor grunt SOBs." He winked at Lux, who'd seated himself on the top porch stair. Standing up felt wrong, like he would be looking down on his old coach.

Bertram leaned forward, pulled the lever that slammed down the foot of the recliner, and turned toward the screen door. "Hey, Billie, you back there? If you can hear me, fetch us a beer," Bertram called. "After all, any boy that's been slapped across the face by a widow-maker and lived to tell the tale can have a man's drink, right, Ace?" The noise startled a small flock of red chickens scratching on the side of the house in a freshly planted flower bed.

"Jesus Christ!" Bertram swore, shaking his head, turning back to the house again. "Rose, get one of the girls out here to pen up these birds. I told you I wasn't going to be able to mind your flower bed and listen to the game." He stubbed out his cigarette, felt around for the volume dial on the side of the radio, exhaled smoke, and looked over at Lux. "Son of a bitch! Clemente's on deck."

"Hey, Lux," Billie Price said, swinging out of the screen door, her elbows sticking out of her blouse as she clutched the beer under her thin arms. She gave two to her dad and one to Lux. Her slim face, dark eyes half-buried behind dark bangs, was all grin. Behind her, with a wooden bowl of table scraps and torn-up bread, Dessie appeared, wearing her sweater, skirt, and knee socks from school. Lux caught Dessie's eye, then turned to look at the side yard, where chickens scratched at the base of fruit trees and lilac bushes had begun to bloom; beyond, the garden had already been hoed into dark rows. Dessie's stocking feet trotted past Lux down the stairs, calling, "Come, chick, chick; come on chick, chick." Hens and roosters, clucking and flapping from all directions, followed her to their pen in the backyard. Lux caught himself staring at Dessie. Her blonde hair hung in waves down her back. Her hips looked soft and round, her legs seemed longer, her pale green skirt flared as she stepped past him. Cheeks flushed, Dessie returned to sit on a hanging swing on the far end of the porch next to her sister.

"Damn, them things are so stupid," Bertram said. He gave up on the volume and began shifting the antenna to catch a better signal from KDKA. Lux began to relax. "They sure is, Coach," Lux nodded. "Especially them purebreds."

Bertram held his hand in the air. It was a full count, and all went quiet while they waited to see if Clemente would come through for the fans. The screen door opened once more for Rose. She was a petite woman, her gathered light-brown hair was streaked with silver around the temples, and though she was more fine-boned and slender than her husband, she had the same ample look. Bertram had often said that if he ate too much, it was because Rose cooked too well.

"Luther Cranfield, how are you? The girls said they saw you at the high school," Rose said in a hushed tone; she wiped her glasses on her apron and waited until Bertram, disgusted, dropped his hand as the inning was over. "How's your father getting along these days?" Rose asked. Her eyes fixed on the eyepatch as if she were trying to decide how bad the injury was, and whether or not to ask about it. It made Lux want to scratch; he rubbed the cold can of beer back and forth between his palms.

"Pa's about the same as ever, Mrs. Price, thank you for asking, and I'm healing up fast, Mrs. Price, thank you. Another couple weeks, maybe, I'll be good as new," Lux said, his voice cracking more than he'd wanted it to.

"Well, it's nice to see you up and about so quickly," Rose replied. She looked over the steel rims of her reading glasses, gazing past Lux toward the side yard. She seemed to be taking stock of the flower bed below. She settled herself into the wide porch swing between her daughters and took two steel knitting needles and a tangled ball of pink yarn out of the pockets of her apron. Something about Rose's round-rimmed glasses, her gray eyes, and the beige ruffles of the apron reminded Lux of a barred owl guarding her nest, plush yet watchful. To Lux's relief, Rose held off on further questions about his eye and about his old man. Billie scanned the ammo box, passed it to Dessie, who turned it over, ran her index finger along its deep creases and folds, and shook her head in disbelief at the way the steel frame was crushed. She stood and handed it back to Lux, then returned to her place on the swing.

Bertram swore under his breath at the baseball score, then lowered the volume on the radio. He and Lux began talking about the chances of this year's high school baseball team making it to the state finals, then switched to how A-1 had a great crew, and how impressive it was that the men had found Lux and cut him out from under that limb so quickly. Lux agreed, adding that he was grateful to Alan Ray, who'd had first aid training in the national guard.

"Tell you what," Bertram said. "Every crew should have somebody who's been in the service or took some first aid training. A fellow like that could save a life in a pinch. Not a bad idea to keep that hard hat handy, too. Not a lot of men would have the good sense to keep a hat on their heads when they cut timber."

"I can thank my ma for that," Lux said. "I gave her my word when I first started clearing timber."

Everyone nodded, and Rose looked up from her knitting. "Lux, I believe Alan Ray saved more than your eye, he saved your life," she said. "It's one of those sayings that is said too often, but the Holy Father works in mysterious ways. He knows why you and Alan Ray happened to be working together that day."

Lux shifted his gaze from Rose to Dessie. "Just what Ma would have said, Mrs. Price. Not saying I ain't grateful, but they ain't saved my eye yet." Dessie had been staring down toward her dad's radio, as if the Pirates game was all that mattered, but now her blue eyes met Lux's. "They might not save it at all," he said. "I'll know more when the bandages come off." As soon as the words came out of his mouth, he wished he hadn't said quite so much. Christ almighty, he thought, last thing he wanted was anyone's sympathy.

Lux felt heat rising through his cheeks to the tips of his ears, the rush of the beer combined with an awareness that he had no idea what he should say next. He wasn't about to dwell on the accident. He didn't feel like talking about the Pirates or backtracking to his years on the mound. *You were the first thing I saw, so beautiful in the morning light, a sign that things would all work out* was too full of weight to toss out there. He wondered if Dessie was happy about him stopping by. They'd known each other for years. She was the girl with bright blue eyes and a ponytail, fun to talk to at practice, willing to set aside her homework, grab an oversized glove to fill in as an outfielder or catcher. At first, she could hold her own, but at some point the boys just got faster and stronger. He'd needled her about her baggy gym shorts, also about throwing like a girl. She could give it right back. If he blew through the signs or if he'd grumbled at an ump's call, she'd mention that kind of thing, not mean-spirited, but with a twinkle in her eye. She took after her dad that way. They both had the same effect, something made him light up, try harder. Lux took a gulp of his beer, wiped his warm face with the back of his sleeve, kept his thoughts to himself, and enjoyed the safety of silence. The hell with it, he thought. She could take him as he is, and that's what she should do.

Billie spoke up. "Hey, Lux, are you going to come back to school now? Varsity could use a good pitcher."

"A one-eyed pitcher?" Lux stretched out his fingers and cracked his knuckles on his right hand, shaking his head, "No. Anyways, I don't need to," he said, looking at Bertram for agreement. "Pine's coming in from Kingwood for framing, hardwood's going out the door as fast as it comes in, cherry and walnut is up, and there's plenty out there to cut. The mines need locust props, too. Boss says he'll find something for me to do inside at the mill next week. That's OK for now, but I want to get back into the woods." Bertram nodded. Lux noticed Dessie didn't look up. She was straightening out knots in Rose's yarn.

Lux finished his beer. "I brung this for you to keep," he told Dessie, setting the flattened ammo box beside her on the arm of the porch swing. He glanced at her; though she kept her gaze down, she had that little grin that was tricky to read. Then, turning toward the Jeep parked at the pull-off along the main road, he said, "Hey, Coach, could Dessie come out for a drive sometime?" The green Jeep stood high on oversized tires. Its top was off, and two squirrel tails hung from the roll bars. Despite sheet-metal patches on the body, it looked clean and cared for.

Bertram crushed the empty beer can between his palms and chuckled. The porch swing creaked as it swayed back and forth. The knitting needles kept on ticking against each other, but Rose lifted an eyebrow and gazed over her glasses across the porch at her husband. Dessie's eyes fixed on the tangle of wool in her mother's lap. Her cheeks had turned almost the same shade of pink as the yarn.

Billie looked at Dessie, smiled broadly, then glanced back at her Dad. "Hey, Daddy, can I go, too?" she asked.

"I believe Lux was asking Daddy about Dessie, Sis," said Rose, "about whether we can spare her, come spring, one of these Sunday afternoons." Rose kept her eyes fixed on Bertram, whose dimples had become more pronounced as his grin widened.

"I didn't know you were allowed to drive with that eyepatch on, Lux Cranfield," Dessie said. She stood, picked up the ammo box, stepped into the house and disappeared. The porch swing rocked as Rose grabbed for her yarn.

Lux watched the screen door spring shut, and then looked back at Bertram. "Of course I can drive! I can even drive the front-end loader and the forklift at the sawmill," Lux answered, staring back at the closed door.

Bertram sat forward in the chair and nodded at Lux. "Well, then, I reckon you're a twice-lucky man, Ace," he said, tapping his cigarette pack into the palm of his hand.

"What d'ya mean, Coach?" asked Lux.

Bertram settled back in the recliner, stretched his legs out, and flicked up the cap on his Zippo lighter, striking the flint. "Well," he answered, "a man that can get work is a lucky man for one thing, and you didn't hear me tell you 'no,' now did you?"

LUX STEPPED over the planks on the Prices' swinging bridge, not wanting to look awkward by making a grab for the cable handrail. The boards swayed under his bootheels as he made his way to the pull-off. He gunned the engine, waved his cap, and headed for home. Instead of taking the blacktop, he cut over the hill on Chestnut Ridge, winding back and forth on a gravel road that narrowed as it climbed until it was little better than a tractor path over the ridge. He wondered whether asking Bertram was the right thing, a needed first step, or was it the wrong approach? He wondered what Rose thought. Now everyone in the Price family, and likely very soon everyone at school and in town too, would know. Screw it, he thought. He was glad that he asked Bertram, not that he planned it, but those words came spilling out of his mouth. Now they were as solid as the steering wheel in his hands, and he could not take them back.

The Jeep's tires skirted the flinty creek bed and climbed toward the ridge. Whenever the road leveled, through stands of sumac and flowering dogwood that had not yet leafed out, he could see fields set back against steep hillsides, homesteads in the full flush of springtime, a few cows or a draft horse or two, pale lilac bushes, a barn, a home, a chimney with smoke trailing upward. The gravel lane crested the wooded hilltop and dropped into a steeper, narrower valley. Further out from town, the road was rougher, folks had moved on. Hand-hewn log cabins and small barns stood empty in fields, siding boards curling away from the framing. Some homes had burned, and some had rotted once the roofs had begun to leak. All that remained were stone chimneys or the barest glimpses of flower-lined paths to sheds or outhouses that had long since sagged into hillsides.

Driving the county back roads, taking it slow, opening another beer, Lux thought about what it took to hold a homeplace together. Some folks seemed to know more than others about making their way on the land. His dad's elder brother, Uncle Ron, pushing sixty now, his sons and their kin, they knew. They could cut lumber, mill boards, put up hay. They had it all, right there, a flock of chickens, a cow for milk, they could butcher their own hogs, set out traps or hunt for meat, even a pond for bluegill and bass. If a man wasn't scared of a little hard work, Lux thought, that man could find himself a piece of land set back on some quiet country lane and have just about every-thing he needed.

Lux turned down a steep cutoff and wound his way toward his pa's place, shifting into low to crawl the Jeep across the water bars and head onto an unpaved lane. Once he'd started working full-time, Lux had thought he'd help fix things up, maybe cut some locust posts, pick up slab wood and framing from the mill, and build a garage or at least a tall toolshed with a wide enough roof overhang to park under and keep out of the weather while working on cars, hang shelves for tools, but Everett had shot that idea down, saying, "I don't want to see a bunch of no-account poles sticking up out of the ground once you figure out you got a real job on your hands," then adding, "I won't have you starting nothing you ain't man enough to finish."

Lux held his tongue. It was risky to take up for himself. The old man's gray eyes turned as flat as the heads of steel tacks. He wasn't above reaching for his belt if he thought he was being crossed. Since Mother died, his old man dug in over the least thing. Well, let him be the ruler over his own sad kingdom. Pa seemed to have let everything go, his tools, his things, his own self. Things don't need to go like that, Lux thought. He had no one to blame but his own prideful self when rain rotted the handles of the tools left strewn in the yard, or when the tractor brakes rusted and seized to the rotors.

No truck was in the yard. That meant Pa's old Ford had started, and he'd taken himself to town, stopping at the ABC store for Rebel Yell and a carton of Pall Malls. With a sense of peace that came over him when he had the place to himself, Lux started on evening chores. He fed the two coonhounds, cleaned their runs, and drew fresh water from the spring. Next, he had to fill the wood box with split firewood. All the while his thoughts circled back to Dessie. When she didn't say no, did that mean yes? What would it take to get her to talk straight to him, he wondered. Usually girls chased him, a working man with money to spend and time to waste. But he was not that man anymore. That man had been staying out too late, wasn't clearheaded at work, had almost got himself blinded, or worse, killed. That man got schooled, got lucky, got a chance to do it right.

However things worked out with his eye, Lux was pretty sure Bertram would take up for him. Marriage was in the air this spring, and a few school friends had summer weddings planned. In some ways, Lux had a head start as a workingman, not a schoolboy. He'd worked part-time at A-1 for three years; he was full-time since the first of the year. Though some of his salary went to his pa, each week Lux added to a roll of bills stashed in a tobacco tin in the eaves. After his injury, the Workmen's Comp paid the hospital, and his boss had handed him sixty dollars in cash. If his eye did get better, he wanted to cut the largest trees for veneer wood, where there was some real money to be made. But even if he'd have to work inside at the mill, it would be steady work. Dessie by his side, and a place of their own, he could make it all work out.

In the dim light of dusk, Lux stood back a good thirty feet from the wheelbarrow and tossed splits of stovewood from the log pile. Aiming with one eye he did just fine, hitting his mark with almost every underhand toss. Lux pushed the full wheelbarrow up the muddy path, stacked stovewood in neat piles in the wood box beside the pantry door, and returned to the woodshed for a final load. The moon was rising. The air was still and warm. With luck, he'd be out with his coonhound before Pa got home.

Damn his old man, and damn what he says about Bertram, Lux thought, setting the wheelbarrow back behind the woodshed. Bertram was a pipeline inspector. He had nothing to do with Pennzoil putting in a right-of-way. What man in his right mind would bite the hand that feeds him? The gas company saved his ass by leasing mineral rights, and Pa spent most of his time in a slat-back rocker on the front porch, swigging whiskey, living off royalties. Plus, Bertram was twice Pa's size and twice as fast. After Pa got up in his face, Bertram pushed him out the backdoor, set him on his ass in a muddy alleyway beside the dumpster, and told Pa that if he didn't watch himself, the law would show up to keep the peace the next time Pennzoil brought a crew up to check the lines.

Pa wasn't hurt, but he was sore. He told anyone who would listen that someday he was going to drop a tree across the right-of-way to keep Pennzoil vehicles off his land. The old fool ought to know enough to let go when he was licked. But he held onto that anger, talking about how he sure showed them, didn't he. When it came to his old man, reason flew out the window. Sooner or later, Pa would find out Lux had his eye on Dessie, but for the time being, the less said, the better. Lux could almost hear his Pa's voice, raising the stakes, saying, *Boy, y'ain't got no business starting nothing y'ain't man enough* . . . Yes, he'd heard it all before. One thing was certain, he was not about to tell his old man that the steel ammo box had found its way to the Price family. Some things Lux couldn't control, and some he could.

IT WAS almost too dark to see, but Lux had saved the best chore for last. Passing the corncrib, Lux took a handful of sweet feed as a treat for his mare and put it in his shirt pocket to see if she could smell it out. With a long, loud whistle, he headed to the paddock. When Uncle Ron had offered him Calamity Jane, right off Pa said, "There ain't no such thing as a free horse," adding that the only thing more useless and wasteful of money than owning a horse was owning one that was ornery and skittish. "Your uncle's only giving you the damn thing 'cause he can't do nothing with her hisself." Uncle Ron had taken up for Lux, saying since Lux's mother Aletha had just passed, it would be good for Lux to have the mare to care for, and that he'd take CJ back if it didn't work out.

That was a couple of years back. At first the mare hung back, hard to catch, and even harder to mount, but she'd just needed some daily attention, and a few treats. Now, one whistle and she came trotting over with her colt Dakota, both of them eating out of his hand. Lux stroked the slender nose of the mare, rubbed her neck under her mane, and gently worked a burdock burr from her forelock. Jealous of the attention, Dakota butted his slim chocolate-brown head between them. Slow and steady, ain't that the best plan, Lux thought, enjoying the night air, the sweet smell of warm horse.

Lux took a final glance to make sure the horses were safe for the night, and gazed up toward the eastern sky, where Venus shone as bright as a searchlight and the almost full moon had begun to rise above the ridgeline. It all felt so right, like there was a reason he saw Dessie, her smile, her wave that morning after the accident. He'd felt something, like that little tug on the crown of his head, like that sense his mother was beside him. Aletha would tell him to pray for guidance and allow the Lord to help. He needed some time alone with Dessie, not standing- around-being-stared-at-on-the-porch time, not even Sunday dinner time. Just the two of them, do a bit of straight-talking, get her to trust him. It was a matter of timing, of figuring out the right thing to say, the right time and place to say it.

THE NEXT day was clear, with a warm breeze that smelled of the richness of summer. Town boys wore shorts as they raced outside after school. Lux sat on the post-and-rail fence at the edge of the parking lot beside the school buses, waiting for junior and senior dismissal. He took a note out of his pocket, unfolded the lined paper, and reread his own tight scrawl.

Hey Good Lookin',

It's past midnight, and I've got Hank Williams running through my mind! I couldn't sleep and I thought about coon hunting but the doc says no shooting, so I went out tonight just to see the moon. It was almost full, there was a silver ring around it, and it took me a while to figure out what I was thinking about. I was thinking about you! I drove up the old logging road beside the gas well to where Lester treed a coon for me last week. Do you know what happened? As I was getting ready to leave, out came that old she-coon from the edge of the woods. I sat there, and soon it called and two twin kits came running out behind it, looking all tiny and squirrelly, running sideways, and I could see it all in the light of the moon. I wished you was there to watch this. Would you come out for a drive? I won't take you anywhere you don't want to go.

Your Friend,
Lux Cranfield

PS. Can l come around for you tonight at dark?

Lux looked up as Dessie came out at last bell. He could see her right off, wearing a yellow-and-white flowered skirt, smiling about something. She looked older somehow than last night, more like a town girl. He began to wave at her, but then he stopped. She was halfway back in the bus line, talking to Jerry Higgs, the teacher's boy with the gold Nova, a senior who'd won a scholarship to WVU. Lux's jaw set, and he turned away. His hand clenched as he crushed the note into a tight ball. He pulled his A-1 cap down low on his face, rubbed at his eyepatch, then headed in the opposite direction. When Billie Price walked over to the fence, Lux had almost reached the Jeep.

"Hey, Lux," Billie called. "Want to give me a lift home?"

"Not today," Lux said. He stared once more at the bus line, turned toward the Jeep, and then stopped. The note felt solid in his right hand. He gripped it and then threw it hard enough to hit Billie on the top of her dark bangs. "Give that to your big sister, will ya?"

"Sure, Lux." Billie fumbled to keep her schoolbooks from hitting the ground as she picked it up. "Nice throw!" she called, but he started up his Jeep and didn't seem to hear.

ALL THAT afternoon Lux drove with the Jeep's top down, sipping beer out of a grocery sack, listening to Top of the Country, WKKW. He passed the A-1 mill, where for almost a quarter mile irregular boards, cutoffs, and slabs were stacked on the side of the road for the taking. He passed the giant sawdust pile at the south end of the chipper, then headed toward the ridge and turned off at the muddy logging road that ran along North Fork into the deep woods. He felt like a green kid for letting himself get torn up. He should've seen that dead limb. Anyone who knew anything would have looked in all directions, including up, and once he'd seen it, he should have planned his cuts before he started up the saw. But hey, Lux thought, bad luck is bad luck, and sometimes your number comes up. Soon he'd find out more about his left eye. From what he could feel, it seemed like the stitches had healed. If he had his way, he'd kick off the cowboy boots and trade them for steel-toe boots, be back in the woods with Alan Ray and the crew.

And then there was Dessie. She must've seen him today at the school fence. Didn't she want a ride home? What was she smiling about with that pissant Higgs? Where were his old teammates? Were they at practice? Last year it would have been him pitching, laying on the gas to see how much heat they could take. Now that was something to look back on, but not a part of him, not something to look forward to.

Lux shifted the jeep into first gear, then second. The sun was slanting lower in the west. He wondered if any girl was worth this trouble, but then again, he'd known Dessie all his life, she was as straight as an arrow, raised right, respected. Bertram wouldn't let her get away with much. Lux popped open a can of beer. As the warm alcohol stung his lips, he remembered how he felt last night, his breath steaming in the cold air, the far-off barking of farm dogs and baying of coonhounds, the light of the full moon, the shadow of the bare branches; then later, staying up all night, how many times he tried to write that note, trying to figure out what he wanted to tell her, trying to get each goddamn word just goddamn right.

He guided the Jeep along the gravel road, stretching out his arms and fingers, missing the weight of his chainsaw, the way it ripped into oak and cherry, the sweet greasy smell of burnt sawdust mixed with chain oil. Most of all he missed the work, the task at hand, each felled tree its own kind of puzzle. Lux killed the Jeep's engine beside a logging cut to listen for the distant whine of the saws, maybe to catch a glimpse of his crew, maybe say hey. But all he heard was the tick of the manifold cooling, the creak of trees in the wind, the cries of distant crows settling in to roost.

THE RISING moon lit the edges of clouds in the east when Lux parked on the wide shoulder of CR 57 and walked over the Prices' footbridge. The golden retriever came out of the doghouse and halfway growled, but when she saw who it was, she yawned quietly and wagged her tail, watching from the end of her run. The house was dark downstairs, but upstairs light glowed in several windows. Bertram and Rose's room, probably, was on the uphill side of the house, back from the road, where a single shaft of dim light slanted back toward the chicken pen. In the front, facing the road, could be the girls' rooms, but where was Dessie? Lux picked up a small handful of gravel, then squinted, stood back in the shadows. He felt like a relief pitcher who'd been called to the mound but wasn't sure which direction to throw the ball. One or two small stones could tap at the base of a window frame, but which window?

There was a way to get closer, and he pulled himself up into the lower branches of a large flowering crab apple tree between two shaded windows. He held onto a branch above his head, straining to listen to the noises in the house. From his perch in the tree, the moon dimmed behind dappled layers of clouds, the air around him was so fragrant he was almost dizzy. It smelled like girls. What was he thinking, he wondered. He was afraid to let go and rub his eyepatch, afraid he might take a sneezing fit. He wondered whether he should get down and leave, just cut his losses. He shifted his weight to get more comfortable, and the limb creaked under his feet.

Suddenly Billie's shadowy profile appeared near one of the shaded windows. She said something to her sister somewhere in the house. Lux focused on the window frame, and even though Dessie was nowhere to be seen, he tossed a couple of small stones at Billie's head, then winced as they clattered against glass. The shade flew up and the window lifted. Billie stared outside, craning her head toward the road. "Hey, Lux, is that you?" she called into the night air.

"Good God, girl," said Lux, "You're loud enough to be heard halfway to town! Where's your sister? Did you give her that note?"

Billie gestured at the next window. "She's a-waitin' for you." Billie's overly loud whisper was like something from a school play. He turned to his left, inching out to get a better look. As he neared the slender end of the limb, the slick soles of his new boots began to slip, the limb bent, then it snapped. He slid down, his boots thudding into the soft dirt of the flower bed below. "Ah, shit!" he said, trying to keep his voice down but not succeeding.

Chickens begin to cackle and cluck from their pen, and a second window opened. A blonde head stretched out. "Lux?" Dessie said.

"Where are you?" Lux waved his cap toward the light above his head. He was afraid to raise his head and see Bertram or Rose. He prayed that they would keep doing whatever nightly things they were doing. He wished the chickens would shut the hell up. He wished his blood would stop hammering at his forehead and temples. Standing there, he saw his pa's face, darkly shaded, but somehow right before his eyes. *"Now who's the old fool?"* his pa cackled.

"Go away!" he finally mumbled.

"Lux, I'm coming down!" Dessie said quietly. "Me too," said Billie from the next window. "You just stay put up here and watch for Mom and Dad," Dessie told her sister, and despite it all, Lux grinned.

A door opened at the rear of the house, and Dessie appeared around the corner. "Hey, lumberjack!" Dessie said as she stood beside Lux shining a flashlight into his good eye. "It looks like you fell out of your tree!" She motioned him away from the windows and toward the darkness.

"Worse than that," Lux said. He shook his head and focused on Dessie, trying to see her eyes. Dessie's face seemed scrubbed and bright, and the rest of her was too dark to see. He pointed her flashlight away from his face toward the crab apple. "I might have broke that bottom branch. And I flattened some of your ma's flowers, and there's some kind of prickly plant." He held his hand under the beam of the flashlight. "Feels like I run my hand into a hill of red ants. I wanted to brush 'em off, and they latched onto my face." The back of his hand motioned upward; fine gold cactus needles spread from his cheeks to his mouth and glinted on the dark of his eyepatch.

"Oh, for the love of Pete, Lux, you got into the prickly pear," Dessie said. She scanned his face. Then she stepped back inside through the back door. As Lux waited, afraid to scratch or move in any direction, she returned with a washrag, a bottle of witch hazel, and a pair of tweezers. Under her arm, she had a can of beer. "Where's your Jeep at?" she asked. "Never you mind," said Lux. He poured the soothing witch hazel onto his hands and splashed at his face. "You just help me out here, and then I'll be going. I'll come back in the morning to help clean up."

Dessie shone the fading flashlight up at Lux's face; his good eye blinked. He wished he could see, he wished the pounding in his head would ease, he prayed that the next sound he heard would not be Bertram busting out the back door. He took a deep breath and instead heard Dessie's hushed tones. "Quiet, Lux," she said. "Set that beer under your shirt and stoop your head down. Hold this light right here. And be still, we better get these spines out first thing." Her hands smelled like the nurse's office. Lux tried to keep his arm from shaking as she worked with the tweezers. Hopefully, Billie was keeping watch. Dessie pulled at thin spines on his cheekbone and along his jaw. Recalling a trick that eased his nerves before a game, he began counting backward. "Ninety-nine . . . ninety-eight . . . ninety- seven," he said, taking a breath between each number.

"What are you going on about, Lux?" Dessie asked, and then, "Can you please hold still?" she said again, holding his trembling hand firmly, for a couple of spines on his knuckles, easing them out. "Ninety-four . . . ninety-three . . . ninety-two . . ." Lux muttered, staring at the outline of the back door in the stark moonlight. Dessie turned off the flashlight, brushed off her slacks, and set the supplies behind the back door. "Let's get going," she said softly. "We can't stay here," she said. "We'll have the whole family out here."

Lux shook his head and started to speak, but Dessie put her index finger up to her mouth. She led the way down the walk to the doghouse beside the footbridge. The hammering in his temples became less noticeable with each stride. The cool dampness of the air near the creek washed over the skin on his arms and eased the sting on his cheekbones. The dog thumped her tail and then let out a whine, but Dessie stopped to quiet her, stroking her on the head. "Do you think we should take Lucy up into the woods with us?" she asked, looking up at him.

She stood on the edge of the field. She looked up from the dog's bright eyes into his good eye. Her face was washed in moonlight, her eyes full of life, the hayfield furrows behind her a patchwork of light and shadow; like the sight of her after the accident, but more like a dream in black and white. Lux stared hard at Dessie to match this image with his memory of her.

He collected his thoughts. "Don't worry. There ain't nothing to be afraid of out there, and anyways, I'll look after you," he said. He stared at her, hoping she would believe this, and then he reached for her hand.

"You're sure about that, Lux?" she asked, her eyes wide with a sense of adventure. A warmth shot through her firm hand into his. Lux nodded. "I am. You'll see," he said. Though he was trying look as serious as possible, a smile played across his face. He took it all in. At that moment, he felt like the future was as clear as the moon, so round, so bright, so close he could almost reach out and touch it.

Dessie paused and nodded, then with a slight grin she spoke up. "Well, I guess I should've brought along a broom," she said. Lux stood back a step, trying to catch her meaning. "What? Why in the world did you say that?" he asked. He dropped her hand. Was she worried about taking the Jeep up into the woods? About getting the Jeep dirty? Was she worried about him? Did Bertram tell her to do that kind of thing?

"OK, not funny, I guess. Uhm, I was trying to make a joke," Dessie said. "You know, a broom? So you could sweep me off my feet, of course." She shrugged, holding back a smile.

Lux smiled back, and looked over at the tall white shape of the Price farmhouse against the dark hillside. "OK, OK. I get it," he said. "Hey, we won't need any old broom."

Dessie laughed. "You sure got off to a good start, Ace," she said, her phrasing an exact imitation of Bertram's cadence and drawl.

Lux looked at her, catching on. He cleared his throat, swallowed. "Hey, I'll give it my best shot, you'll see," he said. Then, reaching out for the thick twisted cable, partly to steady himself and partly to figure out where to set his feet, he took several unsteady strides onto the footbridge, making his way from plank to plank. With a sweep of his arm, Lux waved at anyone, real or imagined, who might happen to be watching them. It was all he could do to catch up to Dessie as she raced over the bridge, caught the roll bars, and swung herself up into the passenger seat of the open Jeep.

TWO

SOMEBODY TO LOVE (1967)

ALL THROUGH NINTH GRADE, BILLIE PRICE PICKED half-smoked Lucky Strike cigarettes out of the living room ashtray and smoked them down to her fingertips without her parents catching on. She rarely got to smoke a whole cigarette because Bertram kept his Luckies in his shirt pocket. Sloppy seconds would do. It was easy enough to collect an almost whole cigarette from the butts that he stubbed out and abandoned, little white crooked swans in the large black swan-shaped ashtray, but in order to smoke them she had to keep out of sight.

After her drama teacher had caught Billie smoking in the girls' room back in September, her parents threatened to paddle her if it happened again. Bertram claimed to believe in "Spare the rod, spoil the child," but he was a reluctant enforcer. But though infrequent, it had happened, and Billie did not want a repeat performance. Rose relied upon logic as well as good old-fashioned Pentecostal guilt. For her part, Billie figured that what her parents did not know would not hurt them or hurt her. Their ignorance would be her bliss, or at least help her avoid her mother's sermonizing. She wasn't worried about stunting her growth or shortening her life. She did not care about bad breath, wrinkles on her face, or worst of all, attracting the wrong kind of male attention. Rose had it all wrong. For Billie, the lure of smoking was so private, so special, a little glamorous gift that only she could give herself, a brief glimpse at the way life should be, instead of the way life was: school, chores, homework, school, church on Sunday mornings, church on Wednesday nights, homework, clothes on the line, clothes off the line, then repeat. One more endless month until the end of June when school let out.

Worst of all, Billie would need a new spot to smoke. She had been sneaking down to the crawl space under the front porch, but warmer weather meant the front porch could be occupied at any time. Other options included the spring house, a little storage pantry in the backyard dug into the steep hillside where seed potatoes and canned goods were stacked on moldy shelves, but that place was as spooky as a crypt; or the barn across the field, but too many stories about fires in barns kept Billie from smoking around dry hay in any kind of weather.

As for inside, Rose was always downstairs fussing around; upstairs, her parents' bedroom was off-limits, and that left only the girls' bedroom, a large rectangular room Bertram had divided using a three-quarter wall to create some privacy. Sound and light traveled over the divider, and smoke would too. A window in the walk-in closet could be cracked open for a few furtive puffs, but lately Dessie was always in that closet, dressing and undressing, trying on blouses, skirts, and sweaters to see what matched, dancing from the closet to the full-length mirror in the hallway, examining each outfit, pulling off rejects and piling them in a heap on the closet floor. Face it, Hurricane Dessie had blown in from some seacoast, and Billie had to keep out of the way.

Lately, every item of clothing Dessie selected contained some shade of green. "Wouldn't you just know that green is Lux's favorite color!" Dessie said shortly after she and Lux started going out to-gether, as if that was a positive attribute. As usual, Dessie had been standing in front of the mirror, rolling up the waistband of her skirt, securing it with safety pins. From the back, Billie saw the hem hang-ing crookedly above Dessie's knees.

With Dessie upstairs, Rose roaming around downstairs, and Ber-tram off running Saturday errands, Billie decided to chance a quick smoke in the crawl space. When she was sure no one was looking, she selected a barely smoked cigarette, strolled down the porch stairs, pried open the rusty trapdoor near the base of the porch, slipped in, and eased it closed so it wouldn't slam shut. On all fours, she crawled to a spot where she could peek out through diamonds of light filtering through the latticework. Billie brushed cobwebs from her hair and pebbles from her palms, reached above her head along the beams, and found the matches she'd hidden on a narrow ledge.

Sound drifted through the kitchen floorboards. The mantel clock that Bertram wound each week with a small brass key ticked. The iron skillet clanked down on the burners, the stove door slammed shut, and floorboards creaked. Rose hummed along with the *Family Hour of Praise* from New Martinsville on the kitchen radio; then the gos-pel choir ended, and a man with a sing-song wheezing voice crowed, "Hallelujah! Rejoice, all you sinners, for your redeemer is come." Under the porch, Billie felt mildly sinful. Was she a for-real sinner? God, who sees all, must be observing these acts of outright theft, pa-rental deception, and disobedience, but at the same time, once some-body gets away with something for a few months, the wages of sin seem somehow to fade away.

Billie pinched the filterless cigarette to straighten out the bent part, lit a match, took a deep pull, and tried to keep from coughing. She hoped she wouldn't be called to help cook, especially so she didn't have to listen to the sermonizing on the radio. She didn't even care what supper was. It would be something boring. She let the smoke roll between her tongue and the roof of her mouth. Maybe tonight she could go to town with Dessie and Lux, to the new Italian pizza parlor, Martino's. Everyone at school was talking about the place. They sold pizza by the slice and served tall icy glasses of Coca-Cola. They even had a jukebox with top forty singles and a dance floor.

Billie drew smoke into her lungs, puckered her lips, and tried to flick her tongue as she exhaled, practicing smoke rings. She knew if she stayed home, she'd have to finish her sewing project for home ec and a pile of earth science homework. That almost made her wish she was the one who was quitting school in June and getting married in September, instead of Dessie. Not that Billie would ever marry Lux, the conceited jerk. All he ever did was pick on her. Lately he'd been calling her "Boney," or "Bag-a-Bones," even "Bonesy-Billie." Last night, when they were all on the porch, Lux came up to her like he was going to give her a hug around the waist. He actually seemed civilized for a moment, talking to her like a normal human being, saying, "Hey, Billie, what'ya been up to?" Then, in front of Alan Ray and Dessie, Lux acted like Billie's ribs were poking into his arms. "Ouch, ouch!" Lux said, backing away as if he was hurt. So Billie took her right elbow and jabbed him in the belly.

She couldn't win. "Watch out for Boney Billie, she'll get y'all," Lux called to Alan Ray. Alan Ray nodded. Then Lux started dancing around in front of her like a one-eyed prizefighter, black eyepatch and cowboy boots, his breath all beery and a stubble of whiskers poking out of his chin.

"Hey, Bag-a-Bones, put up your dukes," Lux called. More than anything, Billie wanted to slap Lux's cheek, eyepatch or no eyepatch. In a sly move, Alan Ray came up behind her and grabbed her wrists, holding them so tightly she could not move either of her hands, not even an inch, and before she could blink, Lux reached out with his right fist and popped her nose. Not real hard, but hard enough to make her eyes water. Alan Ray released her arms, but she wasn't sure whether to elbow Alan Ray in the gut or to punch Lux right back. Lux saw her make a fist, and quickly he called out, "Ouch, ouch, I hurt my hand on that bony nose." He shook his right hand back and forth like it really hurt.

Alan Ray had just laughed, face all red, freckles lighting up his nose and cheeks. "Hey, Lux," he said, "you might need to get that checked out. Bring that big paw over here, I can splint it up for you." He took the bandana from around his neck and started to make a bandage to tie around Lux's hand. Billie looked from Alan Ray to Lux to Dessie. She wanted them to see how unfair that was, how mad it made her, but she sensed it would backfire. Dessie had laughed along with the rest of them. Bertram would say she should probably try to be a "good sport." Whatever that meant. Billie had choked back the lump in her throat and retreated to the porch swing. Could a girl fight back? Boys her age were easy, but older guys were not, and no matter what, it seemed like they always had to get their way. They could be nice if they wanted, but they also could turn right around and ruin everything.

Through the floor above, Billie heard the phone ring out from its cradle on the kitchen wall, then the thumping of Dessie's feet racing to answer it before Rose could get to it. It would be Lux, phoning from Cleve's General Store to let Dessie know when he'd be coming over. Would she be invited to come along tonight? Doubtful. Would she want to go? Possibly. Was it always going to go like this? She never saw this coming; there weren't any tryouts for this new role: Beverlee Ellen Price, tragic and forlorn but perky and pretty, starring as The Younger Sister Who Is a Good Sport.

Billie twirled the cigarette between her fingertips for a last, elegant Hollywood actress inhale. If she were writing this movie, there would be a big scene at the end where a handsome cowboy rode up on a white horse, hopped off, and punched Lux right in the gut so hard that he hit the dirt, swallowed a big old wad of chewing tobacco, and everyone laughed while he sat there, his feet splayed out wide, his mouth open, drooling, stunned, and speechless.

Billie snuffed the cigarette on the ground, crawled out of the trap door, inspected her clothes and knees for dirt, and made her way around the back of the house. Passing her mother's salad garden, she picked some mint leaves to freshen her breath. With luck, she could slip upstairs past the kitchen when Rose's back was turned. Dessie would know something about tonight's plans by now. Billie wondered whether Alan Ray was going, too, and whether Alan Ray even cared if she went. Oh, just let Dessie marry Lux Cranfield, Billie thought. Then they can see each other all they want, and they can all keep away from me.

"HEY, WATCH where you sit," Dessie said when Billie settled onto an empty spot on the foot of the bed. The quilt smelled of Johnson's Baby Oil. Dessie still wore her pink nightshirt, her high school gym shorts underneath, and a white bath towel was coiled on her head like the turban of the Queen of Sheba. She was shaving her legs with Bertram's straight razor, scraping against her pale shin with choppy strokes, holding a piece of broken mirror in her hand to see the back of her calf. Her right foot was propped up on a math book, and her toenails were freshly painted rose pink. Dessie's radio, louder than usual, played the Jefferson Airplane's newest single, "Somebody to Love." Only on Saturdays, over Rose's repeated protests, Bertram allowed the girls to listen to rock and roll.

"Hey, yourself," Billie said, standing up cautiously to keep from shaking the bed. Setting the *Seventeen* magazine and textbooks on the desk, she spread out her home ec project, an apron she was supposed to have already given Rose for Mother's Day.

Billie lifted the roughed-out apron; then she pinned a cutout shape of pattern paper somewhat like an apron pocket where she thought a pocket should go. "I picked this material for Mom. How does this look?" Billie asked.

Dessie nodded approval at the fabric. "It's coming out nice. She'll like those large roses." She paused, and took a second look. "Maybe use a wide red fabric for the pocket and sash? And red thread?" Billie nodded back. She was glad she had not sewn it together yet. She might find the perfect sash material in Rose's sewing box. Billie set it carefully back on the bed, then looked over at her sister.

"Hey, Des," she started. "Did Lux say I if could come along to-night?" Billie tried to sound unconcerned.

Dessie shook her head, said, "Nope. It didn't come up," and turned to scrape the razor at a spot under her knee. Something about Dessie's voice made it pretty clear that she should drop that subject. The music on the radio wailed and swelled, then ended, all the instruments stopping on the same beat. Billie thought that listening to each new song on the top forty countdown made Saturday afternoons feel like being at a party. Carefully, Billie took straight pins out of Rose's little red hen pincushion and folded the hem for the apron.

"Did you know that right after dark tonight, the bright orange spot in the sky next to the moon will be the planet Jupiter, which is 365 million miles from earth?" Billie asked. "My earth science teacher said that."

"Nope," Dessie said, and then, "Did you know that Lux said he could not decide if I was prettier in the sunlight or in the moonlight?"

Billie yawned. "Nope," she said, and turned away. Did everything have to begin and end with Lux? The cover of *Seventeen* caught her eye. She could see the full lips and high cheekbones of the model, long straight brown hair blowing back behind her, long slender legs in a short plaid skirt and knee socks, strolling right off the cover and into an active, fun life, with her long eyelashes and her bright red lips. Thin models were showing up on ads and magazine covers, though everyone at school poked fun at them, said they were flat-chested and undoubtedly undernourished. This could be a part that she, Billie, could try out for someday, The Actress Who Is Also a Cover Girl. She would have radiant and alive black hair that hung down to her waist, high-heeled boots in every color, skirts so short that if she wasn't so famous, so rich, and so popular, she'd be grounded for years. When Dessie set the piece of mirror down, Billie picked it up off the bed and stared at her lips, practicing smiles.

"I hate Lux," Billie mouthed silently, watching the lips in the mirror make words too terrible to say out loud. She looked over at Dessie to see if she'd noticed, but thank goodness, she didn't. Her sister had finished shaving and had begun wiping her legs with baby oil, rubbing her toes, and working her way slowly up past her ankles, calves, knees, way to the top of her thighs and under her gym shorts. Billie caught herself staring and turned back her own reflection, sticking her tongue way out, close enough to almost touch the mirror, moving it around. From that angle, her tongue looked like a slimy sea creature, her face looked like a cartoon, neck stretched behind like a long skinny balloon that some clown would twist into the shape of a wiener dog.

"Lux hates me," Billie said out loud, watching her tongue, lips, dark eyelashes, and the dimple in her chin with each syllable, then smiling into the mirror, not a good sport smile, exactly, but not a grimace of self-pity either. She checked her nose, to see if it was bruised from where Lux had punched her. It wasn't, but it hurt if she wiggled it back and forth with her fingers.

"Huh?" Dessie said. "For the love of Pete! Don't be such a little idiot." She reached out her hand to take back the mirror. "What made you say that?"

Billie tried to come up with an answer, but the words were not in the script. What does the Younger Sister Who Gets Picked On say to the Older Sister Who Loves the Hillbilly-Pirate Bad Guy? "Oh, you know, it's probably nothing," Billie answered, watching her lips make these light and breezy words, words that seemed to miss the point entirely. She remembered how startled she was when Lux pretended that he hurt his hand. As if that was true. He was the one who hit her in the nose. She shook her head and turned away.

Handing the mirror back, Billie rolled down her own ankle socks. Dessie had blonde hair, blonde arm and leg hairs. Billie thought Dessie didn't even need to shave her legs. Her own legs had black hairs, each one thicker, more obvious. No matter what Rose said, these legs of hers would have to get shaved. That way Lux and Alan Ray would have one less thing to tease her about.

"OK, I'll tell you what made me say it. Lux is always picking on me," Billie said.

"Are you ticked about last night on the porch?" Dessie was smiling like she thought it was funny. Dessie's bottom teeth were crooked, actually the two center ones overlapped. Experts from *Seventeen* would agree that Dessie's best smile would be with her lips closed. But Dessie's lips kept on moving. "Oh, he's just ornery. If he devils you, it means he likes you," Dessie's lips were saying. Her head tilted as if it might be a concept a younger sister could not fathom. "Guys want to get close to girls, but they don't know what to do when they get around them."

Lux? Not know what to do? How could Dessie say that about the best pitcher, maybe in the history of Fairchance High, or Alan Ray, who had traveled all over the country in the national guard? "Oh, sure," Billie said. She stood up, held out her sewing project, imagined a finished apron tied around her mother's waist. She checked the hem to see if it was even.

"I really mean it." Dessie said. "You need to act different. Show you don't care about them, and they'll come over and sweet-talk you," she said. Then Dessie lowered her voice. "If you promise not to tell Mama, I'll show you what he does to me." Billie nodded.

Dessie got up out of the bed, and her fingers opened the top buttons on her nightgown. Billie leaned in, stood on tiptoes to see what Dessie was talking about. A few inches below the neckline was a circular pinkish-red blotchy bruise the size of a small peach. Billie gasped. "Did he punch you or pinch you? Did it hurt?"

"No, stupid, it was fun. He did it with his mouth." Dessie's eyes darted back and forth, checking to see if anyone else was listening. "Don't you dare breathe a word." Dessie turned back, her eyes piercing into Billie's. "Promise me. Swear you won't."

Billie knew about kissing, she had heard jokes about sex, but she was not sure how this fit in. This was different than other types of secrets, like faking a headache to skip school. She began thinking about how it felt kind of grown up to share a part of Dessie's new life, like she just peeked through a doorway to a place that she would soon be able to enter.

Billie looked up at Dessie's eyes and made her most solemn promise. "I won't. I swear to God as He is my witness, so help me," she answered, wondering if God heard her say this, if keeping this secret was another of God's tests she had just failed. But Dessie did not seem to be the least bit concerned about God. She seemed more worried about Rose, and for that reason, this felt like useful information, though Billie didn't even know why she thought that.

"Hey, Billie," Dessie called out from the walk-in closet. "Will you look outside and tell me if you see Lux?"

Before she knew what she was doing, Billie lifted the sash of Dessie's window and stuck out her head. Past the walk, past the dog box, midway up the grass of the yard, sat Lux's jeep, the top down and fresh mud splattered halfway up the sides. Billie could see Alan Ray's red hair and long white arms. He was in the driver's seat, shirtless, wearing his army vest with a red, white, and blue bandana around his neck. The Jeep's hood was up. Lux wore his A-1 cap and a black T-shirt. He and Bertram were standing over the engine with tools in their hands while Alan Ray was giving it more gas.

"Yeah, they're here," Billie said. She could hear them calling back and forth to each other over the rush and snort of the engine and the sound of Lux's old-timey country music.

Dessie called out from the closet, "Oh, shoot, I better find something to wear. Can you be an angel and tell 'em I'll be right down?"

DOWNSTAIRS, BESIDE the porch door, Billie halted. She had things to consider before walking over there. Was she just the messenger, the angel? without any other part in this play? What would she do when she got there, say hi? Maybe not to Lux, but to Alan Ray, who usually seemed happy to see her? She wanted to deliver the message, but something made her hang back, to stop and weigh things before she opened the screen door. Angel, devil, devil, angel. She wasn't even sure whether to head down to the Jeep or yell out from the porch to tell them Dessie was coming.

But then it didn't matter. Like a barefooted green flash, Dessie shot downstairs, past the kitchen, straight through the living room. Billie reached to open the door for her sister.

"One moment, Dorothy," Rose called out, walking in from the kitchen, the smell of cornbread trailing after her. Dessie stopped and turned back. She wore a green pleated skirt, hiked up inches higher than Rose would allow, and a green-and-white print blouse with a high ruffled neck. She was carrying her shoes in her left hand, and her wet hair was gathered up with a wide stylish leather clip. Dessie looked at Billie, as if Billie should have known this would happen, as if she should have done something to distract their mother.

"Sit with me a moment, Dorothy, over here," Rose said, wiping her hands on a dish towel and settling onto the piano bench in the living room. Billie could see Dessie's right hand quickly unravel the waistband of her skirt so the hem hung down to the bottom of her knees; then, she sat down beside Rose and pulled her skirt down even lower over her knees, crossing her ankles below the bench. Her eyes were fixed on the outside door.

Rose smoothed her apron and sat up straight, facing her elder daughter who was already taller than she was. She took each of Dessie's hands in each of her hands, bowed her head, closed her eyes, and said, "Dorothy, dear, let us pray. Heavenly Father, please protect my daughter this evening and bring her safely home to her family." Rose blinked her eyes, but kept her head bowed.

"Amen," said Dessie, her eyes cast down at the floor, and Billie said, "Amen," out of habit more than out of conviction. From where she stood beside the doorway to the porch, Billie could hear both the gospel radio in the kitchen and the voices of the guys outside. Billie knew Dessie was ready to bolt. Rose seemed to know this too. Rose continued to clutch each of Dessie's hands in her own trembling hands. On the wall above Rose's silver, braided hair hung a framed print of a painting of Christ kneeling in prayer in the garden of Gethsemane. Rose said, "Father, you have blessed this home with two daughters, and I pray with all my heart that you do not see fit to take them before they can do Your work." Rose's eyes seemed to be about to well up with tears, and the trembling of her hands seemed to increase with each tick of the clock on the mantel. Billie wondered how long Rose would clutch at Dessie's hands. It seemed like she was about to start crying.

"Mother," Dessie said after she could no longer keep silent. "We're going into town. We are going to have something to eat. Then we are going to come right back home."

Rose sighed, her voice hushed. "May it be Your Will," she said, and reluctantly released her hold. She peered above her glasses into her Dessie's eyes. "Stand up now. Let's see that skirt. You know that the Lord has given mothers eyes to follow their daughters wherever they choose to go."

Dessie stood, swirled around, and Billie could see her tummy suck in, letting the skirt's hem fall as low as possible. "That's a pretty blouse," Rose said. "Right proper."

When she had her back to her mother and only Billie could see, Dessie rolled her eyes at the ceiling. Billie tried not to laugh. "May the heavenly Father protect us all," Rose said. She walked Dessie onto the porch, offering her cheek for a good-bye kiss. Then, she added, "Be home before 11."

"We will," Dessie called, dashing down the porch stairs, not turning around.

FOR ONE last brief second, Billie wondered what would happen if she just skipped on down there, following her sister to the Jeep, and in a friendly way flat out asked them all if she could come along. But it was clear as day that she should not do that. Dessie did not invite her to go. And Rose could start in all over again.

Oh well, welcome back to boring. Billie crossed the living room, peeked into the kitchen. Supper was still not ready to set out. Since Rose was unable to see her, Billie searched the swan ashtray, pulled out a medium-sized Lucky, and headed back upstairs.

From the window in Dessie's part of the bedroom, Billie watched Lux ease down the hood of the Jeep, wipe the grease off his hands, and help Dessie up into the passenger seat. Alan Ray sat in the back, a bottle of Coke in one hand, a cigarette in the other, his long legs in green army fatigues stretched out across the whole backseat. Bertram stood on the footbridge watching, his hands idly tapping a pack of Luckies to settle the tobacco. The Jeep turned and splashed across the creek, climbing onto the main road. Black exhaust smoke hung in the air, the rumble and sputter of the engine mixed with the twang of pedal-steel guitars. And then only the wide, wet tire tracks remained.

Billie found the apron, trying to remember where she'd left the needle, thread, and pins. They were half hidden under Dessie's quilt. She'd have to find Rose's sewing box, finish hemming the apron, set the pocket, and then show it to her teacher for grading, so she could bring it home to surprise Rose. The idea came to Billie that since she already had a pattern, she could start another apron as an engagement present for Dessie in green fabric, with some pretty stitching. She could cut out a heart-shaped pocket to make it special.

Though she'd been living in this house for her entire life, sitting on the foot of Dessie's bed, her sister's half of the bedroom suddenly seemed different. It felt like the scenery in a school play, everything almost like real life, but instead, props rolled into place, waiting for the actors. Billie pictured the original room without a dividing wall. Big. Big enough that she could push both beds together and have one double bed. What if she could have that whole closet, which was very likely as big as a model's closet? Billie looked down at the *Seventeen* magazine on the desk, the model's big oval eyes, her smile wide and friendly. *I'm a model*, the model said, sort of telepathically. "I'm an actress," Billie answered back. "Would you like my autograph?"

Yes, please, the model answered. Billie took a pen and wrote her signature, *Beverlee Ellen Price*, diagonally across the cover of the magazine, making sure to place a large swirl for each of the capital letters, so they hooked together in a sort of alphabet chain.

She switched Dessie's radio back on. "Next up," the announcer was saying, "'Light My Fire.'" Billie hurried to close the door, so she could make the radio louder. If Rose heard what she was listening to, she would be horrified. Of all the bands out there, Rose despised The Doors the most, declaring Jim Morrison a demon who'd made a pact with Satan for the souls of girls, although no one explained to Billie how that could be possible.

If only Dessie was there, they could sing along. Dessie could hit the high notes, and she'd take the lower ones. They'd be the performers as well as the audience. Now though, Dessie was further and further out of reach, like the moon, but circling a whole different planet, some different world she could barely glimpse with the naked eye, planet Lux, with his Jeep and his country music. Country boys, Billie thought. Who even cares about being popular with those guys? There are other guys out there. The Jim Morrison type—wild, enticing, too handsome, too shocking—or maybe the kind of guys in *Seventeen*, clean-shaven guys who wore polo shirts, who had sports cars, not Jeeps. Billie sat down on the top of Dessie's desk, opened up the window a bit wider, checked to see if anyone could be watching, and lit up the half-size Lucky.

Across the yard, she could see her father's shape as he walked toward the barn in the twilight. He would clean up the tools, sweep the workshop, come back to the house, and be ready to eat. If she stayed upstairs too long, Rose would come looking for her. Soon, after another puff or two on the cigarette, another chance to practice her smoke rings, soon, when this song was over, she would turn off the radio, wash her face, rinse her mouth, and head downstairs to help set out whatever Rose had cooked up for an ordinary Saturday night supper to the tune of the Family Gospel Quartet.

But not yet. Billie reached for the piece of mirror that Dessie had set on the desk. Her head tipped back, her dark hair settled along her neck, and she parted her lips ever so slightly, rehearsing her most mysterious smile. Her outstretched hand with the cigarette swayed to the music, back and forth in the chilly air. the last few beats of the organ and guitar, the final chords of the number one song in America. The music swirled and drifted like the warm strands of smoke, like those wraith-like, almost O's in the cool evening air, out toward the vast universe, toward the distant planets, then gone.

THREE

IN A FLASH (1967)

Ten

Saturday the twentieth of May, 1967, the morning so hot the sweat drains down my spine, I sit back against the driver's seat, Dessie riding shotgun, and off we go, heading up a logging road to the summit of Chestnut Ridge, stopping after we crest the ridgetop. A field of hay waves in the breeze, spring green, tassels shining, the morning sun above us, not a cloud in the sky and not a soul in sight.

My arm across her shoulder, her arm across my waist, our bodies fitting together, we make our way across the long narrow ridgetop field. From the far edge of the field, a trail weaves through pinewoods. The forest floor slopes down on the right as well as the left. The trail narrows, the trees turn scrawny, finally the woods give over to sky, the hillside drops off on both sides of the path, the soil changes to flat stepping stones of crumbling shale.

We stand at the edge of a windswept cliff. A couple hundred feet below, Decker's Creek shimmers in the sunlight. A red-tailed hawk soars overhead, then swoops a wide circle toward the tree canopy beneath us in the valley.

Nine

Alan Ray sits at the AmVets, holding America's best, a PBR. He is smoking his last Marlboro. The crumpled pack and his last three dollars are on the bar.

He stares at me like I'm off my nut. "Y'already lost an eye, now you want to cut your balls off, too? Go ahead, then," he says. "Just don't let me find out you dropped down on one knee and begged for it." Then he says, "What the hell, it's your life. Hey, I'll buy. Drink up while you still can."

Eight

My mother counted her babes like the months of the year, the ones she had and soon after lost. In January, Peter, in February, Ruth, in March, Mark, in April, April, named after the month she was born and the month she died. All laid out, little graves, fieldstones in a row up the hill, a gate of saplings wired together by Pa, some plastic flowers that bloom forever. Then I came along, the one who lived, the one who sucked her teeth right out of her mouth, as she used to say. She loved us equal, those who lived for only a day or two, those who lived a year, and me, walking on the shoulders of the other four. She called me Luther. She said it sounded holy.

After me, two more gone, Simon, Eliza, and then the stones were laid side by side for her and the one who did not receive a name.

Seven

Bertram stands beside his workbench in the barn. He and I puzzle over how to get the carburetor off the International Harvester, in the hopes that we can replace the fouled intake manifold and get the old SOB to keep running once it starts.

He cracks a grin, tells me, "You can't have just her hand, Ace, you got to take the whole package."

Later, with Bertram at my side, Rose sits on the piano bench. A narrow silver cross made from hand-hewn framing nails is mounted on the wall on a pine plaque.

Her gray owl eyes meet mine. She says, "There is a right way and a wrong way to do these things, Luther." Then she says, "Do you mean to be a proper Christian husband to Dorothy? Will you be baptized in the name of the Father, the Son, and the Holy Spirit, and will you take the Lord into your life as your Savior?"

Six

As a boy, I used to race to keep up with my mother. I used to watch the backs of her legs, her straight-seamed stockings knotted at the knees as she knelt in the church pew, the tied bow of an apron behind her waist as her Sunday heels clacked from room to room on our milled pine floor, swirls of dust in shafts of light.

As I grew older, both she and Pa began to change. Her fingers shriveled like bent twigs. His steel-gray eyes narrowed to slits, as if the light of day would scar them. Her slim face sagged, deep grooves chiseled her brow, hollows dug into her cheeks. His beard grew white in shapeless strands. Bit by bit, the knotted cord that held her slight form together began to fray.

One night a month before she passed, Pa took the cast-iron pan to her when she served supper too cold, and I laid into him. By that time I was almost fourteen, as strong as he was, a head taller and sober. I knocked him flat and drug him into the Ford to sleep it off, locking the house door against him. I cleaned the floor, wiped the walls, set her down with a cool washrag on her brow. From then on, I slept with a baseball bat under my bed, although I was not afraid.

The day I first felt fear, the day the pounding in my chest began, was the day I lost my compass and began spinning free. It was the day my loving mother died.

Five

We take it all in. She holds my hand tightly, a little out of breath, but pleased to stand beside me. I could tell by her broad smile, the excitement in her eyes. She would be the one to take me forward into life. I could no more stop than I could stop my own birth, than I could stop the locust limb that took my eye, than I could keep my mother's spirit in her body, than I could stop loving this sweet girl.

I reach for it all. I say, "Des, what if we wanted to get us some land?"

She shakes her head like she was trying to get the sense of my words. I feel bold to even try. I feel scared to get it wrong. I feel the weight of each beat of my cowardly heart.

She looks up at me. She says, "Lux, what in the world are you going on about? Do you mean like a business? Like we buy us a little farm somewhere?"

I know what I have to do. I have to say the words, to make it real. Under the bluest of all skies, in the brightest light of high noon, and the spirit of my mother with me at all times, I look at Dessie. "Well, I suppose, we would probably have to get married then," I say, stepping back up the trail a good yard or so, to give her room, not because I wanted to, but because the words push me, they drive a space between us, a space as solid as my fear.

She is quiet. The breeze holds off. The air is still, the only sound the drum of a woodpecker on a hollow tree behind us. "Lux, you did just say what I thought you said?" she asks.

Four

No one knows for sure what took my mother's mortal soul. They think her heart gave out. She laid herself down in the middle of the day, pulled up the quilt, and passed from this earth on the tenth of September, 1964, while Pa was on the porch in his rocking chair, swigging from a bottle, and I was at school, too far away to hear if she cried out for help.

That fall, Pa slept on the porch in his rocker, swore he wasn't asleep when I tried to wake him to come to bed. When the moon was right and he was well, he and I went coon hunting, a momentary truce, us halfway up some logging road or setting out the night beneath that hit 'n' miss gas well, drinking and waiting for the hounds to bay and the chase to begin. He'd run on about fighting in France and Italy. Though he would never admit it, the more time we spent together, the more I knew that he wanted me to take on his place, make his untended acres produce once more, take him on too, prove to him that he could trust me, keep him from himself, agree with him that everyone was trying to get the better of him. I never knew what would set off the stick of dynamite buried in his gut, but I knew it had a short fuse.

My mother would tell me that she passed from this earth into the arms of her Savior. Maybe it's true. Maybe it's for the best. She would tell me that when I find my Savior, there I will find her. I know she left when she could no longer stay, that she did everything she could. I failed her, but she did not fail me.

Three

On the prettiest day of the prettiest month, under the bluest sky, my sweet, beautiful blue-eyed girl says, "Yes." There is no other sound like this, not even the sound of a perfect strike, the way it hits the glove of the catcher. Her one word, "Yes." I have pitched a no-hitter. I have hit grand slam homeruns, the ball soaring over the stands and into the junkyard beyond the centerfield fence, kids scrambling, the ball bouncing off the roofs of rusted-out sedans, but I have never known this feeling before or since. She looks at me, she gets quiet. My chest pounds. Maybe she will change her mind, but she doesn't. Instead, she says, "Lux, we have to do it right, marry in a church."

My Dessie, whose mind is clear and steers my heart. "I will do it," I said, the pounding in my chest the sound of the gears of my heart reaching for the gears of her heart, I swear it.

I will stare into the eyes of my Pa, and I will set this before him, one man to another. My best girl, I have nothing to be afraid of with you by my side.

Two

I reach into my shirt pocket. I have a treasure. It is a perfect soft gray bird point, an arrowhead, chip-flaked and as sharp as it was five hundred years ago. I braided a buckskin cord into the notches at the base of the point.

I tell her, I was a boy, walking behind my mother on the ridge trail, on the way to pick wild blackberries. I saw it among the broken rocks at my feet. It stopped me in my tracks. I bent, picked it up, raced to catch up.

Dessie places my gift over her lovely head. This ancient gray point against her skin, resting in the hollow of her neck.

Mother, you came to me, tugged at the hair on the crown of my head, you guided my hands as I braided this cord.

One

My name is Luther, but only on my paycheck, my hunting license, my birth certificate, and in my mother's mouth, as it will be on my baptism certificate and my marriage license. My name is Lux.

Things can change. I know that to be true. I have been spinning free, a wheel with not a cog to hold it; then, in a flash, I am a part of a great machine, spinning like a gear that drives another gear and so on, until the world is put right.

They will take me to the river and they will wash me clean from sin. My mother who art in heaven, hallowed be her name, she called me Luther. I will be saved for you, Mother, saved for you, my Dessie, the light I carry in my heart.

My girl and I stand together. The world is wide open, the world is new, for our new life together.

In a flash, things can change. I know that my eye was the price I paid. I once was blind. I could say that it was like watching my old life slip through my fingers. Now I can see. It feels like reaching for a second chance.

My hair will be so short that my head will feel naked. My shoes will be so tight that I will barely feel the earth beneath me. Water will stream over my forehead, it will seep under my eyepatch, and it will fill the socket of my eye. It will remind me.

FOUR

BIRTHDAY (1969)

TWO YEARS AND TWO MONTHS AFTER HE GOT MARRIED, Lux traded his eight-year-old dappled gray, half-Arab mare Calamity Jane to his friend Alan Ray. In return, Lux got Alan Ray's .30-06 Remington 700 rifle and a German scope, and to sweeten the deal, Alan Ray added a rebuilt Gravely rototiller. Alan Ray had hinted that if he proposed to Billie, CJ would make a dandy engagement present. That's when they shook hands on it.

Lux felt like he should have been happier about the trade, even though for the past couple of years he'd felt like he owed something to Alan Ray for his quick thinking after the logging accident. This trade could even things out. Alan Ray would be getting an even-tempered, well-trained mare. CJ was sure-footed on trails, and unlike some horses she never tried to unseat her rider by galloping under low-hanging branches or balking at fallen logs across the trail.

Alan Ray was happy as a boy on Christmas morning. He'd also offered to buy CJ's colt Dakota for five hundred dollars outright, but Lux refused. Now that Dakota was old enough to be ridden, everything should have worked out differently, the mare would be for Dessie and the young stallion for him, the two of them riding together, so the colt could learn from the mare's example. But that plan fizzled after Lissy was born. Whenever Lux mentioned riding together, Dessie declined, giving one excuse or another. She might've let her sister or mother babysit, Lux thought, but Dessie held back, reluctant to ask for any kind of favor.

Then, once she found out she was expecting for a second time, Dessie wouldn't even enter the paddock to help feed or brush down either of the horses. She said she'd heard a story about a girl in Reader who'd been kicked in the belly by a mule and lost her baby, and she wasn't about to go taking any foolish chances. Lux had the good sense to know a good horse, and he almost told Dessie how silly that seemed. But an inner voice told him to let it go, that women who were expecting might have some kind of protective instinct, not quite rational but worth heeding. He thought back to his mother, living through so much hope and loss. How much did she know about the life inside her, even the one that eventually took her?

Lux knew that Alan Ray had his eye on Calamity Jane for some time, and he knew he would make good use of the Remington. But almost as soon as Alan Ray had loaded CJ into his trailer, Lux began to miss having that mare. CJ was a gift from his Uncle Ron. She was shy and hard to catch when Ron first bought her, but took to Lux right off, trusting in his steady hands as he rode her the four miles back home. A few months later, when she went into season, Lux rode her back to Ron's house to breed her to Ron's dark bay Morgan stallion. Uncle Ron was pleased with how CJ had settled down under Lux's care. Lux was in the paddock eleven months later with CJ when she'd delivered Dakota, waiting up all night, and just after the colt was able to stand, breathing into his nostrils before he was even an hour old.

LOOKING BACK, Lux would say that those few months after his accident, the world spun faster than it ever had, life had charged past and all he could do was hang on tight, hope for the best, and give pieces of his life a nudge here and there, so they could fit like an unfinished puzzle. There was Pa, a soon-to-be reckoning about his future. There was Dessie, the promises they'd made to each other, the moments of joy at coming together, the pangs of being apart. There was bad news about his eye, a total loss, and with that, setting aside his chainsaw and beginning a new round of training as a millwright. Work days flew by, taking measure, tracking lumber, gaining more know-how and business savvy, the last man each night to leave the shop. Out in the paddock, Dakota thrived, his weight and girth increasing by the day, a dark bay colt with a snap in his step and a star on his forehead. But at his pa's house, with each day Lux felt more chained down. He could wait to marry Dessie until late August when he turned eighteen, but why? His old man could sign legal consent for him and the wait would be over.

One evening, about a month after Dessie said yes, and a couple of weeks after he'd received the blessing of Bertram and Rose, Lux could wait no longer. After chores, he joined his old man on the front porch. The breeze picked up as darkness began to fall. The light lingered in the west for what seemed like hours. June bugs crawled up the cabin wall and darted headlong into the screen door to get at the light bulb in the kitchen ceiling. Lux settled back against the porch rail, holding out a tin of Copenhagen tobacco for his old man, taking a pinch for himself.

"There's something I been meaning to talk to you about," Lux said, staring at the darkening features of his old man in his slat-back rocker. Everett tugged at his cap, setting it back on his head, and reached out for the snuff. Lux waited several minutes for a response. "Ain't that just how your ma used to talk," Everett said, startling Lux, loneliness in his voice.

Lux rubbed the snuff between his lower lip and his gums, spit into a coffee can at his feet. It had come to this. "Truth be told, a few months back I got my heart stole by a girl," Lux said. "I want to do it right, to ask consent and all."

"Do ya, then?" Pa said. "So, you'll be bringing her up here one of these days," he said. It was a statement more than a question.

"I don't know, I don't know about that," Lux said, caught a bit off guard, drawing out his words while he figured out his next thought. The tobacco put a sour taste in his mouth. He spat it into the tall grass. "I expect we'll get us some land of our own, maybe work something out with her pa."

In the waning light Lux couldn't see his pa's face well. It seemed like his eyes were shut, like he was only halfway listening. Lux wondered if his pa would ask for any more information, or if he was off in his own mind barely heeding Lux's words. An owl hooted back in the woods, and a pair of bullfrogs called like the twangs of a banjo along the stream banks. Lux heard the creak of his father's rocking chair on the planks of the porch.

"Well ain't that something. Will you, then?" his pa said suddenly.

Lux nodded slowly. He stared at the tree line. He waited.

Pa spit into a Coke can. Then he cleared his throat. "Who's the lucky girl?"

Lux winced. The air had darkened, the old man had taken his time closing in. He could walk off the porch, head out for the night, he could head for the Jeep and be gone. It could have gone like that. Lux's legs would not let him move. His fingers gripped the porch rail beside him. His own body did not know how to dodge this question.

"Dessie, ah, Dorothy Price," Lux said into the night air. His voice seemed too loud, like it had its own echo. He rubbed at his eyepatch.

"Taking up with that Price girl?" Everett reached down behind his chair for his knife and sharpening stone. "It's a wonder she'll have the likes of you." Everett slid the old Bowie knife from its leather sheath. He stroked the edge of the thick blade with his thumb, then slid the blade along the stone, a practice so ingrained that he needed no light at all. "So that's how it goes around here," said Pa, his eyes cast down at the knife or possibly the round of oak he'd been resting his feet on, or maybe the planks on the porch. "Why you just go on then. You always did follow that son-a-bitch coach of yourn like a pup. You're to be eighteen in a couple months. Ain't nothing I can do about it."

Some things do not change, Lux knew. Bertram had gotten the better of Pa, and the old man was never going to let it go. Lux had the sudden awareness that he had just stepped across the enemy lines, that both he and Dessie, and Bertram and Rose, too, would stand forever behind a closed a door in his old man's thoughts. Lux had stepped through that door, he had chosen, and his old man had latched that door behind him. "Well, good riddance to all of you'ns," his pa said, breaking the silence. Lux wiped the sweat off his forehead. "Reckon I can sell them horses once I'm shed of you for good."

His old man never made anything easy. Lux shifted, started to speak, and held back. *That ain't how it is*, he wanted to say. *It don't have to go like this.* But then he thought, *Yes, old man. There ain't a damn thing you can do about it.* Everett moved his feet. He sat forward in his chair, spat into the Coke can, and stabbed the thick-bladed knife into the oak log. A bat circled and wheeled just past the roofline. The steel blade and rivets on the smooth handle of the Bowie knife glinted in the darkness.

THOUGH HE did not speak of it that night to his old man, Lux had other plans for CJ and Dakota. There was a scrubby quarter-acre section of hayfield on the Price property that was too steep to cut with the tractor, and Lux had already mentioned to Bertram that he would sure appreciate it if he could bring his horses over and set them up on that strip of pasture. Dessie had added that she'd wanted to learn to ride, too. Bertram hadn't considered keeping horses, but he suggested that if he and Lux made a paddock large enough maybe they could both make use of it, and that way he could also raise a calf for meat.

Lux gathered some men from A-1, and in no time they dropped off a truckload of locust posts and poplar boards from the mill. With the help of Alan Ray and Bertram, and Uncle Ron's posthole digger, in a few weekends they built a corral with an open tack shed at the back of the Price property. The paddock was close to where Lux and Dessie soon would set their trailer, and it was easy to drive over to with a bale of hay in the back of the Jeep. The horses moved onto the Price homestead even before Lux did.

Dessie had taken to riding like a natural. Her long arms and legs made it easy for her to reach up to the pommel and hoist herself into a western saddle, and Calamity Jane responded to Dessie's steady hands and the light pressure of her knees. Soon Dessie was cantering across her father's hayfield, her hair in a ponytail flying out behind, one hand on the reins, one hand on the neck of the gray horse just at the base of her mane. Calamity Jane's head lifted up, her neck arched, and her silver tail waved out as she picked up speed. They were a sight for anyone to behold.

One of those perfect October afternoons soon after their wedding, the idea came to Lux that he could buy the forty-acre piece of land at the head of the Goshen Road on a land contract from Bertram, and as soon as Dakota was old enough to ride, he and Dessie could spend their spare time on horseback, side by side, exploring the lay of the land and planning out a future homestead. Though he hadn't discussed it yet with Bertram, he mentioned it to Dessie. All she said was "That's fine, Lux," with a nod and a wistful smile.

SO MUCH for those plans, Lux thought. So much for trail riding beside the prettiest girl on the prettiest horse, so much for warm summer nights. Autumn sneaked up on him. He had a sweet little baby daughter, another on the way any time now. He couldn't ride both of the horses. Yet right away, the trade with Alan Ray began to needle him. Lux thought Dessie would've been tickled to have the garden tiller and to get him a good reliable hunting rifle, and happy that their money would stretch a bit further. But lately Dessie never seemed too happy about anything, especially this last month as she got closer to her due date, and she hadn't even looked at the tiller or at the rifle. All she said was "That's fine, Lux," with the same reassuring nod. At least he'd held on to Dakota, Lux thought. The colt needed a firm hand and a training routine. By rigging a makeshift scabbard to his saddle, Lux could take the Remington along as he rode through the woods on old logging roads to the highlands above the farm, crisscrossing the overgrown fields at the head of the Goshen Road, scaring up grouse and turkey, looking for deer sign, and planning for gun-hunting season later in the fall.

IN THEIR trailer Dessie eased her pregnant body into the rocker, set her feet up on the milk crate they used for a coffee table, and took a few minutes to rest up before starting to put supper on. She placed her hands on her swollen belly, trying to figure out the position of the baby she was carrying. Little body parts, maybe elbows or feet, punched and kicked at her ribs. Each day, her skin felt more stretched and tight, the time closing in.

She hadn't wanted to think about this, but she couldn't keep the memory from flooding back, the strange, glaring white walls of the Fairchance General delivery room, a room of stainless-steel counter tops like large shiny mirrors that she couldn't quite see herself in, surgical implements she couldn't figure out, arrayed like silverware next to the metal sink, and male doctors and orderlies that set Lux off into a jealous rant whenever he drove her to the clinic for a checkup. *Did that man touch you? Did you let him look at you?* She did not know how to talk to Lux at times like that. She knew that she did not trust them all that much herself, strangers all of them, using words that made no sense, *epidural, Fallopian tubes, forceps,* always in a rush. She remembered the astringent smell of the delivery room, how the double glare of an adjustable spotlight had shone in a young doctor's glasses; she couldn't see his eyes or his mouth under the mask.

Shaking the memory out of her brain, she looked over at the uncooked supper of white beans and collards she'd set out next to the stove. She should get herself up and get started on that. "Michael row the boat ashore," she heard a voice sing; startled, she realized the voice was her own.

Fourteen-month-old Elisabeth Rose, Lissy for short, sat at Dessie's feet, ripping Kleenex into tiny pieces. In her wide, dark eyes and straight black hair, Dessie could see her daughter's resemblance to Billie, and in her long pudgy legs and fingers she could see hints of Lux's athletic build. "Michael row the boat ashore, hallelujah," Dessie sang again, absently. Lissy grabbed hold of a tissue in the box and pulled with both hands until it came up out of the center. Each time she got a tissue out, she squealed and waved it in the air; then, piece by piece, tore it into bits and let the pieces fall like the leaves that blew down from the trees outside the window.

Dessie leaned forward in the chair and held out her hands. "Come up here to Mama, that's my big girl." Lissy clutched more tissues in her right hand, and a wet smile lit up her face. She crawled over, then held up outstretched arms. Dessie gathered Lissy up and settled the child on her hip, careful not to put any extra pressure on her tight, stretched-out belly or her diaphragm. Breathing had become harder, the trailer was stuffy, and the hot spell in the past few days hadn't helped. Today a throbbing lower backache made it even harder to get out of the chair. At least now that October was here, the air cooled down as night came on. Dessie wondered if she should call her mother over from the farmhouse next door before the pains in her back got any worse. It felt almost like cramps but not quite; the pain shot from her lower back to her hip. Must be all this extra weight, Dessie thought, straining to lean forward in the chair.

"Are you going to help Mama when the new baby comes? Can you be Daddy's little girl?" she asked Lissy. "Da, da . . . da, da, da, da" said Lissy, looking up at her mom, her eyes wide, drool running down the center of her pink lower lip, her little swollen gums raw where two bottom teeth had begun to pierce through. Her pudgy fingers held up a full-size tissue. She pushed her face back and forth into it, then held it up to her mother's nose, and Dessie smiled and sneezed loudly on cue.

THERE WAS a softness in the damp earth, and Lux had caught the fresh tracks of a large deer. The trail crossed the muddy ruts of the old Goshen Road; horse and rider followed bean-shaped scat and trampled ferns on the forest floor. Then broken stems, the remnants of scrapes on sumac, and more deep two-toe depressions in the mud on the north side of the creek, then the trail narrowed into underbrush. Through the low thicket, Lux held Dakota to a slow walk. Sumac branches scratched at Lux's arms, blackberry brambles caught against his eyepatch and pulled at the Remington in its scabbard. Lux kept Dakota in the creek bed until they emerged into the sunlight; he had a hard time seeing past the overgrown wild grapevines and scrubby crab apple trees that had sprung up over time in the untended field. Lux pictured clearing this scrub to turn it back into a field: first a machete, then a chainsaw, then piles of brush drying, sinking into themselves. What a job this would be, the landscape a three-dimensional set of problems that needed to be solved correctly. Old tires and brush piles, he thought. They burn good and hot.

Dakota moved forward, perhaps by instinct or perhaps because his height allowed him to see the remains of an old logging trail. On a knoll between some aging cedar trees and the fence posts that marked a Smith family graveyard, the young stallion braced his front legs, stopped, and shook his head. His brown ears straightened, and his nostrils flared. Lux reached down and stroked his neck. "Easy, boy," he whispered. "Easy, Dakota." Across the narrow field of timothy and orchard grass, under a row of scrappy apple trees, Lux heard deer chewing fallen apples. Dakota's front hoof pawed at the ground and the noise vanished. When horse and rider stepped out from the cover of the cedars and into the sunlit grass, the white warning flag of the deer's tail waved up out of the scrub; from the saddle, Lux could make out a flash of wide antlers.

Lux reached back with his right hand to find the Remington, and though the buck was just out of range and he knew he shouldn't, he gripped the reins with his left hand, then shot the new rifle straight into the air. Startled, Dakota reared up, and the saddle slid back toward the rump of the horse. The rifle sailed out of his right hand, and Lux hung on to the reins with his left, then grabbed for the colt's long black mane. Dakota came down trembling with his front feet splayed wide.

"Goddamnit, Dakota, you big asshole. Don't try that again." Lux hung onto the horse's mane long enough to steady himself, then, managing to get his feet out of the stirrups, he jumped free as the saddle kept sliding, sideways now, toward the colt's belly. Lux jerked down the reins, grappled for the horse's halter, and glared into Dakota's eyes. The he lashed the reins to a nearby tree trunk.

"You little son 'a' bitch. I'm just glad for your sake you didn't bolt." Grabbing hold of the cinch, Lux reset the saddle blanket and the saddle, cinching it hard against the horse's belly, making sure this time it was too tight for the saddle to slip. The surprised colt tried to turn his head and bare his teeth, but the bit yanked into his mouth; he breathed out short rapid snorts. "That'll learn you. Settle down. You might as well get used to it; I'm going to win these battles," Lux said, picking up his rifle and snapping it back into the scabbard. "Just you wait, little man. We'll get a shot at that buck one day soon," he told the colt. But on the far edge of the narrow field, the large buck had already bounded away into the wooded hillside. Lux thought his white tail waved in triumph and victory, not a bit like surrender.

DESSIE SAT up in the rocking chair and pulled a blanket over her arms while she waited for her mother to come over from down the driveway. With each pain in her back Dessie had become more on edge. She could not get comfortable. She stood on her front step and rang the dinner bell. That was the family signal. She needed Rose, Billie too. What was taking them so long?

By now, Lissy's birth was all Dessie could think about: the white-coated delivery room doctor, the aides and nurses exchanging glances, no one meeting her gaze, but instead staring somewhere below the starched heavy white sheet, between her restrained legs. She'd been half blinded from the bright lights, bathed in sweat, exhausted. Her head pounded, her legs shook from straining, from the effort; it was the hardest thing she'd ever done in her eighteen years. The doctors and nurses told her that she'd delivered a girl, but she couldn't listen. Her ears were ringing. She wanted her mother, her sister, or Lux, but she didn't recognize anyone. She couldn't understand it. She had wanted all along to know what was happening to her, but the strangest thing was, through all that straining and pushing, she'd never really felt the baby coming. She remembered that all she did was follow someone's orders to push, "push now, now stop pushing, now push again"; and then it was over. Where was her baby? The man in a green mask took it away. Was something wrong with it? With her? Why hadn't she seen her baby? She remembered how cold her fingers turned, how her teeth began to chatter.

"She's in shock," some nurse had said. "She tore badly, and she lost a lot of blood." They had added something to the tube in her hand, and she could not move her fingers. She felt a burning pain in the lower part of her spine. Where's my baby? Is it really over? Why couldn't I feel it? Dessie blinked into the light. An older, broad-faced woman in white looked into her eyes. "She's waking up," someone said. "How are you feeling, honey?" Dessie opened her mouth, but her tongue was so dry it was almost impossible to speak. "Cold," she said finally.

LUX TURNED Dakota back toward home, and they slowly worked their way down the shadowy road. Despite his eagerness to return to the barn for feeding time, the colt placed each hoof carefully. Dakota took after his mother, sensible and surefooted on the steep, dirt and gravel road. Back at the paddock, Lux dismounted and led the horse through the fence and into the corral.

Bertram's plan to raise a calf had not yet materialized, and Lux was secretly glad, even though Bertram was easy to work with and generous. A man needs his own land, Lux thought, and with the raise he was promised when he became a crew boss at the mill, Lux hoped that before long he'd have a down payment and be able to move his family up to the head of the Goshen Road. Once the dirt road was graded, ditched, and graveled, the trailer should be able to go right up, or maybe he could sell the trailer and use the money to build a small farmhouse. He'd found a nice level patch of ground to clear, a fine house site near a stand of sugar maples, not far from the apple orchard; there was a spring to develop for fresh water, topsoil for a garden, and the creek flowed all year long for livestock.

Steam rose off Dakota's back as Lux removed the warm leather saddle and the Navajo-style saddle blanket. Dakota held still as Lux brushed him down, and in the waning light Lux lifted each hoof to pick out the bits of mud and small stones. After he was sure the colt had cooled down, Lux fed the colt, adding a little extra grain for the cold night. It was expensive, but Dakota had earned it. The sun was almost down, and across the field the full moon had begun to rise in the east, the bright October hunter's moon, a cloudless sky, deep dark blue and clear. Lux's fingertips stung in the cool air. Tonight would be the first frost, the killing frost. He headed back toward the trailer to see about supper. He would also need to find some old tarps and maybe a sheet or two to cover the long row of late tomatoes before the frost hit.

INSIDE THE stuffy trailer Lissy squirmed to get out of her grandmother Rose's arms. She was hungry and fussing for her mother to feed her. Billie stood in the kitchen, barefoot in cutoff shorts and an oversized sweatshirt. She'd boiled up instant cereal in a small enamel saucepan and was cooling it down with milk. Another woman was in there with her, a friend of Rose's, Olive, an aging country midwife who had delivered Dessie and Billie two decades earlier. Rose had called Olive and asked her to stop by and check on Dessie. As soon as Olive heard that this was Dessie's second baby, she came as fast as her ancient green Studebaker Wagonaire could carry her. "Honey-girl, you best stay put and hunker down," Olive insisted, as soon as she began to time Dessie's cramps. Dessie could forget taking the drive to the hospital. "This baby's a-comin',' hain't a bit a' time to dawdle."

Olive sent Rose back to the passenger seat of the Studebaker for a basket with various supplies and a thick pile of towels and linen sheets. Bertram walked with Rose back to the trailer and stood in the doorway, but he would not set foot inside. He said he'd just make things worse for everyone when he passed out, and then they all would have to look after him instead of Dessie.

Dessie smiled from the couch as her mother pushed her father out the door. Almost immediately Dessie's smile turned to a grimace; she could only concentrate on bits of the conversation between contractions. She had no time to panic; she just had one goal at a time, stand up, hold on, wait out the contraction. Stand up, hold on, try to make it to the bathroom. Stand up, hold on. One more strong contraction and her water broke. Hold on, ease back down to the couch, relax.

WHEN LUX walked in, Dessie, Lissy, Rose, Billie, and Olive were crowded into the small living room. The women circled Dessie, whose eyes were closed as she more leaned than sat on the edge of the couch, propped up with every pillow they owned. Billie sat on the rug and stroked Dessie's feet, and Olive held her hand and cackled over old birth stories with Rose. Lissy stood barefooted on the couch between her mother and her grandmother, wiping Dessie's wet face with her small fist full of tissues. "It's amazing," said Dessie, looking up into the wide brown eyes of her daughter. "We can feel our new baby coming." Dessie placed Lissy's small hand on the tightly stretched skin at base of her belly as the contraction began to hit. All of a sudden Lissy raised up her hand, jumped back. She looked up at her mom with a giggle.

Clean sheets and towels were draped over the furniture; to Lux their living room looked like something out of some kind of movie set or a hospital TV show. From the doorway he watched his round-bellied wife with amazement. Her hair was down, and all she wore was her old nightshirt and slippers. When Dessie saw Lux she tried to stand up on her own and walk over, but she wobbled back and forth like her legs would not support her weight.

He walked over to her, and she stretched her arms up, as if she was moving in slow motion. "You smell like warm horse and gunpowder," she said, burying her head into his neck, clutching at his shirt collar. He stroked the beads of sweat on her forehead, and her fingers relaxed and she smiled. Then he could see the pain rise over her face like a wave, and she had to stop moving completely. They stood there together, her eyes shut tightly. "OOH," Dessie moaned.

Lux wasn't sure what to do. His brown eyes narrowed, and he scanned the room for an answer. He wanted to take his cap off and sit down to supper, but there wasn't any food ready, and there wasn't even a chair. His mother-in-law Rose, his sister-in-law Billie, some lady named Olive, and little Lissy stared back at him, and in return he focused his eyes down at his wife, her flushed cheeks, her damp forehead and brow. As she held onto him, Dessie swayed a little, tipping the two of them backward. Her eyes opened, but they could not seem to focus. To Lux she looked as drunk as she did on their wedding night.

Lux's eyes found Dessie's. "What have we here?" Lux asked when they stopped swaying and he could think of something to say.

"Hey, Lux," Dessie said, as soon as she was able to breathe enough to speak. "The girls say it's a birthday party, d'you want to stay?"

"Not really," he said. "This here's a hen party, and this rooster wants out." He shuffled her over to the couch and eased her slowly down onto a clean sheet. Her nightshirt was soaked with sweat. Dessie settled back, breathing deeply as Lux let her go. *So this is it,* he thought. *So this is it. Oh, Mother up in holy heaven, please protect the lot of us.*

"Y'all holler if you need me," he said, "Ring that bell, something." He didn't know what else to say. The longer he stood in the doorway, the more useless he felt. Then, remembering the tomatoes, he turned down the driveway to Bertram's porch to get a tarp, or a few old sheets off their clothesline. Bertram waved, flashed the porch light, beckoned to him from the window.

A great flock of black starlings rose up out of the dark field as Lux headed to the garden to cover the tomato plants. Dakota trotted over to the corral fence, whinnying for some attention. In the moonlit garden, Lux reached between the foliage to pick some of the largest green tomatoes to bring into the house to ripen. He shook the folds out of the tarps and spread them over the tall tomato stakes and the bushy green peppers. Steam came out of Dakota's nostrils as he watched from across the fence, his head shaking with each snap of the tarp in the air. After a bit the colt grew calm, and he moved along the fencerow, even with Lux.

Lux took his time, making sure that each staked tomato plant was covered down to the bare ground. When he finished, he reached down and pulled up a couple of the last remaining carrots. He started over to wait for news with Bertram at the farmhouse, but then Lux turned back to the paddock, walked to the fence, and held out a carrot for the colt.

"It's all right, Dakota, you're a good boy," he said when the horse reached his long nose over the fence. "We both miss her, don't we," he said. "It's you and me from now on; we'll be a good team, won't we?"

While the horse chewed, Lux's thoughts drifted past the garden, past their trailer, and past Bertram's house, and over to the steep dark lane that led up the hillside toward the start of the old Goshen Road. The autumn constellations spread across the sky, Orion came sharply into focus in the east, and to Lux it seemed like the whole valley had become silent, not the hoot of an owl or even the chirp of a cricket. He snapped back and remembered what he'd been thinking about earlier. "Think we'll have us a baby boy?" he asked the colt, his voice the only sound in the still autumn air.

FIVE

JACKSON CHILDS (1970)

THE YEAR I TURNED EIGHTEEN I HAD THE TWO WORST
experiences of my life. I went to jail and got married. Don't get me
wrong, it wasn't Alan Ray Munn, who I did marry with all my heart
and soul, for better or for worse. It was the wedding that was so wrong
in every way. I swear it was all my mother's fault, though she'd never
admit it. I know she'd put it all on me. I guess she'd be hard-pressed
to forgive me for what I done to her, too.

Jail wasn't so bad. The food was take-out from the Washington
Cafe, scrambled eggs, bacon, and toast in the morning, a cheeseburger
with the works for dinner around two. It took them five days to lower
down the bail, and my poor dad had to put his house up to the bonds-
man. Of course, he got it back. Alan Ray promised him that he'd take
the bond fee out of his pay, a paycheck at a time. What was bad was
how I got to jail, how I fell for a six-foot, long-armed, fast-talking,
blond-haired, motorcycle-riding dreamboat named Jackson Childs.

Jackson Childs breezed into our yard on his Yamaha 650 one late
summer day, stopping at the house to ask for directions. He had a pup

tent slung over the sissy bar, a gas tank painted like a sunburst, and an army-issue backpack that was as gray as gravel on the road. He was going to be camping out, looking for a cheap piece of land to buy, somewhere he could settle his weary bones for a while, he said. Well, his bones didn't look so weary to me in those cutoff blue jean shorts. In fact, they looked as fit as a fiddle.

Before I knew it, he drove through the creek, hopped down off the Yamaha, and had it setting on a kickstand alongside the dog box. "Where's your folks?" he asked me, and I told him Daddy was off at work for Pennzoil and Mama's TOPS meeting was way over at the First Apostolic in town. "What town?" he wanted to know, and I said, "Fairchance, of course," and he thought a moment and said, "Oh, of course, Fairchance! I've been there! It's halfway between good chance and no chance at all."

At that I started laughing, and he smiled wide open and natural, like he was tickled with himself. You could tell he wasn't from around here. No local guys like Lux or Alan Ray had the guts to laugh at their own jokes. They got insulted if I didn't, but that was their problem.

I TOLD Jackson Childs where to pitch his pup tent in a peaceful spot behind the reservoir dam. He came by the house the next day to tell me that it was all he needed out of life, a place in the woods next to a lake, and a pretty girl like me holding onto his middle as he gunned it down the road. Also that he got a job working roustabout at the county fair at night on the midway. Then he kick-started the bike and took off, the engine roaring in a cloud of dust and gravel. Around two that morning, just as I was lying in bed awake, wondering whether I would ever see him again, I heard Jackson Childs drive his motorcycle up the road, past the front of the house, then head up to camp out behind the reservoir dam.

Nobody but me knew it was Jackson. My folks were asleep for one thing; for another, I recognized the sound. I was in bed, thinking about how to arrange to get to the fair to see Jackson, but also thinking about Alan Ray, which I sometimes did at night, wondering if Alan Ray was ever going to kiss me again or call me to go out again, wondering if he was going to admit that he really liked me, wondering what I would say if Alan Ray proposed to me, and thinking about our splendid wedding at the Katy Fire Hall with three bridesmaids and a two-tiered chocolate cake, and the two redheaded boys and two dark-haired girls we'd want to have someday.

It was the kind of hot night where a person could hardly get to sleep. All the upstairs windows were wide open, and the shadows of branches made spooky patterns on the window screen. Damn if I couldn't hear something, coming closer, over the sound of the crickets, around the bend, slowing up, revving the motor, going past the footbridge. Vrooom, vroom, just like the song "Leader of the Pack." The second night, my late-night thoughts of Alan Ray began to get crowded out by thoughts of Jackson Childs in his pup tent. I tiptoed to the window as soon as I heard the Yamaha coming. There he was, Lord have mercy, no helmet on, long blond hair blowing back from his face, slowing down at the bend, then heading up toward the dam. On the third night, I told Mom I was sleeping at Coral Hine's house, and instead Coral Hine dropped me off at the fairgrounds right before closing time.

IT WAS eleven o'clock. The fair was supposed to close, but all the midway lights were still on. The night air was warm and steamy; each little light on the booths and the rides glowed with a fuzzy halo. A thunderstorm was rumbling somewhere; heat lightning behind the haze made bright flashes above the Tilt-A-Whirl. Under the covered part of the main stage, a gospel group was singing their old hearts out, working themselves up to a big finish. It was two men and two women, piped over the main loudspeakers, the female voices first, high and twangy, singing, "Be ready when He comes, Oh Lord, be ready when He comes," then the male part, almost as high and twangy: "He's comin' again real soon"; then all together, chiming in: "Don't let Him catch you on the barroom floor, laughing and dancing like you done before, be ready when He comes, Oh Lord, He's coming again real soon." The few folks left in the audience were singing along, swaying back and forth; some of them down front were actually on their knees on folding chairs.

As I passed the stage I began to pray too. First I prayed that I wouldn't see Alan Ray, and I prayed that I would find Jackson Childs on the midway somewhere, then I prayed that I wouldn't see my relatives, or none of the folks from my mother's church circle in the assembly gathered round the stage, especially considering that I borrowed a tight blue sweater from Coral and her push-up bra, and I used her lip gloss and blue eyeliner, too.

Walking the midway I began thinking about a different song, the one where Mitch Ryder sings "Devil with the Blue Dress On." The lights were still flashing, and folks were still milling about, and it was closing in on midnight. I saw a few kids from the high school, boys in white tees, black slacks, and high tops, their hair greased back and their pants too tight, with their girls' hands on their hips. Other townies, too, people I didn't hardly ever notice, but maybe knew from Cleve's grocery or the laundromat. They think they knew me too, that they've known me since Sunday school. Like the stooped-over lady, her face as white as a china doll's, with her little squeezed-together slits for eyes and pulled-back hair who was working at the wiener stand, and like the grizzled old-timers at the picnic tables chugging beer from cans in brown paper sacks right in public, waving and staring at me like they might have once worked on the Pennzoil crew with my dad.

I saw Jackson Childs at the far end of the midway. He wore a black T-shirt with white letters that said, "Eat the Rich," and he paced back and forth inside the penny-pitch booth, just him and a big square table with a red-and-white checkerboard tablecloth and a goldfish swimming in a tall cider jug. This jug had a narrow hole on top, hardly wide enough to slip in the goldfish. Pennies and dimes lay all over the table, with only a couple of pennies and dimes in the jug. "Wanna get lucky?" he was calling to no one in particular. "Don't gotta be strong, don't gotta be good, just gotta be lucky."

"Hey, Jackson, what do you win?" I asked him. A big smile broke out all over his face to see me. And I felt myself grin back. "Billie girl, most everyone wins the fish, of course, but if you win, you get the granddaddy of all prizes."

"What's that?" I asked, rooting around in my purse, thinking, OK, I'll pitch a couple of dimes; it will give me something to do, so I won't look nervous.

Jackson cozied up next to me, leaning his long body over the rail and ducking his blond head down so he didn't smack it into a big white giraffe that was hanging from the top of the booth, and he said, "Well, sweet thing, for you and for you alone, if you sink this here copper in that there jar, yessir, you get the extra special, the one an' only." And he took a quick jump up on top of the table, near upsetting the fish in its jug, and he bowed deep and low on one knee.

I was trying not to show how I knew he was acting so hokey on my account. I didn't want to look overly surprised, either. "Good," I said, "I didn't want a fish, anyway."

"Nobody does," he said, "That's why they throw all that money. They want to win, but they don't give a rat's ass if they get the fish. And a goldfish is a filthy little creature. You wouldn't believe how it dirties the water in this jug. It takes a special kind of person to enjoy that kind of dirt." He grinned.

"Well, that's not why I don't want a fish. I don't want a fish because it's just going to die, and that would be sad," I said, showing him my sensitive side.

"You bet it will die," he said, not the least bit sensitively. Then he leaped over the edge of the booth. "Come with me," he said. "Anyways, I don't work here. I work up at the stables cleaning stalls. I was just watching this booth for that lady over there." He pointed over at a skinny lady in a red, white, and blue shirt with fringes on the arms and across the chest, and tight black Levi's tucked down into her white boots. Even her boots had a row of fringes on them. I looked back up at Jackson.

"She was going to get something to eat and go to the can, and she didn't want none of these redneck boys around here to steal the fish or the jug," he said in a loud enough whisper for everyone to hear.

For some reason that struck me as ridiculous, all that money laying around loose on a table and someone gonna steal a fish. But as Jackson explained, with one jug and one fish a person could make all that money and then some. We walked back across the midway, and he told me that he was from Baltimore, the home of the Orioles, and that he'd been to college in western Maryland for a couple of years. He was studying business. He was interested in making money someday, but just now he didn't think he wanted to go back to school in the fall. Jackson said he wanted to live life instead of reading about it in books. I told him I felt the same way. But he said no. He was jealous of me, I had it good, he said. I had something that he didn't have. I had a real life. I was part of the land, I was in touch with the earth and could take control of my destiny.

No one ever said that kind of thing to me before. And that made me think about my life, and what I wanted to do with it. I flipped through the pages of my dreams like the color photos in a *Life* magazine. Actress? Model? Movie star? Well, the fact was, I was eighteen, I got my diploma, sometimes I babysat Dessie's two little ones and worked the garden for Mom, and one day a week I watched my old aunt Nelda for pay on the nurse's day off. She broke her hip but was still pretty sharp for seventy. I was ashamed to admit to Jackson or myself that I had not gotten started on any real plans at all. I didn't even have a driver's license. I had thought that all those plans could wait until after the summer. But here it was, almost the end of the summer, and I felt so stupid, so trapped, living at home, having to make excuses and sneak out to go to the fair. Dessie had her own house by the time she was eighteen, her own life; she had her babies and everything.

"Hey, you!" A large woman in a polky-dot blouse that hung out over the top of her polky-dot pants yelled over at us. "Stop a minute. Hey, you kids," she yelled again. I stopped dead still and looked at her, instantly feeling a stab of something, the heat lightning coming down from the sky splitting me in half, or maybe she was going to scold me, to tell me I didn't belong here, or that my sweater was too tight, or I should be home at this hour. It must have been half past midnight by now. But, amazingly, she didn't. Instead she asked us if we were hungry, if we wanted some leftovers before she put them in the trash and cleaned up for the night.

"Sure," Jackson said, smiling his bright white smile. She dished out two big paper plates piled high with Belgian waffles, whipped cream, and topped with strawberries, maybe even twice the regular amount. That was when I knew I had died and gone to heaven. Every year, when we passed by that booth, I begged for Belgian waffles. One year I cried tears for Belgian waffles, and Dad got so mad at me, he took me right home.

Praise be to God for small miracles and heavenly signs. Jackson and me sat down on a picnic bench away from the lights where no one much was around and watched the sky go from bright to dark to bright again. Maybe Jackson Childs was a magic charm, I was thinking. People wanted to give him things, to treat him nice, to wave and smile and offer him food. He seemed like the kind of guy could do anything he set his mind to. The waffles were cold, but the sweet cream and strawberry sauce was the best thing I had ever eaten in my life. I ate 'til I was stuffed full. There was too much to finish. Then I started watching Jackson, who was holding his whole waffle in his fingers. He hadn't even tried using the fork. He had a white whipped-cream mustache. I laughed out loud. I couldn't stop myself, I liked watching him eat so much.

"Just who are you laughing at?" he said, and I said, "You."

Just as I was thinking about how I could never have laughed that way at Alan Ray, Jackson Childs popped the last bite into his mouth, then leaned over and kissed me, for what seemed like a very long time, all the while wiping his whipped-cream mustache everywhere over my lips. And I kissed him back, getting into the fun of it, taking licks of the whipped cream off his cheeks and his chin. This was not the way Alan Ray kissed me at all. Alan Ray's kisses were hard presses against the lips, serious, usually over pretty quick, only one or two and then it would be good-bye till next time. He never even seemed to want me to kiss him back. But Jackson's tongue felt like it was checking every bit of my mouth for hidden bits of waffle and cream.

Suddenly Jackson stopped kissing, and he got a serious expression on his face. "What would you do with your life if you could do anything?" he asked.

"I don't know," I replied. What I thought was, I'd keep kissing you. But I could tell that he wanted a thoughtful kind of answer. So I wiped my mouth and said, "I'd have a farmhouse, maybe some animals, like a horse and a dog. I'd have children, too, and I would teach them important things, like how to garden, and how to live by the golden rule, and how to ride horses, too."

"How are you going to get that stuff?" he asked, and I shrugged. "Do you have plans?" Jackson asked.

"No," I said, "not really, not yet. Do you?"

"You bet I got plans. I got great plans," Jackson said, and he was going to let me in on them. There were things he wanted out of life. Things he wanted to do. He was going to buy him a cheap piece of land back here in the hills, and have a little homestead, live a simple life, and make a huge profit from an amazing cash crop.

"An amazing cash crop?" I asked. "Tobacco?"

"Nope. Better. Just come with me," Jackson said. He led me up to the horse stalls, where he'd been working cleaning up after the prize Belgian pulling horses, the cutting ponies and the 4-H lambs, past the shaggy goats and fancy long-hair rabbits, and the pink-and-black piglets grunting and sucking at their mother. He waved friendly-like to the few farmers and the livestock owners that were bedding their animals down for the night. "What do you see here?" he asked me. One of those mares we'd passed was Chance, the mare that Alan Ray had got off of Lux Cranfield. I knew Alan Ray'd brought her down here; I'd heard that Alan Ray was going to ride her in the barrel racing on Saturday afternoon. I didn't mention Alan Ray or the horses, instead I looked around and my eyes caught the hog pen.

"I don't know," I said, "I think it's some kind of registered sow."

"No, silly," Jackson said. "I mean all over here, this whole barn." I shrugged. I mean I knew the answer, I thought. At least I knew that there was some pretty expensive livestock in this barn. And I was starting to feel nervous now, like Alan Ray might show up any time to feed and water his precious Chance. I mean, I was starting to like Jackson Childs pretty well, but I had two good years built up on Alan Ray, and one guy doesn't just wipe another guy out of your mind that quickly. But then again, Jackson was not your average guy.

"No, no," Jackson said. "You don't get it, do you? Not these animals. I'm talking about all the shit. All these animals crapping their little hearts out, chowing down on all this good hay and feed. I'd just bet you that people might even pay me to haul away all that shit."

I was stumped. What the heck for, I wondered. But I didn't have to wonder for very long. He could hardly wait to tell me. Back at the end of the livestock shed was his motorcycle, Jackson said, and locked into the saddlebags was a coffee can full of the best pot seeds from the world over, Hawaii, Turkey, Mexico, Jamaica, even India. His plan was that he would clean out stalls, all the hog pens and horse stalls in the county, even come back each year just to clean out the stalls. He'd figure out any way he could to get truckloads of shit, and make all that shit into new dirt. "Have me some great big compost piles, and let Mother Nature do the work," he said. And then with that soil he'd grow the best reefer in the state. He could sell composted topsoil as his cover, meanwhile sell primo reefer to all his college friends in Baltimore, who paid top dollar, thousands of dollars a pound. "We'll be rich, girl, rolling in dough, before one year is out."

And I looked down the long livestock barn, at all those animals, each of them just chewing away, and I thought about thousands of dollars, and I didn't doubt him for a second.

WE SET out for home on Jackson's bike, and the summer storm was finally beginning to look as if it meant business. There was lightning in every direction, but so far there wasn't much wind, and the tree leaves hadn't started to turn over yet. Sometimes we'd hear a real loud clap of thunder, and once Jackson turned off the motor of his bike to listen to where the storm was coming from. "Where to, girl?" he asked me, and I thought, we could actually go anywhere. We could drive around the country, from Texas to Florida to Alaska together. I could send everyone postcards of state capitals. And so I said, "I don't want to ever go back again. Let's go out to your tent. Let's sleep outside tonight."

And the storm broke as we rounded the last hill before his campsite, and it was glorious to watch from Jackson's pup tent as the lightning split the air over all that water in the reservoir, and each time the world flashed brighter than daytime. And we didn't sleep a wink that night, and by the morning, sitting awake, watching the sky go from pitch black and full of stars, to a rosy haze, with just the morning star Venus shining in the east, I was sure I wanted to marry Jackson Childs instead of Alan Ray.

JACKSON WOKE up with a smile on his face and eggs and sausage gravy on his mind. As soon as we made it to town to get us some breakfast, a squad car pulled up to the Biscuit World and the two deputies, Forrest and Lamarr, arrested me and Jackson. I heard later that Alan Ray had stopped by my house looking to take me to the fair, and when he heard that I was at Coral Hine's, he went there. I sure was surprised to hear that. He must have really wanted to see me. Then he went back to my dad, who went to the town police. They'd looked for us all night.

When the law found us, at first they were going to get Jackson for kidnapping a minor, though I wasn't kidnapped and wasn't a minor. Then they were going to get us for illegal camping, and that wasn't any worse than a ticket, but when they searched his stuff they found his coffee can. It was a stroke of dumb luck, but they really had something to haul us away for.

"Don't you worry about nothing, my sweet little missy," said Jackson Childs, looking worrieder than I ever seen him. "My daddy's got a lot of pull in this state," he said right before they took me off to the woman's detention area, and then I could hear him say to Deputy Forrest, "If you pigs fuck with my bike, you're all going down."

After two days and nights in jail, Alan Ray came in to visit me and proposed marriage, telling me how it had come to him that it was all his fault that I went off with a lowlife like Jackson Childs, and that if only he'd've spoke his mind earlier and declared his intentions to me, this thing would never have happened. He looked like his eyes were brimming over, and he smelled like he about took a bath in beer, his face as red as his hair, standing outside the bars, reaching his hand inside to hold my hand, and not letting go for the longest time. He must have spoke his mind to my parents, too, because him and them had my whole marriage planned out before I knew what happened. And what could I say but "Yes, I do."

Jackson Childs's dad came to bail him out. The deputies said he was a famous doctor from Baltimore. I was still in jail, waiting for my pap to get the bond approved on his house. I was hoping Jackson would have to come back for trial, but from what everyone told us, even though we both had charges, it would be hard to make them stick on me, and hard to prove that Jackson was going to sell the coffee can of seeds. After two days, Deputy Forrest said that all the charges would be dropped against me, that Dad did not need to put his house up for bond after all. I heard the charges would be reduced to a five-hundred-dollar fine against Jackson, since he owned up and said they were his seeds.

The bad part was the wedding, like I said, which had no church or organ music, no matching bridesmaids in lilac. My mother said she didn't want the day turning into a three-ring circus, a chance for all the nosy biddies in the church to attend, acting happy or friendly and meanwhile saying, "I told you so" about any number of things. Like Mom said, the ink was barely dry on the first piece of news.

So we had a short and sweet courthouse wedding the day they let me out of jail, Deputy Forrest standing by to keep the peace. Then we all went back home. Dessie baked an applesauce cake, Coral Hine was there, and Lux who stood up for Alan Ray at our wedding, and Alan Ray's parents were in from Moundsville, and his aging uncle Herman, who seemed to have a pretty good time talking to my aunt Nelda about the time they ran the scrap drive during World War II. After supper, four of Alan Ray's guard buddies from Moundsville showed up with a case of beer in the back of their pickup. They called us out of the house and stood beside the barn, shirtless, with polky-dot beach towels draped around their waists like skirts while they sang "Stand by Your Man."

Alan Ray and I drove back to his little apartment in downtown Fairchance. It was in an attic of an old house, with three floors of stairs to get up there and a view of the downtown buildings lit up all night, including the Washington Cafe, Sutton Drugs with the loafers' bench, and wouldn't you know it, the jailhouse, those little windows on the second floor, all that cinder block and black steel bars. Alan Ray took the day off work so we could sleep in together. And my only regret, though I love Alan Ray dearly, and though he has put me back on the straight and narrow, and I swear I'll never stray, is that the last I ever saw of Jackson Childs was from behind those bars of my little jailhouse window as he loaded the pieces of his Yamaha, tailpipes to motor, sunburst paint job gas tank, handlebars, chrome sissy bar, all of it, into a U-Haul-It with Maryland plates, and that I never got to kiss him good-bye.

SIX

THE GOSHEN ROAD (1971–75)

What Love Is

My mother used to say I was so hardheaded that no one could tell me anything. It was her daily declaration. When she got herself worked up, she would cry out to the Lord above that there wasn't a human being alive that could save me from myself, it was up to Him and Him alone to do something with me. Dad said things like, "For the love of Pete, Dessie, if it ain't broke, why the hell are you trying to fix it?" But me and him had an understanding about these things, and especially if I got him alone, he'd give his big old head a shake and agree with me that experience was the best teacher. If I look back, I can say that although I was raised up right, whatever choices I made were the ones I wanted to make. I do not blame either of them in the least for how things turned out when we moved to the head of the hollow, up on the Goshen Road.

I never paid my mother any mind, not even as a child. I must've been born that way. I did know that she meant the best for us girls, that she never wanted to see us work too hard or struggle in life. Growing up, she told us girls to marry a fellow with his mind set on a profession, or one who came from good stock, and that if we did, we would never have to lift a finger. There was something so irksome about the way she looked at life, I'd as soon stop up my ears than listen to Mom's version of happily ever after. She was by my side, with her loving and watchful care, with her dreams, but she never realized that all the while I was already struggling. I was struggling against her motherly goals for my life of idleness and ease. I wanted to earn my keep in this world, work hard as I needed to, to see the results of my work and to be proud of them.

Through the spring of my junior year in high school, my mother prayed that God would lead Jerry Higgs to propose. I heard her morning and evening, adding that plan to the sad, sweet list of bedridden relatives and community members she prayed for. Praise God, if He was listening, He did not show His will in that regard. That prospect filled me with dread. Jerry Higgs did not impress me. To spare my mother distress, I pretended to like talking to him, but whenever I said anything, it didn't feel like me talking, the real me. Every word that came out of my mouth felt pitiful, like a script from a TV show or phony words from some book written fifty years ago for only girls to read. It did not make a bit of difference what I said to Jerry Higgs anyway, I barely got a word in edgewise.

One afternoon before I started going with Lux, Jerry followed me to the bus line and asked if he could drive me home. He had a gold Chevy Nova that his daddy, Jerry Sr., a hotshot at Consolidation Coal, had bought him for Christmas. His mother was my math teacher, and it entered my mind that things could get uncomfortable in class if I refused to take a ride from her son. I also knew my mother would want me to. Jerry revved the engine, popped the clutch, and the wheels of the car spun mud and gravel all over the school parking lot. I swear he thought he was Steve McQueen, speeding around corners, never paying attention to any of the road signs that showed speed limits or twisty roads up ahead. All the while he ran his jaw about how he was headed to West Virginia University and planned to go on to medical school. Seemed like he never cared to hear what I had to say back.

Halfway home, Jerry stopped at a pull-off on the top of Peckinpaw Ridge and began to slide himself over to my side of the front seat. I inched away until I was crammed against the door handle on my side of the car. He acted like I should let him put his pudgy roamin' hands up my skirt because someday he would be a medical doctor, and because he had such a shiny new Chevy to drive around in. His breath smelled sour like overripe onions. Worst of all was this blank, greedy look in his eyes that put me in mind of a boar hog, ready to gobble down his evening feed before he even checked to see what was set out before him. I crossed my arms over my chest, and my legs clamped themselves together. Then I said, "Take me home right now, Dr. Higgs, or I will walk and get there just fine on my own." Those were the last words I ever said to him, but I did not only blame Jerry Higgs. I blamed myself, too. The time for make-believe was over.

I married the man I wanted to marry. There was just something about Lux, and I knew it from the time we were kids on the ballfield. Nothing held him back, not losing an eye in the accident, not wearing an eyepatch. I longed to be close to him before I even knew what that meant, or what longing was all about. I loved the man he turned into—a hardworking hilljack of a guy, smelling like Copenhagen snuff, chain oil, and wood smoke, skin tasting like salt, long arms as wiry as hackberry limbs, a man just as hardheaded as me. I must have shattered my mother's dreams, or maybe gave her more things to pray about. Lucky for me, I could tell that Dad was on my side.

Moving up the Goshen Road was an adventure. It was our adventure. We were overrun with the place, the joys of it, the work of it. If we didn't try, if we never tried to take that chance, who would we be and what would we know about life, or about ourselves?

Here's what I mean when I talk about how it was for me and Lux.

I remember back before we were married, when Lux and I first started going together. This was maybe a couple of months after his stitches came out, on one of those hot, steamy summer afternoons. He pulled his Jeep up to the house right after he got off work. "Let's go for a ride," he said. "We can cool off from this heat. You might want a towel."

We rolled up to a pull-off near the dam, where the local kids always liked to swim. It turned out he had something else in mind. He led the way along a footpath through the woods above the dam to a cool, shaded break in the trees, just beside a small waterfall on Buffalo Creek. It was me and him, standing on a rocky ledge, must've been ten feet above the creek, looking down onto a flowing rush of cold water, and that rushing water had carved out a deep, wide pool—a perfect, private swimming spot.

Lux said, "OK. You're going to see something, and it ain't going to be pretty." He stripped off his shirt. Then he stripped off his eye-patch. I did not know what to look at first. His face, chin, and throat and his long arms were tanned dark ruddy brown, but his slim, lean chest was white as a pillowcase, speckled with a few black hairs around the base of his brown neck and under his arms. OK, that did look kind of funny. But his left eye, under the patch—the stitches had closed into scars around the eye, and his eye was sewed halfway shut. Lines of red shot out toward his temple from around his eyelid as if some great wolf had clawed at his face. "It'll do," I answered, as I could tell he wanted me to say something, but all the while thinking that it might not be pretty, but it was real, and real was better than pretty.

"OK, then," he said, nodding. "You ready?" Then he turned his back, scrambled from branch to branch up a nearby pine tree, reached for a thick braided rope that someone had hung over a branch about twenty feet above us, then worked his way down the rope, arm over arm, toward me, until he stood beside me on the rocky ledge, a foot or two away from the rushing waterfall.

Then he stripped off his pants, stood in his boxers, and said, "Catch the rope when I swing it back to you, and do what I do." I watched his arms grip the rope just above a great knot at the base, saw his legs skip backward a few steps, then he launched and swung his body way out, releasing, arcing out into the deep water below the rocks, hitting the water with a splash, coming back to the surface with a big old grin. On its own, the rope came right back to me, exactly where I was standing. I reached out and caught it. I looked at the water below. Then it was up to me, in my shorts and T-shirt. I looked down there at him, paddling backward, making room for me to land in the deepest spot.

I'd never before clenched anything as hard as I held on to that rope. I hung on as high as I could, my arms trembling with the grip. I stepped backward, still hanging on, then ran forward, pushing out over the rocky ledge, gripping tighter now. I held onto the rope until my body was all the way out over the water and starting to swing back, all of a sudden knowing that I had better let go.

Then I let the rope go. It was just me, out over flat rocks on the bank of the stream, the feeling of flying, knowing that if I did not get it right, I'd know soon enough, those rocks looked closer than I expected. All the way down, my legs stretched out below me, the rope swung loose above. I forced my legs to swing out, to hit the deepest spot of the swimming hole. The water was warm at first, then cold, cold and deep. I held my breath, hit the cool, sandy bottom with my toes and pushed off. My head rose up out of the water. I opened my eyes and saw Lux paddling over with his broad smile. "Ain't that something," he said.

It was everything. It was the whole world. It was all I ever needed.

I never wanted to hear that girls did not do these things. I never wanted to sit on the sidelines and watch. How do you know when to let go of the rope? You know that if you hit the rocks, you could break bones. You know that if you hit the muddy spots on the edge, you have to get back up, wash the muck off your legs, and then you will have to climb back up to that ledge and do it again, and do it right this time. Or you can grab the rope, swing out with all your strength, shoot for the sky, and when that thick piece of rope arcs all the way, drop into the deep, and there you go.

That is the secret that people who sit around and watch others do not know anything about. I know that I have been lucky sometimes, unlucky other times, and the Lord might have had something to do with that, although He works in mysterious ways and His lessons are not always clear. Don't tell me you love me so much you do not want me to jump. Show me what to do and give me the rope.

The Goshen Road

My mother never wanted me and Lux to move up the hollow. The road scared the daylights out of her. My dad might have had something to say about it, but he kept it to himself, as he never wanted to get between me and Lux once we were wed. Lux said it was really the road's fault that we had to leave our land and our dreams behind and move back down to Dad's. Though I didn't agree entirely, I came to see his point.

That rocky, rutted, backcountry dirt road, the Goshen Road, was twisty, steep, and narrow, with Barker Mountain rising up on the north side of the road, and a dark, deep-set gulley below on the southern side. It was a mile and a half drive uphill to where we would build our cabin, and I knew every inch of the way between Dad's farmhouse and our property line.

For the first quarter mile, we had to splash the Jeep through the creek and climb steep jagged layers of shale rock. This was a test on the best of days. The road flattened out, then rose steeply again, then flattened out at Barker's and finally rose once more, following the Goshen Creek until it arrived at our parcel of land at the head of the hollow, the end of the line. In the winter we could hear layers of ice crunching underneath us from frozen mud in the rutted tire tracks. Through the road, I could feel the living cycle of the earth, freeze and thaw, damp and dry.

Late winter, coming onto spring, the creek was as high as the wheel wells, the water flooded down the rocks in the daytime, but at night that water froze in sheets. To get out of the hollow, we had to slide the Jeep down those sheets of ice and pray the road was banked correctly. I never mentioned that to my mother, trying to spare her the grief, I suppose, or maybe not wanting to add to her doubt about our choices.

Some winter days, coming back from town, just before heading back up the hollow, we made a stop at Dad's to give Lux a chance to set chains on the tires. We could visit for a spell, let Mom spoil the kids with hot cocoa or milk and cookies, then off we went, winding out low gear, grinding through the snow like an army on the move. In a hard rain or a snow-melt, water overflowed the ditches on the up-hill side, flooded down the tire ruts into the hardscrabble in torrents, and the cliff face turned into a waterfall. Come summer, the road was drier but narrower, as wide as a tractor path, briars and low tree branches scraped at the doors of the Jeep. One of us had the brilliant thought that we lived on a one-way street just like in town, but the one-way arrow was pointing whichever way we happened to be traveling at the time.

For three years Lux drove, I held my breath and clutched Lissy, Ronnie, and eventually Little Lux, and thought about how we did it before, so we could do it again. If we'd have broken down or gotten stuck by sliding backward into a snowbank, we would've had to hike clear back to the bottom to get Dad or Alan Ray to help winch us out of there. It would not be the end of the world, I told myself. It would all work out, I thought. Get tough, I told myself, get real. People faced a lot harder in days gone by, when this land was first settled using mules and horses. Look life in the face, I thought.

I thought of this road like I thought about all of life. Running away from a problem does not make it go away; a person is only going to have to face that problem again some time, in some other way. I don't know why I knew this, I just did.

NO ONE else lived on the Goshen Road between our land and Dad's place when we began building, though two families had lived there in recent memory, Barkers and Smiths. Decades earlier, the Smith family farmhouse had stood on what would become our house site. Old-timers said it was as pretty a place as they had ever seen, with a pond full of bass and bluegill, pasture, gardens and fruit trees. Wooded hillsides rose up in a ring around our meadow. Dad said the apple orchard came right from Johnny Appleseed himself.

The Barkers still held onto a parcel of land halfway between Dad's and ours. It used to be their family homestead, but all that remained by the time we bought our land was a caved-in tar-paper shack and an outhouse behind it. Sometime after the Second World War, the Smiths sold their ninety-acre farm to the Barker sisters, although they retained access to the Smith family cemetery. The Barker sisters bought the land, then sold the Smith farmhouse right off its stone foundation. The story goes that the buyers set the floor joists of the farmhouse on rails, loaded it onto a flatbed, and hauled it to town. It stands to this day near the post office in Fairchance. After that, the Barker sisters sold off all the prime hardwood timber and locust trees to A-1 lumber. Finally they let the Smith parcel go to the county for back taxes. Then they moved on.

By the late 1950s all that remained up at the head of the Goshen Road was an overgrown field, a half-caved-in cellar pit made of hand-hewn stones that had been the foundation of the Smith farmhouse, and an old cistern-type well with a rusty pipe that stuck out of the ground. At some point the county abandoned all road maintenance. The Goshen Road became an "orphan road." Anyone who owned property had a right of way, but it was not worth the cost to the county for upkeep.

Dad grabbed up the ninety-seven-acre Smith property as soon as he saw the notices in the *Telegram*. Even though it wasn't worth much, once it was his he could hold it or sell it, and if he sold it he'd be the one to decide who lived up the road from him and Mom. He was all smiles when Lux asked him to sell it to us on a land contract. Dad said he was so pleased to keep it in the family that he would have given it to us. Lux insisted he pay, and they worked it all out. Dad did not ask for a down payment. Just a smile, a handshake, and a pat on the back, and it was ours.

FROM THE start, Lux and I used to ride horses up there and scout the property, talking about where to put the chicken house, the corral, the gardens, the tack shed, and, of course, our little cabin that Lux talked nonstop about and would build himself. At those moments, joy flooded through his words into me with an open sense of possibility and wonder. It was like we were the painters and saw this wide arc of fields and wooded hills as our canvas: this field with a barn or a chicken house, that hillside cleared and fenced and turned into pasture, this spring that already flowed with clear water should be fine for Dakota. The orchard was overgrown but still bearing bushels of fruit, and the dark, steep trails led into the lush shade of the deep woods, where turkeys called in the spring. We'd crest the last hill and cross onto our land, and the wide world would open up in shades of green. Our horses trotted through waist-high wild oats and clover, crows called out a welcome. We'd canter into the apple orchard, and I thought that this must really be paradise, this gift—to have a real chance to shape our lives and the lives of our children.

But it wasn't until we began to move up there that it struck me how little I knew about how to live way back in the woods. Oh, Mother, dare I say it? You might have been just a little bit correct there. That first year, once Lux drove off to work, I didn't have any way to get out of that hollow other than hiking out with a child under each arm. Lux eventually bartered his spare western saddle to his uncle Ron for an old four-wheel-drive Bronco with no reverse gear and the hubs permanently locked in. It took guts and sheer will, but I learned to drive that ornery son of a bitch, winding out first gear as I tried to get it up the hill, or riding the brakes all the way down between our place and Dad's. I was the first female in our family to drive a car, and I wore that like a medal.

Dad gave me the thumbs-up whenever he saw me, but if Mom was impressed, she did not show it. She always found something else to point out, some other aspect of my life that caused her the heartburn. There were things I knew better than to mention, not to Mom or to Billie, who was known to spread a rumor or two in her time. For instance, though I had kids and critters to watch over, and there was always something to do, I was lonely sometimes up there, with Lux at work all day, and for the most part no visitors. I didn't mention it because after all what good would it have done to bring up the subject or cause Mom more worry? It's just that I didn't quite expect how different things would be, with no vehicles passing by, ever.

Billie came up, not that she would hoof it, but if Alan Ray was off work and he felt like taking a walk in the woods, he'd drive her up. Mom and Dad's Lincoln would have bottomed out in the ruts, so they didn't risk it. Truthfully, there weren't many folks wanting to risk that road, even in the best weather.

Once a year a family of Jehovah's Witnesses made it up, in a spanking new four-wheel-drive Jeep Wagoneer with off-road tires. They must've known what they were in store for, going in and out of these hollows. Two families at a time would drive up to our little cabin, the boys dressed in little business suits and the girls in little matching pinafores, like a little flock of chicks circling a mother hen. My front walk was usually so muddy I was embarrassed to have company, but I could hear a vehicle coming, then a second, then slowing down when the road got steep, the rumbling engines getting louder.

I was actually sort of glad to see them. I'd take their *Watchtower* magazine and offer them whatever cookies or cake I had baked and some tea or instant coffee; after all, they were doing the Lord's work. But I wouldn't ever see things their way, as I tried to tell them, and neither would anyone in my family. While my Lissy and Ronnie had their crayons and toys all over the floor, their quiet little ones stood around in their Sunday best, raised so strict in that Witness faith. It seemed like they would have to break with their own parents if they wanted to play on the floor with dolls or toy trucks. I felt a little sad for the children. Maybe after they drove down out the hollow, those folks felt sorry for me and mine. They look at our practices as sinful, but I believe people ought to worship God in acts and deeds and with a joyful noise. People ought to sing out their love for the Lord, to shout it out, or speak in tongues if the Spirit calls. Some of that comes from how I was raised, but some of it comes from deep within me and was not something I heard in a church pew. I believe in moving if the Holy Spirit calls you to move, and I believe in signs and wonders that come down to us from above. They are there for anyone.

This Dream of Witches

I remember when the Lord first sent me a sign that we shouldn't be moving up on the Goshen Road. It gave me the shivers, like a cold hand gripped me in the belly, like something deep in my gut already knew what my dream was going to tell me. I knew. I had this feeling, like the past and the future are all the same thing, like we sense what will be, what the Lord wants for us, and it's no different than if it's already happened.

On the last three nights of August in 1971, right around the time that Lux hauled the first load of lumber up the hollow to set the corners for our first building, which would soon be a little toolshed for Lux and a little chicken house for me to keep some laying and brooding hens, I dreamed the same dream.

The dream was so clear I could watch myself in it. I was standing in our field at sundown. Lux hadn't mowed yet, so flowering stalks of queen of the meadow and Joe-Pye weed were almost as tall as me. The light- and dark-purple flower clusters swayed slowly back and forth in the breeze like bridesmaids, bowing left to right. In the dream, I couldn't quite see the sunset from where I stood. The row of round apple trees still heavy with leaves and fruit was between me and the pink-and-orange sky. It was right before it starts getting dark, when the whole sky brightens in the last rays of the sun. The field was almost glowing, the light seemed to settle just above the tree line. Then two wrinkled-up, chubby witches formed themselves from the shadows cast by the trees and slowly circled on their flying broomsticks, around and around in the swirling air.

I watched, and I saw myself. I stared like a child at a carnival watching a ride spin. The broom riders looked like the Barker sisters, or what I remembered them looking like. They were all in black, as witches are, but with tight black stretchy pants on, and black capes and hats, with stringy black hair, bad skin, and crooked front teeth. As I watched, I wondered how they stayed up on the broomsticks. They were large people, all of the Barkers. I knew better than to laugh at this sight, as something solemn and unnatural seemed about to happen, a ceremony, or a ritual that I was only just getting a glimpse of, but something that had been done many times before. They saw me, too. They saw me watching them, and they sort of flaunted themselves in a trashy way, laughing at me, circling in the shimmering air, and chanting loud enough for me to hear. "Go away, go away, go away. This place is not your place, this here is our place."

"Who are you? Who are you?" I asked them, in my dream. But they refused to answer, though they knew I was speaking right to them. Lord God up in Heaven! If that didn't beat all, I thought to myself. But I remembered something about the Barker sisters just then. Their house had been a little ways down the hollow, not on this exact place at all; still, they just appeared, swirling up out of the field. I watched them circling and taunting until it became too dark, until the very last ray of sunlight turned to a single spot of ruby fire in their midst.

The first time I had the dream, I was spooked. After the second night, I know I called out in my sleep, "Who are you? Who are you?" Then Lux woke next to me and held me, shaking, to his chest. I was ready to tell Lux that we should reconsider, maybe hold off on starting our little chicken house, but something kept me back from telling the dream to him. I pondered on telling Mom, but I could already guess her response. This was just one more thing that I wanted to puzzle out for myself. I thought about it all day, turning it back and forth in my brain.

After the third night of the same dream, I got to thinking I was just replaying some fearful childhood nursery rhyme in my head, a tale Mom might have told me about witches in the woods. I told myself that we should take ahold of our destiny as a family, and that living people are way more powerful than ghosts and dreams. Just maybe it was up to us to show those Barkers that they could not keep what they never had. So I kept my mouth shut and tried to push that dream into the background, under the surface of my mind. But it smoldered on, a little flame that wouldn't quite snuff out.

The Barkers of Barker Mountain

Over the years the Barkers were a subject of conversation in the family. Until I was about five or six they still lived up the Goshen Road, and the sisters and Wade would drive out of the hollow in a rusted-out, faded, two-tone gold-and-cream Ford Fairlane sedan. Dad would go to the window and watch to see if they could make it safely across the creek and up to the blacktop. Mom would say, "There go the big, bad Barkers." I did not ever ask why she said that, but it seemed like there was just an unfriendly air about them.

The Barker sisters were born and raised on the Goshen Road. They never married, they lived in the small tar-paper-covered cabin, halfway up the hollow between our place and Dad's. Which one had that boy, Wade Barker, I can't recall. The two sisters and Wade stayed on the Goshen Road until their old shack of a house began to fall apart. That was the last anyone saw of them, until about five years later. Wade came back for about a year, a grown man, living in that cabin off some kind of disability from a steelyard accident and the money the sisters had made by selling the Smith house and all the hardwood timber. He moved away again when I was about eight or nine, which was about the same time Dad picked up the Smith property at that county tax sale.

Wade's cabin, what was left of it, set against the back of their narrow field, just before the last steep rise of the road that led to our property line. Some of the roof, most of the walls, and a caved-in front porch still stood, and behind it a little shed and outhouse, but parts of the roof had slumped down flat on top of the ceiling. Window glass, handrails, a wringer-washer, and an old dog box were strewn out front; half-buried pieces of crocks, slop buckets, rusty cast-iron skillets, tree limbs, and scrap lumber lay in the yard. Once, riding past on horseback, Lux and I looked through the busted-out windows of the house to where cobwebbed bed frames and a dresser were piled in one corner that seemed to keep dry. Lux said we ought to check to see if anything looked useful, but I wouldn't have us touch any of that Barker stuff. I've heard folks out this way scout these old places to see what they could use or trade. Lux saw the waste of it. Tools and crocks should be used, he would say, but I felt that every old farm tool carries a story, that we should allow the rightful owners to reclaim what is theirs. Abandoned places are common in these woods, but they are a piece of somebody's life and family story, beauty and sorrow mixed together.

They say bad things happen in threes, and I put the three dreams mostly out of my head, hoping that the past would eventually bury the past. We had one sign of good luck in an odd way; we got lots of help building our house that fall. The A-1 mill had temporarily shut down while the miners in the central part of the state were on strike. Lux was home, and Alan Ray and some loggers came around every day. By the end of a month they had the first part of our cabin built. It bothered me that the spot Lux chose for our house site was square in the middle of that field where I'd seen those witches circle, but Lux wanted to center the house over the old well to keep our water pipes from freezing.

When is the time right to listen to these hints and signs? Where are the ones who say they've been here before, who tell us the meaning of these things, the dreams and intuitions that come seeping into our brains from who knows where? And if they flat out spoke to us, would we listen?

House and Home

Though it seemed like it took forever to get our whole house built, it suited us in the way it went together. We planned that we would build it in two parts, the first part, a two-story section, with a little front porch, a kitchen, mudroom, and living room downstairs and two small bedrooms upstairs. We bought a Warm Morning wood stove and ran the stovepipe up through the second floor for extra heat. As a gift, Dad had the electric company set poles and run power. Mom insisted we have a phone, and we agreed it was a good idea. Me and Lux had a laugh about that, as we knew that most of the phone calls would be from her. We bought an old wagon wheel at a junk store, and Lux wired that for a living room ceiling light.

Everything that we needed seemed to come to us at the right time, like there was bounty in every direction, although we knew that our final house would never be the kind of place that my well-meaning mother had envisioned for me to live in. We used green milled poplar from A-1 for the framing and beams and more poplar planks for a board-and-batten-style siding, and set the whole house up on used telephone poles that Dad got us from Pennzoil. We knew we would be adding on to the back, so we left that unfinished, and just stapled up tar paper. That was sort of an eyesore, especially as we walked out to the outhouse, but so what? It was our eyesore, perfect in its own way because it was waterproof, snug, and held out a promise for the future.

For the first two weeks in September, after the corners were staked out and the house was square, all the men did was dig postholes. Every few feet another post was set into the ground. Then they built from the floor up, first a platform four feet high in the air, like a landing pad for aliens stuck out in a field, then they raised the walls and built trusses, then a scaffold to start nailing on the roof.

In October, after the tin roofing was nailed down and the windows set, Lux and me, Lissy and little Ronnie moved our furniture from the trailer to our home-in-progress. It sunk in that we actually had a place of our own when Mom and Dad and Billie and Alan Ray came up, and all of us sat around our living room one Sunday afternoon in late October, warm and cozy from the woodstove, and listened to Curt Gowdy call the game as the Pirates beat the Orioles and won the 1971 World Series. Dad bet Lux that Clemente would be the MVP, Lux said it would be the pitcher, Steve Blass. I recall that Lux took Dad's Lincoln to the carwash the next day.

I watched to see what Mom thought as she looked around our cabin. I could tell she was starting to set aside some of her misgivings, although she could not resist a suggestion. She went right to the top. After the World Series, as soon as she returned home, she called up to the house and made me hand the phone over to Lux. I watched while Lux nodded his head and said, "Yes, ma'am. I will, ma'am. Don't worry." The next thing I knew, he built a little gate that circled the wood stove to protect Lissy and Ronnie from accidentally bumping into the hot cast iron of the woodstove. Things like that went a long way to show Mom that my choice in a mate was not entirely wrongheaded.

THE SECOND part of our cabin, which took more than a year to get started on, would eventually have the indoor bathroom, a pantry and laundry room, and upstairs our bedroom, with a view of the sunset looking out over the orchard. Lux surprised me when he announced that he had plans to put a commode in the downstairs bathroom. Mom never did like using the outhouse, and neither did Billie, and they were thrilled to hear it. As Dad said, "Indoor plumbing beats the heck out of three rooms and a path." I swore I would never take a flush toilet for granted again. Only Lux said he would miss the privacy and the view from the little outhouse window, the span of blue sky and wooded ridgetop.

As we were building our home, Lux was still off work, and though there wasn't much money coming in, we had lots to do and the time to do it. Is that some kind of rule of nature? The more money, the less time, and the more time, the less money? I have never known the luxury of too much time and too much money, but I guess I had something to be thankful for, since real trouble starts when a person has neither. I could help when the little ones napped, each task a chance to gain skills, learn what to do and what not to do.

Together Lux and I set posts for Dakota's paddock, built a shed for tack, and suddenly there was a fenced horse yard alongside the winding creek. Lux developed a spring, and we found an old claw-foot bathtub, which looked silly but held running water all the year round for Dakota. For a while Alan Ray and Billie kept Chance there, too.

We did not always have time or money, but we did have friends and family. Lux would head down to the house some Saturday afternoons and fetch the folks, and he and Dad hung drywall in the bedrooms while Mom and I cooked, fixing whatever the men shot along with whatever came out of the garden: squirrel, grouse, venison, rabbit, wild turkey, collards, turnips, tomatoes, sweet potatoes, new potatoes, corn, and beans, canning the leftovers for the winter. We sat on the porch after supper watching families of does and fawns browse the edges of the orchard in the front yard at sunset. Lux used to say if he was patient, he could feed his family year-round from his front door and no game warden would be the wiser.

On rainy days I stapled up insulation inside and hung shelves in the kitchen for plates, pots, and pans. We had a stack of planed poplar boards from the mill, each with their own pattern of sapwood and heartwood that ranged from light tan to yellow to brownish green. Weekends on the way to town for groceries, we hit the garage sales. Lux would not borrow tools from anyone, even Dad, and he scouted for anything he could put to use, from a shovel or a mattock to old chisels and files. I learned to use an axe, a sander, a staple gun, a drill, a tape measure, and a level. I could countersink the head of a screw and putty over the hole. The chainsaw never bothered me, but my hands shook whenever I tried to use a circular saw. I left that for Lux. Our first Christmas, we asked Mom and Dad for Sears Craftsman hammers.

When Alan Ray was off on a rainy day, or if his crew quit early, he'd drive Billie up. Alan Ray would head into the woods, look for ginseng to sell in season, set out some rabbit boxes, and check for turkey or deer sign. He didn't have to look too hard. Some mornings the toms came right into my yard and fanned and strutted for my penned-up turkey hens. By then Lux and his crew were back to work. Billie and I had the house to ourselves to work and gossip about the outside world. With the kids' help, we painted the bedroom walls, then Billie sketched out a red pickup truck on Ronnie's wall and giant purple flowers for Lissy. Sun-soaked afternoons, while Alan Ray was in the woods, Billie and I took the kids for walks to the henhouse to collect eggs, or we played in the sandbox Lux had set up for Ronnie. He had all his Tonka trucks laid out like a miniature road crew on mountains of sand. Ronnie could say "dig and dump" perfectly, but when he tried to say "dump truck" it came out like "dumbfuck." Alan Ray made Ronnie say "dump truck" over and over, wherever we were, and everyone howled except for Mom. Her face blanched white and she shook her head.

Ronnie would make such a mess out of himself, I'd have to draw and heat water and set him into the washtub as soon as he was done playing. At that time we were still using a hand pump for water. We had to save up to buy an electric water pump and water heater, and we had yet to run the water lines. But the place kept warm as winter came on. Even Billie said so, and though she was warmer from being pregnant, she was so thin that she usually was chilled. When it was too wet to be outdoors, Billie set up her portable record player on the kitchen table, and the four of us, Billie, me, Ronnie, and Lissy, pretended we were on Dick Clark's *American Bandstand*. We awarded prizes like homemade pickles to the best dancer, the kids outdoing each other, inventing new dances. Lissy practiced cartwheels; Ronnie hopped in circles until he would fall over face down on the rug. We sang along to "Maggie May" and "Me and You and a Dog Named Boo."

Eventually Alan Ray wore out his welcome. I still can't figure out whether I did something to put the wrong idea into his head, like maybe I laughed once too often at his pitiful dirty jokes. Late fall, one afternoon while the kids were in the house with Billie and I was out splitting firewood to fill the wood box, Alan Ray walked out of the woods, came up behind me and locked his long arms around my arms, and said, "Girl, ain't no one ever taught you the right way to swing an axe?"

I pushed my way clear of his arms, shoved him back with my free hand, and cast a glimpse back toward the house. Neither the kids or Billie could see him or me, as I was behind a corner of the tack shed, but I looked at him square on, saying, "What in the world are you up to, Alan Ray?" He kind of stumbled backward, and I realized that he was flat-out shinnied up, that he'd been hitting a flask that he kept in a back pocket of his jeans. He sort of smiled at me, licked his lips, and blew me a kiss. "Didn't mean nothing, don't you know."

I turned around. It might just be that he was trying to be helpful, but I wasn't so sure about that. Just to show him I knew what I was doing with the axe, I took it up, and swung it as hard as I could into the chopping block, where it lodged itself solidly.

Next thing I knew, he stood right in front of me. "Up to some mischief, I guess," he said, looking at me. He was bare chested; he'd stripped off his T-shirt and army vest. Sex was written all over his face. He walked back a few steps, motioning to me to come back behind the shed with him. "You know you been wanting it," he said. "I just know you been waiting on the right time and place."

"You better keep your hands to yourself, Alan Ray, or Lux is going to come beat the tar out of you, and it won't be pretty. Where in the world did you get the idea that I was that kind of girl?" I asked him, scowling at him as seriously as I could manage.

"All girls are that kind of girl, right time, right place, right man," he said back to me. He rubbed at the bulge in his pants. I tried not to look, stared back up, straight into his bloodshot eyes, trying to shoot him a glare that would settle him down. He was not taking the hint. He held out his hand to try to get me to take hold of it, so he could pull me closer. "C'mon Dessie, you 'n' me, come on. A little bit of fun. No one has to know. I ain't had none for weeks now. Billie ain't interested since she's expecting. All she does is push me away."

I walked back to where Billie could see me from the house, just in case she happened to be standing near a window. I wished Lux would come blasting up the hollow, surprise us, home from work early. But the road looked about the same, just a slip of gravel cutting between the apple trees and heading west, downhill. I thought about what to say next. "Alan Ray, don't come 'round here, acting like that. You ain't my type of man, and you never will be," I said.

"Oh, I get it. Ain't you just like your mom?" he said. "I get it. Go ahead, be a bitch, why don't you? You been fucking with me, leading me on all this while. Well y'ain't any better than anyone else round here, you know."

"That's a load of hogwash and you know it," I said back to him, wondering if I did something wrong, and when I did it, but thinking it could be a trap, too. Like my mom? That gave me pause, but only for a second. "You got the wrong idea," I said. "Or else you don't know nothing at all about me."

I turned my back to him, pulled the chopping block forward, so if he wanted to talk to me he'd have to stand out in the open. Then I took up the axe by the handle and yanked on it, hoping to hell that it would come free of the block. It did. I set a wide, round piece of poplar firewood on the block, thinking all the while, Alan Ray, you are a real snake in the grass, aren't you now? My jaw clenched and my hands shook. I raised the heavy axe and split that round chunk of poplar clean in half, one swing. With each log I set on the chopping block, I took aim for the block below the log, not the log itself, raised the axe again, and watched that blade slice through the poplar like I'd been doing it all my life. Then I set it all into the wheelbarrow. When I looked up, Alan Ray was gone.

I checked to see if he was hanging around, but he had gone to the house and rounded up Billie. All I could see was the tailgate of his red pickup headed down the road. The sun was low in the sky. The cool air helped me breathe, to look at each piece of wood, and think only about the spot on the top of the log where the axe would fall, the spot on the bottom of the log where the axe would wind up as the wood split apart. I could inhale, pick up a log, set it on the block. I could breathe out as the heavy head of the axe fell.

I tried to figure out whether or not I should tell Billie or Lux, Mom or Dad, or keep it to myself. Lux would be ticked off, so ticked off there would be no telling what he'd do or say. I thought about the kids, about how quiet they got when he flew off the handle. Mom would blame the Devil himself for putting wicked impulses into the human heart. Dad, well, much as I wished someone would punch Alan Ray in the nose, I was too old to run to Daddy. But mostly I thought about my sister, wondering if she knew the true nature of the man whose baby she was carrying. Even worse, I wondered if Billie might think I played up to Alan Ray, and that, as he claimed, I'd led him on. It was too much weight to put onto all of their shoulders. I filled the wheelbarrow with as much split firewood as I could, and I headed for the house.

I kept these thoughts to myself, but I saw less of my sweet, beautiful sister that autumn. Alan Ray said he was too busy to make time to drive her up. The kids asked for Auntie Billie, wanted her to bring up her records, sit cross-legged on the floor, and cut out paper dolls, but I told them Uncle Alan Ray was busy and Auntie Billie's legs hurt too much to hoof it, and I helped them find other games to play. I missed her too, like there was a little less sunshine in our day. There are lessons to be learned here, I thought, lessons about what to say and when to say it. Not every problem has an easy solution. For better or for worse, as winter came on, I kept it all under my hat.

The Price of Love

Sometimes the real world drives away dreams, and sometimes it brings them into sharper focus. I might have forgotten all about my dream if it wasn't for seeing so many snakes. Opened the front door one sunny April day and I thought I saw a piece of washer hose just lying on the porch, but as I got closer to pick it up, it turned into a black snake, six foot long if it was an inch. It saw me and started forming a rippling letter S in slow motion before my eyes, slinking toward the edge of the porch, blending in to the dark beneath. All I could think about was how many we'd seen the year before. It was not that I wished it any malice or harm. I just wished it gone.

That was only the beginning. As soon as the ground warmed and trees began to bud out, seemed like snakes crawled out from under every rock outcropping or wild berry bush, especially the first year. It didn't make any difference that Lux mowed the grass around the yard and kept all the stacks of unused lumber away from our outbuildings. At first Lux didn't believe me, because I only saw the snakes during the day while he was off at work. But one summer night when the Jeep rolled up into the yard, a copperhead struck at Lux's work boot as he stepped down. After that, when we'd been out for a trip to town, I didn't let Ronnie and Lissy out of the Jeep without Lux getting out first and walking a circle around the tires for me and the kids. Lux shook his head and called it the Price of love.

I wouldn't let the kids play out in the yard without me, since even nonpoisonous black ratters will bite. And they are stealthy, for the most part, though timber rattlers will warn a person. They will rattle to protect themselves. But copperheads will not. Copperheads will strike anything, and to me that feels like spite. Neighbors of Dad's once had a penned-up 150-pound prize sheepdog with a shaggy coat that got attacked while it slept and died on the way to the vet.

I saw so many copperheads, I began to wonder whether they were real. On the way to feed my little banties, any type of snake could be stretched out along the path in the sun, or under the chicken house trying to figure out how to steal an egg or snatch a baby chick. I never knew when I'd see them, but each time my heart about seized up in my chest.

Hard to say if it was bad spirits, bad luck, or bad planning. The day Lux and his men started digging the postholes for our house, they dug into an old cellar wall from the Smith house site. I learned that there is nothing that snakes like better than a half-buried rock-wall cellar. We did not know it was there, though we had seen some exposed stones, a couple of limestone corners that broke through the ground near the base of our house.

I knew it wasn't rational, but I began to think that the snakes were those Barker sisters' fault, that we must have unearthed some Barker family crypt. Other things made me wonder, little things, like if a hen was broody but none of her eggs hatched out, or if the potato vines were fine but the potatoes had black rot, I would remember my witch dream. Maybe it was a sign or a prophecy. Maybe this place was not our place.

I fretted so much over snakes that I wouldn't wear open-toed shoes. But Lux didn't fret. He just killed them with whatever was close by: shovel, hoe, or switch. I could never bring myself to kill one, even though on my way to and from anywhere, a snake would stop me dead in my tracks, a two-inch-tall hurdle that was impossible to jump over.

On this matter Mom and I agreed. A mother's duty was to keep her children away from snakes at all times. Thank God the children didn't get bit, is all I can say. I saw how bad snakebite could be for full-grown man when a copperhead struck Wade Barker on his pinkie finger. That was the following year, and I'm getting ahead of myself, but Wade told us he was picking up a flat rock on the ground to fill a deep puddle on the road, and a small copperhead had been coiled underneath. At the time, Mom said, "A snake will charm people till they stand stock still, and then strike them down dead." That was a new one on me. Where in the heck did she get those sayings?

But Wade insisted he got charmed and that's why he froze and couldn't take his hand away. Lux said Wade was probably drunk at the time. He always did move slowly, being overweight and because of his bad hip. Wade limped out of the hollow straight to Dad's, his little finger looking like an angry red egg got stuck onto his dirty scabbed up mitt of a hand. If not for Dad speeding all the way to the emergency room, Wade might've died. It is possible that the Lord spared him for a reason. There's no way to know how to read that kind of sign, though Dad took it upon himself to do the right thing when a man's life hung in the balance; still, Wade moving back onto the Goshen Road was the beginning of our troubles.

AFTER OCTOBER'S hard frost the snakes disappeared. As November came on, I was grateful for the frozen ground, and the way the tall grass had died down on the paths to the paddock and chicken house. Our first Christmas we were snowed in for a week, and we only saw the sun from about 10 a.m. to 2 p.m. The scant light lingered in sort of amber glow on the ridgetop for a few more hours. Lux hunted, following tracks, brought home turkey and rabbit for supper. The kids and I baked gingerbread cookies and made our own books out of construction paper and crayons. We kept the animals watered and kept the fire burning.

Lux managed to drive out to the mill no matter how deep the snow. It piled up on the roof of the tack shed and capped each rail and fencepost. Icicles hung from Dakota's shaggy coat and clinked together as he walked. We trudged a path to the outhouse. With each snowfall, even if it was pitch black outside, Lux would throw his work boots on over his long johns and rush out to shovel, so he could turn the Jeep around. Sometimes, when the snow was too deep to drive back in, Lux would stay overnight with Dad and Mom, and Mom would call us about every hour to make sure things were OK up the hollow. It seemed silly, but I looked forward to hearing the phone ring.

With the January thaw, our little family could drive out of the hollow together. Lux would drop us off to visit Mom and Dad or Billie and baby Bertie and then head to work. Mostly Mom kept her critical comments to herself, but every so often she would tell me how she was praying for us, trying to keep us in the sights of the Lord, hoping that He would protect us and save us. "Yes, Mom," I would say. "Don't worry yourself sick. We are fine," I would say, though what I did not say was that it was kind of nice to have a warm house to pass the time in, even if it meant watching reruns of *Gunsmoke* or *Bonanza* with Dad. Lux would take us back home on his way up the hollow, but I knew that since no one was home all afternoon to keep the stove going, we'd be coming back to a chilly little cabin.

I think that these were the best times for us. I know that one of those snug and cozy winter nights, I realized I was pregnant again. It came over me, like a spell was cast. A sense of joy and peace, a fullness. But like everything in life, things change, and as the saying goes, you don't have to go looking for trouble—trouble will find you.

Wade Barker

Whenever there was a story on the news about a forest fire, Dad told us kids about how during a very dry summer back when Dad first got home from the war, Wade Barker set fire to the woods on the Goshen Road just to see what would happen. When he was growing up, Wade was a big skulking boy about ten years younger than Dad. Wade started the fire with leaves and brush on the edge of the road; then all of a sudden, acres of woods were ablaze. Dad said, "Clouds of smoke and heat reached down to within a few acres of his place. If not for the creek that ran along the road, it might have caught the whole valley on fire." Volunteer fire departments from two townships came with pumpers, and neighbors came with shovels. By the grace of God, they put out the fire and saved the rest of the valley.

Wade denied it to the fire marshal, but later he bragged about it to let everyone know just what kind of dangerous character he could be.

The strange thing was, the Barker homeplace wasn't touched, though fire charred a ring of huge pine trees around their house. Those great, scorched, barren trees still stood after all these years.

That second year, driving in or out of the hollow, I got used to seeing a large black dog limping around, so skinny I even thought about putting out some dog food. I never saw that dog again after Wade Barker came back in the flesh, a little over eighteen months after we moved in. By then, Billie and Alan Ray'd paid us for the trailer, set it up near the barn on the western edge of Dad's land with a little picket fence, and settled in. Lux took the money that Alan Ray gave him and traded in the Jeep for a black Ford four-by-four pickup. Then he hired Edgar Sutton, Dad's friend who drove a dozer for Pennzoil, to widen the road, set culverts, and grade and gravel it. Edgar made the road smoother, and he even cut some ditches alongside the rocky part of the road, so not quite so much water would run down the road and freeze in the winter.

The best thing that Edgar Sutton did was to set a couple of two-foot-tall steel culverts on the steep rise above Barker's, keeping the water from washing down the road in the wettest part of spring when our little creek spilled over its banks as it worked its way down the hill. The worst thing that Edgar did was improve the whole length of the road enough for Wade Barker to be able to move back up on the Goshen Road. Word gets out, it seems, when someone fixes up a road.

Wade Barker was unmarried, unwashed, slow-moving and even slower-talking, and built like a fifty-five-gallon drum with a head stuffed on and a smudged-up Weirton Steel cap, so dirty I couldn't tell what color it used to be, atop that ruddy, scrubby head of his. He said he was in the "haulin' business," and he left it at that. Within a few weeks he had a group of buddies up there, helping themselves to his beer and any other consumables offered by his relief check. Someone came up with the idea that using Barker's beat-up old bald-tire flatbed truck they could haul whatever logs he could buy in the area and sell them to A-1.

In a few short weeks, during the rainy, early spring weather, Wade Barker undid most of the good that Edgar Sutton had done with his dozer and grader. Wade began driving in and out of the hollow with that old rear-wheel-drive flatbed truck. Its back tires slipped and ground in the mud, its engine raced and smoked. Then it would stall out, slide backward on the steep road, and start up and begin to try to climb again, breaking down the road surface and churning up more soft mud between Barker's and Dad's, especially the spots that Edgar Sutton had recently improved.

Lux began driving his Ford pickup down to the lower creek near Dad's yard after work, to shovel loads of rocks and creek gravel onto his truck bed. He stood in the creek, pant legs so full of muck that I couldn't tell where his overalls left off and his work boots began. From that point on, we were always working on that road, Lux mostly, and me, too, when my back wasn't bad from carrying the children. As the weather got nicer we all went with him. Lissy and Ron's heads barely reached the top of the tailgate, but they stood on tiptoes with their tennis shoes in the cool creek water and threw stones onto the truck bed to help their dad. Ronnie picked up crawdads from under the stones and threw them in a bucket for me to boil up, too.

Once the truck bed was filled, Lux'd take the kids to town and buy them a soda at Cleve's. On the return trip, Lux would set the largest stones into the holes on the road and stand in ruts over his ankles, scrape shovelfuls of the creek gravel out of the truck bed, and set it in place with a steel tamping bar. Lux always said that crushed limestone would have been a better way to fill the ruts, but creek gravel was free for the taking.

EVEN THOUGH Wade Barker got over his snakebite, he never again threw a bit of rock onto the Goshen Road. He and his old drinking buddies acted as though they didn't have to. But sometimes, when Wade was heading in or out of the hollow and Lux was standing in the creek with the kids, I could hear Lux get on Wade, just loud enough for all of them to hear. He'd say, "Throw any rocks on the road today, boys? how 'bout you, Wade?" But Wade's fat hairy arm would rest on the open window, the brim of his cap would hide his eyes, and he would just drive on by, his truck smoking and chugging, wheels spinning the creek gravel right out of the tire tracks.

Road work took time, but Lux made that part of his daily chores. Evenings, Lux drove home from the sawmill with his truck bed full of rocks from rock slides off the shale cliffs on CR 57. Weekends, we drove to town for groceries with a shovel and a tamping bar sticking out of the bed. Alan Ray told Lux that he worked harder than the state roads crew. But then again, Alan Ray told that old joke about "What's yellow and blue and sleeps six during the daytime?" and, of course, the answer is "A state roads truck." Alan Ray used to devil Lux about mud splattered up to the windshield of his truck, and he always made a special point to tell Lux to make sure he took off his boots before he came into their trailer, but teasing never seemed to bother Lux that much.

What dug at Lux was Wade Barker. When Wade moved up, he started clearing, probably to keep back the snakes. Soon Wade and his buddies had taken the junk out of the yard, an old wringer washing machine, torn-up couch springs, car parts, old fencing, crocks, anything they couldn't burn, and tossed it all into a little ravine on the side of the Goshen Road, just uphill from Wade's house, right before our parcel of land began. It is possible that Wade also got paid to haul trash and scrap, as more and more junk began to fill up that ravine. Lux watched Wade remove the shingles from the roof of his house, and then add those shingles to the pile.

Whenever he saw Wade, Lux would stop his truck, get out, and tell Wade that all that garbage would slip down the creek one day and clog up the culverts that Edgar had set. In return, Wade said Lux got on his case for no good reason. Wade waved his hands around, said Lux acted like a worried old lady, said that Lux was off his rocker, said that when Lux paid the taxes on his land then Lux could tell him what he could and could not do with it.

The only one who could get anywhere with Wade seemed to be Dad. When Dad talked to Wade, Wade said he had pension money coming, and he was going to really fix the road up. He'd truck in eight tons of limestone at a time, and he'd have Edgar lay a new road over the old one, with larger culverts the whole length, and maybe even build a bridge. "He's a real concerned citizen," Dad said after Wade had left, and then he threw his head back and laughed. Mom told us she prayed that the Lord would keep Wade away from us and guide him to move back to wherever he came from. Mom was one of the most welcoming people I knew, but Mom never invited Wade to set foot into her home.

None of us ever suspected how bad it was going to get.

Soon enough, Dad found out that Wade didn't really have much money coming in, just a very small disability settlement. Lux predicted that Wade and his friends would just drink up whatever money he got. Lux couldn't stand the way Wade's friends stared at me if they were out when we drove past. Only Alan Ray got friendly with Wade. No surprises there. Billie told me Wade and his friends had cases of beer and jugs of moonshine in the old root cellar behind his shack.

By the second winter after Wade moved back, our third full year up there, Lux'd had it with Wade Barker. December and January, as the days turned cold and rainy, Wade moved his hauling operation closer to home. He started timbering his own property. He probably needed the extra beer money. All the real timber had been sold off by Wade's mother and aunt years earlier, so he and his friends cut scrub locust for props for the mines. It was a pretty crummy operation, just Wade and a couple of men and his truck, clear-cutting the hillside above his house and throwing the brush down into the same ravine, on top of all the other junk.

In January the road was frozen, and Wade's flatbed running up and down wasn't too bad, but with a wet snow, or a warming thaw, the road surface softened, and Wade's tires slid, spun, and dug their way up the hill. Wade's pension came and went, and nary a bit of gravel showed up on the road to fill in the ruts he'd made. February was just overly wet and snowy. The wettest days, Alan Ray could not cut timber, so he would show up with Billie and Bertie, leave them with me and the kids, and take off into the woods and end up down at Wade's, shooting the bull, having a couple of beers, coming back to our house late in the afternoon to drive Billie home.

Lux worked inside in the mill, so he had to show up every day. The rocks that Lux laid into the ruts of the road got churned under the mud by Wade's truck. Even with a four-wheel drive, it got more and more difficult to get back home unless the road had frozen the night before. Lux bolted a heavy wooden railroad tie to a steel I-beam and tried to level out the road by dragging that beam behind the Bronco, scraping the soft mud off the hump in the middle to fill in the ruts. But it didn't last. New ruts and puddles appeared, and Lux could not keep up. The rainwater and snowmelt kept running down the tire tracks instead of in the ditches on the side of the road.

Day Full of Holes

Weekdays, about an hour after Lux left for work, I drove the old Bronco out of the hollow to Dad's bridge so Lissy could meet the school bus for preschool. Since the Bronco had holes in the floorboards and didn't have any heat, I kept a woolen blanket so Lissy and the boys could bundle up and keep warm. Some mornings Mom would turn on the porch light for me, so that I'd know she was up, in case I wanted to stop by for coffee. Though I didn't want to hurt her feelings, I rarely stopped. Getting down the road was easy, it was just that I wanted to be sure that the trusty old Bronco could make it back up the hill to get home, since the mud on the road had gotten so deep and slick.

"The hog needs feeding," I'd say, so I didn't hurt her feelings, or, "I'm checking on the chicks." In winter I turned a light on in the henhouse to keep those hens from freezing. Mom used to say I had the only electrified henhouse she ever heard of, but she admitted that

I had the first eggs of the season. When the temperature dropped into the teens and the road froze, I knew I'd be able to get back, so I'd stop and visit with Mom for a spell, and her parting words would always be the same. "May God lead you safely back to my door."

EACH TIME Lux and I passed Barker's on our way back from town, Lux used to say he was going to have to "get serious with old Wade." I never had the guts to ask him what he meant by that, too afraid that he'd do something that would get him thrown in jail, and if that was the case, it would leave me with three kids, up a hollow and on my own. I knew that no one would help us keep the road up. We were too far away from town for zoning laws, and it was not a county school bus route. It was us, and it was Wade Barker, and there was axle-deep mud churning away under our tires, potholes getting deeper and wider each day as we drove in and out.

When it rains in West Virginia, folks have been known to leave the "s" out of "West." On one of those rain-soaked gray afternoons in late winter, on our way home, Lux drove slowly up the hollow, splashing through the water-filled puddles and potholes. Three-quarters of the way up to our house, he eased the truck to the side of the road in front of Wade's yard, and stopped when he saw the lights were on and Wade was outside. It was still getting dark pretty early, and Alan Ray, who was drinking a beer on Wade's porch, later said he could see Lux's headlights over each rise in the road, just the two foggy beams streaming out of the darkness, heading up the hollow, way before he heard the slow grind of the engine or the splash of Lux's tires slipping in the muddy ruts, but by the slow way Lux was driving, he could tell something was up.

From the driver's seat, Lux looked over at Wade's shack, which was half covered in billows of smoke from the woodstove and foggy rain.

Lux turned to me, pulled his cap down on his head, slid his work gloves on, and said, "Might be three, four guys on the porch, might be more. How many do you see?" I wasn't sure how he could tell that. I rolled down the window, blinked back the rain in my eyes, and craned my neck to see Wade's porch. I could not see anything but shadowy forms. Lux stepped out of the Ford, pulled up the collar on his coat, and through the beam of the headlights I only made out his hands in his pockets and his cheekbones. His jaw was set, steam seemed to rise off the brim of his cap. The rain had been pouring down for the third day in a row, and the patches of snow and reddish-brown mud were so slick that Lux's work boots kept getting stuck as he walked up to Wade's porch.

Alan Ray stepped half off the porch and held out his hand to Lux, but Lux walked right over to Wade. I could hear Lux, shouting to be heard above the clatter of the rain on Wade's steel roof, say, "How much will you take for your truck, Barker?"

Wade started mumbling, shuffling his weight back and forth, looking at Alan Ray and at his group of drinking buddies. "I don't really know, mister," said Wade. Wade seemed a bit surprised, but he never was too quick to reply to any question.

"Well, then," Lux said. "By God, I'll give you five hundred bucks and my old Bronco to quit your logging, park that truck of yours, and, tell you what, you say the word, and I'll also give you five thousand to sell me this here piece of land." As I heard this, I wondered how Lux thought he'd make that kind of money, with us still needing a hot water heater and the house still needing flooring in some places. I pushed those thoughts to the back of my mind. What was I thinking? We did not need the flooring as much as we needed the road.

"Five thousand?" Wade said. He took that old cap off and he scratched at the top of his stubby hairline. "You got five thousand?"

"I can pay it on time, a thousand a year for five years." Lux looked around at the men on the porch. One of them began to laugh. Lux took a step forward, closer to the porch.

Alan Ray spoke up. "You boys don't think Lux's good for the money?" That shut them up.

Wade stood there with the rain hammering against the metal roof of the porch, the steamy rotten smell of wet wood smoking out of his chimney. Finally he shook his head. "Look here, mister," he told Lux, "you drive up and down this road every day, same as me. Your pretty little blonde-headed wife drives up and down this road, same as me. You don't get out and say 'Hey.' She don't get out and say 'Hey.'" Wade looked over at his friends as if to say those same men have sat there for years now, and they'll swear to it. "I'm an old man. I may not live five years. But I'm a Barker, I am. This here's Barker Mountain. I'm a Barker."

Lux pulled his A-1 hat down on his head and turned back to the truck. "You simple son of a bitch," I heard him say, over and over again, more to himself. "Where are you going to be when you can't drive that piece of shit flatbed truck of yours in or out the hollow, Mr. Barker of Barker Mountain? You ever think about that?" He didn't look at me. The windshield wipers slapped back and forth. Wade and the rest of them on the porch started laughing, repeating Lux's words. "Ain't you the simple son of a bitch," they called back at Lux, laughing.

Lux climbed back up into the truck, and the engine raced as he hit the gas. I turned around and looked out the window, and saw Wade Barker stumble back to the porch with the men. But Alan Ray held his beer and stood in the rain in the road, like he didn't have the heart to return to Wade's porch while we could see still him.

Lux didn't say anything else. He just revved up the Ford and gunned it. He started up the hill as fast as he could, spinning mud out behind his tires and sliding back and forth, in and out of the ruts that were already on the road. I held onto all three of the children, the baby in my lap, the other two by whatever parts of them I could grab. To me, from the passenger seat, it almost seemed like Lux's pickup wasn't going to make it up that slick hillside, like the Ford might slide sideways into the ditch. For a brief moment, I worried that Lux would have to get all those drunks to push him out if we got stuck. But one of the tires finally grabbed on to something solid, and we got going.

Then the noise of the swollen creek rushing through the culverts and the splatter of the rain drowned out all the other sounds, and we made it back onto our little turnaround spot in front of our house.

I don't know whether it was the sound of the rain, the noise of the creek, or a message, but that night I had one of those witchy dreams again. I dreamed the whole house was bewitched, that it was spinning in circles, like the ground beneath was a whirlpool. I was alone in bed and holding onto both sides of the mattress and trying to figure out what had caused this great spinning. In my dream I looked out the window, and all I could see was black, and then I knew. It was like we were shrunk down, wee little, and house and all, we were inside a great iron cauldron. And the spinning was us, being stirred faster and faster by the giant hands of the sisters. I could hear them laugh, I could hear the rush of the wind, I could hear their smoldering fire as it hissed and popped.

The next morning as the fog broke I could see that it was just barely raining. Lux had left already, and I set some wood into the stove. I could hear a different noise in the yard, and without even thinking about it I knew the narrow Goshen Creek had come up out of its banks in the night. In the icy mist and haze of the morning, I opened the door of our house and saw a different world, a view unlike any I had seen before. The creek had flowed up high enough to surge halfway up our yard, a roaring wake of water, rushing close to the house, almost to our outhouse behind the back steps. It rose halfway up the planks of the chicken house, and all my little setting hens had drowned. The poor girls wouldn't leave their nest boxes. They were so tame they used to eat crumbs out of Lissy's hands.

Lux went out at six as usual, but after he got to the end of our property the road was completely washed away. Each piece of Wade Barker's discarded junk had come sliding down the hill with the rising of the creek. The sheet metal and garbage wound up clogging the large culvert pipes that Edgar Sutton had put in. Once those culverts got crammed full of junk, the water from the creek bed rushed over the top of the culvert pipes, then onto the road, and then up, onto the field beside the house. By morning the creek had cut a new creek bed, through the center of what used to be the road between our place and Barker's, but was now rushing water with chunks of rocks and garbage in its wake. If Lux hadn't stopped the truck at the end of our property, above the flooding creek, he would have totaled the truck.

The strange thing about this was how, after washing out that section of road, the creek rushed back into its proper bed. All the damage happened on the hillside above Barker's house. His yard and his homeplace weren't touched.

Alan Ray must have been watching for Lux to come out of the hollow. When Lux didn't come, Alan Ray drove up the road to see if he could help. Wade and his drinking buddies were not stirring yet, he said, but when he passed Barker's place and started toward ours, there wasn't enough dry ground for him to drive on. Alan Ray parked his Blazer at Barker's and hoofed it through the woods up to our house.

I went to the door when I heard Alan Ray knocking. "Bring a couple of blankets, a couple of shovels, a bottle of whiskey, and meet me at the property line between your place and Barker's," he said.

I settled the two older kids in front of some early morning cartoons, told them to stay in the house, bundled Little Lux into a woolen blanket, and followed Alan Ray's instructions. When I got the Bronco to the brink of our land, I saw Lux, no shirt, no eyepatch, up to his thighs in the freezing churning water, pulling any piece of garbage or scrap metal he could grab hold of out from those two steel culverts so that the water would run through the culverts again and stop gouging out what was left of the road.

"Stay back, Des, keep away from the water," Lux called out to me. I could see him fighting for footing, bracing himself against the edge of a thick piece of cable and some old tires that stuck up out of the water. Alan Ray had stripped his shirt off and jumped in to help. I kept having visions of one of them getting washed into one of those culverts and hemmed in between the junk, winding up under water.

"Do you want a rope?" I called down at them, thinking that maybe if they tied ropes around their waists, it would keep them from getting swept into the deeper water.

"Nah," said Lux. "Just keep them kids away from this mess. Stay back, Des, I mean it."

I stood back, watching for what seemed like hours, there, on the uphill bank, that day at the edge of our field. I could hardly believe my eyes. A raging river had appeared where once there was a little stream. By midmorning the water had begun to recede, and I brought the kids down with me and told them to stay in the Bronco. For once, they listened. I drove that Bronco back and forth to the house and the toolshed for anything that seemed useful: hammers, picks, shovels, axes, hoes, mattocks, pry bars. By lunchtime it had just about stopped raining, and I allowed them to stand behind me and watch. It must have had a strange effect on Lissy. In one hand, she held up a large green umbrella, and her other hand clutched Ronnie's little hand so tightly, it looked like she was scared he would race down to the water and get swept away. The water was so loud I realized I was shouting to her, just to tell her she could put down the umbrella.

Lux worked like I have never before seen a man work, in silence, as if speaking would just cost more energy. I expected him to be furious, that his rage would push me and the kids back up the hill and into the house. I thought I needed to be watchful, wary, to keep from getting him more riled up. But the time for rage was over. Instead, he had a steady, grim expression, as if he had seen this all play out in his mind and had almost expected it to happen. With each piece of roofing, with each busted two-by-four studded with nails, and each hubcap and car axle he dug out and threw downhill for Alan Ray, he did not crack a smile. He was all business, all arms, all legs, all of his body and all of his brain.

Alan Ray stood on the bank, taking whatever piece of garbage Lux tossed at him and piling it in the bed of his pickup. He'd reach his long arms down, pull Lux out of the water, blue and shivering, and wrap him up in a woolen blanket. Forgiveness flooded over me for Alan Ray in a way that I never would have expected. Lux needed Alan Ray at that moment, and like a friend was supposed to do, Alan Ray came through.

Dad had called some friends from Pennzoil, who brought picks and mattocks and chopped away at the rocks and trash and brush from both ends of the culvert pipes. Billie and Mom finally got a ride up from one of Dad's crew, and they stood on one side of the creek as I stood on the other. We just stood and shivered, watched each other, and tried to shout back and forth. At one point I saw Mom sink down onto the passenger seat of the Blazer and weep, but I could not get any closer to console her.

Finally, when Lux had cleared enough of the garbage out of the culvert, and most of the creek water flowed back through the culvert pipe instead of flowing down the road, we could see what the flood-waters had wrought. What once was a graded road full of packed limestone, clay, and creek gravel was now a grooved-out gulley. Small ridges of shale, boulders like stepping-stones, deep gouges of clay and mud, water-filled sinkholes, but not a bit of roadbed remained.

Some of those sinkholes stretched six feet long. Alan Ray said there was one you could've parked a whole VW Beetle in. It took two days more, but Dad, Lux, and the crew from Pennzoil filled in all the holes on the road. Edgar Sutton brought his dump truck, rounded up the roofing, old motors, and the rest of Barker's junk to take to the county dump. Then they busted rocks off the cliffs and picked up boulders from the edge of the creek and cracked them with picks until they filled the gaps in the road. Wade and his friends never showed their faces once.

Finally, Alan Ray was able to drive the A-1 company four-by-four across the new stretch of road. When he reached the top of the two culverts, he stopped. Lux got out and shoveled the last few heavy slate rocks out of the truck bed into a low spot on the surface of the new stretch of road. Then Lux stomped them in with his soaking wet work boots and a tamping bar. It was starting to snow big wet flakes, but by then the creek was down to its usual flow in its old banks. Lux climbed in and Alan Ray drove the quarter mile up to our house. Billie and me carried the kids and followed behind, only stopping at the chicken house to throw out a couple of handfuls of corn for the remaining few banty hens, who must have perched on the top of the henhouse to ride out the flood.

And Yet

After that, every morning when I brought the kids down for school, I didn't care so much about going back. Once Mom asked me, "Shouldn't you be getting back up there now?," but I couldn't answer. I guess I really couldn't think of a good reason. And I could barely bring myself to pass that Barker house. Soon Billie started coming over to Mom's, and we drank instant coffee and watched the game shows and soaps. By the time the little ones woke up from their naps it was time to meet the bigger ones off the bus again.

Sometimes Lux would get home from work early, and then we'd all stay for supper before we headed up the hollow. Dad would come home and kick us out. He said he wanted to have his house back to himself, but the kids liked having their cousin Bertie to play with. We just carried on like one big family.

One warm Saturday in late spring, well after the road had dried out, Dad and Mom and Billie and Alan all drove up the hollow together to our place. Dad would never drive his Lincoln up there, of course, so he and Mom rode up with Alan Ray. When they got here Mom had a camera. She took pictures of the gardens, the toolshed, the chicken house, and of all of us in front of the cabin. Then, while us women and the kids watched, Lux, Alan Ray, and Dad pried the roof and siding off our tack shed, so they could move it back down the hollow to rebuild it up against the hillside, where we'd once lived in our trailer, next to Mom and Dad's. Dad found us another trailer and we set that up, just about in the same place our first one had been, and we moved in during the summer, making short trips up the hollow while the road was dry, gradually taking apart our cabin, stacking the wood in piles, and thinking about how we could reuse it all on projects down at Dad's place.

Wade stayed on until the next winter, when the road got bad again, so bad he could not drive himself in and out. Then he blew the engine out of his flatbed. He hoofed it out of the hollow, one of his friends gave him a ride to town, and he never came back to live there again.

The next spring, as Lux walked up to the head of the hollow to have a look around, he told me how he found Wade's rusty flatbed truck sitting in the middle of his front yard, with spiderwebs on the door handles and grass growing out from under the tires. When he got up to our old place, Lux said, all he could see was a single line of daffodils that I'd set out where the front porch used to be, and strange-looking telephone poles sticking up out of the ground. In the cool of the late afternoon, Lux piled up all the scrap lumber left from the house and the outbuildings in the center of our field, right about where our house was, perhaps around the spot that used to be our living room. Then he poured gasoline on the pile, stepped back, took a match to a piece of rolled-up newspaper, and tossed it into the center of the lumber. With his back to the east, with the apple trees between the sky and him, he sat down and watched the pile burn until the sun went down.

Mom, if you are listening, if there is anything I can say to you to show you why this was all worth the effort, there are some lessons here, I know, but they escape me now. I look back, I recall the patterns of life at the head of the hollow, pathways we created through the fields to the chicken house, the outhouse, the barn and orchard. I remember the way that we marked the seasons by the cries of each different bird, by the shifting colors of the deep woods surrounding us, by the evening constellations above. For now, I can only say I understand what you wanted and how your love must have burned inside you, a mix of worry and grief. For I too am a mother, I have my beautiful children. They too will strive, I know, and they too will fall.

SEVEN

MR. CLUTCH (1977)

IT STARTED OFF LIKE A PICTURE POSTCARD, THE SNOW drifting down in big feathery flakes, weighing down the boughs of the spruce trees along the drive. A circle of brown earth ringed the base of each tree, and bright red birds clustered around the feed corn I'd set out, hopping around from the pines to the ground and back up again into little pillows of snow, twirling and swooping like a redbird ballet. Before long the snow came down so fast and thick I couldn't even see the pines, much less the road or the woods across the way. I stood at the window, stew simmering on the stove, watching the sky go from gray to grayer, wondering where those poor little birds were going to hide to keep themselves warm, and wondering when my husband's red Ford pickup would be coming up the drive. This was the second day in a row that Alan Ray was late getting home, the darkness creeping in and the roads a blanket of snow; the plow might not hit this road for days. I had no way to know where he got himself off to unless he picked up a phone and rang up to the house, and Alan Ray Munn just did not do that kind of thing.

Last night I fed the boys, bathed them, and had them in bed before Alan Ray showed up, almost 9 p.m., his hair flying every which way, and his flannel shirt buttoned in the wrong places. He walked in, tossed his coat in the direction of the closet, rumbled around in the fridge, popped an Iron City, set himself down on his La-Z-Boy, and fell asleep with a Marlboro burning down to the filter while he held onto the can. But tonight, Wednesday, there was weather, wind tearing through the pines, clattering the window panes, knocking the TV cables against the outside of the trailer, the rattling and howling about to make a girl lose her grip.

Long after dark, a good five inches of snow had fallen already, and it seemed like more on the way. With him up in the hills with a crew of loggers who don't have the good sense to quit when snow starts to fall, with his almost bald tires, and the way these steep roads glaze over with ice, all I can say is that I was about at wits' end by 7:30. I called up to Pap's to see if he had any ideas about where that husband of mine had got himself to.

The headlights came on in Pap's Lincoln across the long field that separated our houses, and it hit me that the snow was probably too deep in our driveway for him to drive up to our trailer or to turn around if he did get the car up the drive. I set out supper for the boys and told them to stay put. Out I went, with a garden spade and mud boots, and I started shoveling even though it was almost too dark to see. I could not get so much as a path dug before Pap pulled off to the side of the road. That garden shovel could barely hold a teacup of snow; times like this, I wished we had a decent snow shovel so I could dig a proper turnaround spot. I hurried down to meet him, needles of snow darting in his headlights.

Keeping the car running, Pap asked if we needed anything, and promised that he'd run through town to see whether Alan Ray's truck was parked anywhere. I hated to make him head out like that on a night like this, but if he could be found, Pap would find him. Pap said that he'd be back before long with news, and that anyway he needed a pack of Luckies, some Coleman fuel for the lanterns, and Mom needed some Pepto-Bismol. I knew Pap well enough to know that he got restless now that he was retired, and that he liked having a job to do. Pap said not to worry, Aunt Nelda had a police scanner, and no one had wrecked in Fairchance so far tonight.

Two hours passed. The cable went out, and all we could see was crazy static on the tube. Snow outside and snow inside, I told the boys for giggles. The lights flickered off, we hunted for a flashlight and candles, they came back on. The boys sat at the table, melting candle wax into little blobs, saying "poop" and laughing, making faces at each other and poking their fingers into the flame. I swear, if they asked me once more when their daddy was coming home, I would've lost it. Around 9, the boys finally in bed, after I'd once again swept the snow off the stairs and cleared a little path from the drive to the door, the Ford came sliding up, one windshield wiper going like mad and one stuck on the upper edge of the windshield. Alan Ray kind of waved, he sort of slid out of the pickup, a can of IC in his hand; all he had on his feet were socks. On the main road a short distance behind his truck was a second set of headlights with snow drifting in the beams, Pap's, but he turned off before our place, at his own driveway.

Right then I realized I was between a rock and a hard place. Oh, I could ask Alan Ray where he'd been these last two nights, and get him riled up, or I could not know and just be glad Pap had got him back home. I knew I'd never get anywhere asking Pap, so I bit my tongue while Alan hung his wet socks on the back of a chair next to the space heater, while he shook the snow off his cap and set it down on the counter, and while he filled the kitchen sink with warm water and about drowned his face into it. His bare feet left tracks across the floor. Without a word I set out his supper and handed him a dish towel.

He slapped me on the butt and disappeared into the bedroom without giving the stew a second glance. Fine, I thought. Just fine.

Starve yourself, I thought. But still not a word. I wished I had a hobby, something I could be doing to ignore him, like cutting coupons or quilting, but instead I wiped up the table, put away the dishes, and sat and smoked, kept my questions to myself, then headed to the bedroom. Alan Ray was sprawled across the bed, face down in his union suit, all of him on top of the bed quilt, long arms and hairy legs taking up both sides of the bed, smelling like a brewery and snoring like a chainsaw.

Next day the sun was out, and Dessie rang up at 6 to tell me the sawmill and the schools were closed due to the heavy snow. The drifts were over the tires of the truck. The boys were still asleep, so I took some time to make a path so the boys could get out to play in the snow. As I walked back in, Alan Ray rose up, moaning about how every bone in his body hurt. He looked halfway to pitiful in the way he shuffled his feet so slow. He sat at the table in his union suit and his army vest, smoking his morning Marlboro and drinking his morning Coke. I trod softly. A wife can pick a fight when her man is in a weakened state, but sometimes it comes back to kick her in the ass. Finally I could stand it no longer.

"You going up in the woods today?" I asked Alan Ray, starting with an easy question, one I was pretty sure I knew the answer to.

He looked back at me with a cockeyed smile on his face, a bristle of red stubble on his chin. He squinted at the one cracked fingernail that had half come off. "Nah, they ain't going to cut timber today. Too slick and wet up there. Hell, the skidder's in the shop for busted hydraulics. This weather's tore the hell out of the heavy equipment." He stubbed out his cigarette into the lid of a baby food jar. "Maybe Lux will be called in to the mill, but none of the crews are going into the woods for the rest of the week."

Another week's paycheck coming up short, I thought, but did not want to point out. Good thing I had set a bit aside for gas, cigs, and a few groceries. "Are you sick or just hungover? You look like you got run over by a tractor-trailer," I asked him, but stopped when he shook his head. He went to the sink, squinted into the mirror, soaked a dish towel in cool water, and covered half his head with it, just a crooked grin, a bristly chin, and an Adam's apple sticking out below. "Don't start, woman," he said.

Hmmm, I thought. Don't "woman" me. What's a wife to do? Moments like this, I think I hear two voices in my head. One voice, the one that sounds like my father says, "Speak now, or forever hold your peace," and the other one sounds like my sister Dessie, saying, "Bite your tongue and wait and see; ain't nothing you can say or do will make a bit of difference anyways."

Yeah, right, I answered myself, we been down this road last spring, and I saw where it led. Alan Ray, walking in at all times of the night, chasing that lowlife barmaid KaraMay McAddams from Reader, finally one night showing up with a black eye and a bloody nose from her truck-driver boyfriend, meanwhile Alan Ray telling everyone he fell off a four-wheeler. And I believed him at first, both me and Dessie did, but we're not going to fall for that again. I'll never forget a Dear Abby column a few years back, where the husband wrote to ask whether it was a good idea to come clean and tell his wife he was stepping out on her. Dear Abby told that husband to keep it to himself if he wanted to keep his marriage. Dear Abby probably did not have her man showing up late for supper night after night, and her finding out the truth a month later from her sister's husband. First time, shame on him, second time, shame on me.

Just then the boys came tearing out of their room, barely able to hold still long enough to get their pants on over their pj's and find their boots to play in the snow. Alan Ray held them, first Bertie, then AJ, while I stuffed their feet into plastic bags over their socks and then stuffed their pants into their shoes. They kept hugging on their dad, which made me almost want to bawl, the worry and the joy like a windshield wiper, beating back and forth in my brain.

I gave the boys some feed corn to set out for the birds and told them to stay in the yard where I could see them and come in if they got cold. Alan Ray headed outside to shovel out the truck, wearing an old pair of work boots that flapped around at the sole. I offered him some bread sacks to line his socks too, but he shook his head no. I kept it to myself but I was sure those old boots of his would soak up water like a sponge. Good, I thought, serves you right. Where the hell has that man been these nights? And where the hell had his work boots gone? What if one day he just did not come home? How would I ever raise these two hellions without their dad around? What's that old joke? Why is a wife like a mushroom? 'Cause they keep her in the dark and feed her shit all day long. A man can live with anger, but a woman lives with mad.

IF THERE is one thing I cannot abide, it is someone telling me what to do. You want me, I'll be there, but don't be telling me I have to be there, or you won't see me at all. I heard it nonstop when I was growing up, every teacher saying read this, Alan Ray, write this, Alan Ray, all of it just a bunch of nonsense. If you write something five times, you ain't gonna care about it any more than if you write it one time. I heard the same thing from my pa, especially when I got into high school and closed in on the end of eleventh grade. What are you doing with your life? Join the Army, join the Navy, join the Marines, get a job in the steel mills, be a man. My pa ran with some guys from the mills, and ain't a one of them what I would call happy. All they did was bitch about their bosses and bitch twice as much about the union stewards. Shit. Two sets of bosses. I knew a couple of guys went into the marines, and them guys did nothing all day but follow orders, and once they got out, they drove down the road with their noses in the air, not a look back at their own people. That's why I picked the Guard. First thing I asked the recruiter when he came to Middletown is if I had to finish school to join up, and he said not at all, if you're eighteen, you don't even need your folks to sign. I signed then and there, as I'd turned eighteen that month, and in two weeks I was out of that school building and into the fresh air, drilling and driving a

Jeep around, with a new set of clothes, a new pair of boots, and a cap to keep the sun out of my eyes.

I liked the Guard and the Guard liked me! So what if Pa ragged on me about keeping the family tradition with the infantry. Maybe some men can join the service and save the world, I wanted to stay put and help out my neighbors. We got plenty of action, sandbagging Decker's Creek when it flooded, helping out with first aid and evacuation when Camille hit Mississippi. The best thing about the Guard was artillery training drills out behind the barracks, packing clips with shiny new rounds, the stink of the burnt gunpowder, and the sergeant calling our shots, then cleaning our weapons, then hanging around waiting for supper playing basketball. I liked basketball, too. I wasn't the fastest, but I was one of the tallest, and those guys could count on me. When I got in the zone, I could shoot from anywhere, and when I wasn't shooting, I could always block a shot or pick up a rebound. No one had to tell me what to do on the basketball court. The second best thing to sex, seeing a ball drop right into a basket from near half-court, everyone stopping dead in their tracks and staring as the hoop opened wide and swallowed up the ball.

I don't know whose idea it was, but the other day we couldn't get nothing done in the woods so I stopped into the AmVets for a cold one. A few older guys from the Korean War stood around, but I just could not sit at the bar and listen to the same crazy stories about half freezing to death halfway across the world. I headed into the rec room, mostly to blow off steam. I guess Coach Campbell could see right away I had talent, just a little rusty, that's all. It's about time the AmVets decided to round up a team, play other teams across North Central and up the Ohio River, the Moose, the Lions, the Eagles, maybe for charity or just for beer money. I say they're just waiting to be schooled. So I said, "Hey, I'm in!" It ain't hard; get me the ball. The Gunners can show them other teams how it's done. When it's too cold or wet to cut or when the equipment is in the shop, I can stop in to the AmVets and get in some practice. As we say in the Guard, "Always ready, always there!"

FOR THE first time all week, temperature climbed a bit, and the frost on the windows started to melt in little circles, just enough for me to see Lux's pickup as it splashed through the slush on the road on the way to the mill. Three days of snow and ice, three days of my man disappearing a little before noon and not coming back until way past dark. On the good side, even though he was late, he still was coming home of an evening. On the bad side, he did not seem to care whether I had a clue where he'd been keeping himself. I knew he wasn't working because he did not ask me to pack a lunch pail. I knew the bills would be piling up and the groceries would be running out, and I had to stretch out everything from the Cheerios to the washing powder. I knew Alan Ray's work boots showed up, because he wore them home. I knew he had blisters on his feet, nosebleeds in his sleep, and he woke up a couple of times a night with coughing fits, rolling over to spit into a coffee can on his side of the bed.

Around dawn, Alan Ray rolled over in bed, but he didn't hurry to get dressed, saying he might stop by the mill around noon to check on things. He woke up in the best mood he'd been in all week. "Come on over here," he said to me, in the way of his, a smile on his face that says he had something he wanted me to see. "Hey, you," he said. "Come on back to bed."

Here's my chance, I thought. "Alan Ray," I said, holding my ground. "If I ask you something, will you tell me the God's honest truth?"

When Alan Ray smiled, I couldn't help but smile with him. "Depends," he said, but I could see that he wanted something from me, and he wanted it bad enough. "I get to ask you something first," he said.

"Fair enough," I answered.

"What's the best kind of wood there is?" he asked.

"Alan Ray, that's a trick question!" I shot back.

"Morning wood," he said. "Check it out." He started to pull the quilt down, but I grabbed it and pulled it back up, taking a quick look to see if the boys were stirring.

I geared up. "Where you been, then, these past three nights?" I blurted out, almost afraid to hear the answer.

Alan Ray looked at me, his blue eyes full of sleep and sex, his side of the bed looking tempting and warm. "If I tell you, will you promise to quit talking for five minutes?"

I nodded, feeling like my heart was about to bang out of my chest, but somehow hoping that this was one of those times a man might not be able to lie to a woman.

"OK, then." he said. "I been reporting to basketball duty with some o' them boys at the AmVets. We got a game coming up tomorrow and we've been practicing up. Now will you shut the bedroom door and get back into bed?"

"You been reporting . . . ?" I asked, but he put his left hand under the covers and his right hand over his mouth and made a zipping motion with his index finger. I almost asked him if KaraMay McAddams had got herself a job as a barmaid there at the AmVets, but I had a feeling I had got all the information out of him that I could get for one morning.

THE FIRST thing I asked when they told me I was on the team was if I could be number 44, just like Jerry West, Mr. Clutch. It's my lucky number. Coach Campbell said they didn't have any jerseys with that high of a number on it. They did have a number 4. That would do just fine, I told him, close enough. We found a dozen guys in no time, the only requirement being that a player was in some branch of the service. We all took a few free throws for practice, took the ball down the court, that kind of thing, next thing I know, Coach asked me to play power forward. And I said, "If you got the time, I got the game!"

That first night I swear I was on fire at practice, blocking, shooting, stealing the ball. I felt like a kid again. The guys on the team were from age eighteen to about fifty, with me somewhere in the middle, but I played my ass off, to show them kids how it's done. Next day I was a little stiff, had a few blisters, but a couple beers and I was right back on the court. Every time Coach looked for someone to take the ball, I was there.

Best thing about the AmVets is you never knew who was going to show up, buying rounds for the team. There was always some kind of food at the clubhouse, chili, beans and cornbread, sloppy joes. Hell, a man has to wake up and go somewhere; he can't just hang around the house like an old woman. I look back at my life after the Guard, and I feel like I have been the guy who wakes up, goes to a job, comes back home, and does it again the next day. But what kind of life is that? It might be OK for some, for Lux, maybe. A guy like Lux, he don't take no time to smell the roses. Where does that get anyone? You work yourself to death, and you still can't afford to pay the undertaker. The joke's on you. As I always said, "All work and no play makes Jack a dull boy."

THE SNOW started in again on Saturday, the day so cold, bleak, and gloomy that it seemed like the birds were afraid to fly out for their corn. I waited in the doorway of the trailer just long enough to see the redbirds hopping around, feathers all fluffed out, and the little black-and-white ones, too, coming down in flocks to get the corn and stay warm. I'd been holding my breath that they did not freeze to death in the cold air overnight.

I phoned up Dessie to see if she could take the boys for the day, since Alan Ray had a basketball game in the afternoon and he'd asked me to come along to watch. I did not want to bring those boys to the Moose Lodge to see the game; who knew what kind of people sit on a barstool all day at a place like the Moose, and besides, it seemed like a good way to break this cabin fever after being a shut-in all week. I got the boys dressed and fed and packed a couple of extra of everything, socks, tees, bibs, underpants, pj's sweatshirts, hats, mittens, the little

Tonka dump truck and the Hot Wheels that my folks got the boys for Christmas, in a grocery sack for the day. Bertie liked Oodles of Noodles, AJ liked Skippy and saltines; Santa had put packages of instant hot cocoa into the boys' stockings, and I'd set those back for a special occasion, but I threw them into the sack too, enough that all the kids could share some, a thank you to my sister.

Dessie was a good sport about watching the boys, but six kids running around could get old fast, and I didn't want to ask her too often unless I could return the favor. She was still sorting out after moving back down the hollow, still living out of boxes. I'd meant to head up to her place to help her. I made myself a promise that I'd get over there once this weather broke. Alan Ray spent the morning digging out the driveway, again, and the boys and I trudged across the field, or really, I trudged across the field and they raced up to the trailer like their pants were on fire, so happy to see their cousins.

Dessie opened the door, just a crack, to keep the warm air in, and hustled us into the house. "Alan Ray has got a *what?* A basketball game?" Dessie'd asked, her eyes squinting, trying to keep from laughing and looking at me for confirmation. "He a bit old for that kind of thing?"

"He don't think he is," I answered. "Might keep him from chasing women, I guess." Dessie shook her head and shrugged her shoulders. "I guess! Since you're going, you can keep an eye on him." She gave me a look, and I knew that she knew that this was exactly what I'd been thinking. "Let me know how it goes," Dessie added, scooping up the boys, one in each arm. "Hope they beat the pants off those old drunks from the Moose."

THE SNOW blew drifts across the road, and I never did get that one wiper to work right, but Billie hopped up into the truck and we headed for town, no boys, some spare change, some rock and roll on the radio, ZZ Top, Allman Brothers, just the two of us out on the town, taking it slow, not much traffic on the snowy roads. She even said she'd be my cheerleader, and I had a good laugh, both of us long out of high school, but hey, look at Jerry West, playing ball for all those years, high school, college ball, and fourteen years in the pros, older than me and still making his shots. I don't know why we never did this kind of thing in all the years we been together. Seems like one thing or another, and then the kids came along, and Billie always wanting to have the kids with her wherever we go, and one or the other gets to screaming or throwing a fit, must have a candy bar, you're taking up my side of the seat, no I ain't either, and that nonsense can kill a perfectly good afternoon in town.

When we got to the AmVets, the snow drifts were a foot deep, and some of the boys who said they'd be able to play could not make it out of their driveways. Turned out seven of us showed up, plus the coach, enough to play and rotate a couple guys from the bench. We sat at the bar, having a shot of whiskey for the road, and Coach Campbell handed out the jerseys, red, white, and blue, sponsored by the Fairchance AmVets with help from the squad. I couldn't have been prouder than if I was back in active duty, just the sight of that eagle with its wings spread wide across the chest, my number 4 on the back in honor of the greatest basketball player who ever lived.

Then we geared up and got on the road. Coach's station wagon led the way, most of the other guys in a car or pickup with their friends or their girls. We drove down to the Ohio River, taking it slow, past Dallison Lumber, past Sistersville, Paden City, Tyler county seat, glass factories, feed stores and Dollar General stores, trainyards; the little towns along the way, wood or coal smoke coming out of the chimneys, looking like Christmas cards come to life. For some crazy reason, people seemed friendlier in the snow, old-timers and shopkeepers leaned on their shovels, waving as we passed.

The Loyal Order of the Moose, Lodge 931, stood three stories tall in the heart of downtown New Martinsville, a block from the courthouse and about three blocks from the Ohio River. It was a red brick building, about ten times the size of our Quonset hut AmVets.

But we know what they say in the Guard, "It ain't the size of the dog in the fight, it's the size of the fight in the dog!" We might've been the few, but we were also the proud! On the streets of town, every block looked empty as downtown can be on a snowy Saturday afternoon, streetlights changing from green to red without a single car lined up to watch, just some tire tracks and footprints down the middle of North Street.

Once we opened the door to the Moose, we knew where the whole town had got itself to. Men and women of all ages crowded around the bar or sat at long tables, three bartenders, barmaids about jogging back and forth with trays full of orders, kids racing in and out of the place, tossing around snowballs in the back parking lot. I'd seen the AmVets full of people, say on Veterans' Day or after a vet's funeral, but this was a Saturday afternoon in the dead of winter and the place was jammed. A head of a moose, must have been a yard or more long, stared out from a giant plaque on the wall opposite the bar. The damn thing was twice the size of the head on the bronze elk statue that stood outside at the Elk's lodge. The building seemed even bigger from the inside. Me and Billie walked around the place, found the gym down in the basement. I thought I would size up the competition, but no one was shooting yet, so we headed back up to the bar to check on the rest of the guys.

Back in the kitchen behind the bar, Coach Campbell was already pitching in, circling back and forth from the fryer to the grill, each part of him in motion. "Hey, Alan Ray," he said, "grab a plate so I can set up this order." He shook the oil out of the fries, and before I even had a chance to think I grabbed a dinner plate off a stack. "We can split the take if we help out in the kitchen," he said, and as the game did not start for a good hour yet, it seemed the perfect way to kill time. I bought Billie a Coke and a pack of Marlboro Lights and saw her set our stuff down at a table in the corner next to some of the wives and girlfriends from our team. I didn't want to stand around, so I kept busy in the kitchen, lining up the orders for the barmaids. That got me some big smiles from some of the prettiest girls I'd ever seen in any bar.

Everyone seemed to know everyone else, the bar was a mile long, and cans of Miller and Iron City were fifty cents each, laid out in giant coolers just beneath the bar. At one end of the bar, two large pickle jars with signs were stuffed half full of money. One said TIPS and one said SWEARS. A couple of beers went down pretty easy, but as we walked downstairs to shoot and run drills before the game, a knot formed in my stomach that did not ease up until sometime during the first quarter.

Coach called us all together on our side of the court, right before tipoff. "I want a clean game," he said. "We're vets. We served our country. There's been lots of people these days talking trash about the service. You know and I know that there could be some of them people in this crowd today, might have something to say about the Vietnam War. None of us don't want no trouble. Now let us pray."

We bowed our heads, each of us thinking the same thing. *If any of these Moose starts a bit trouble with any one of us, we are brothers, and that is where it stands.*

THE GUNNERS were standing around in the kitchen, cleaning up with the Moose guys after the game. Coach Campbell scrubbed down the grill, emptied the grease out of the deep fryer. Alan Ray wiped down the counters, limping a little. He was still peevish, I could tell, since he didn't want to talk to anyone yet.

I watched this show of male industriousness in the kitchen. Never thought I would see the day that a man would wash a dish, much less wipe down a griddle and a fryer. That was surprising, but an even bigger surprise was that the Gunners made it through the whole game and won, 26–21. Crazy thing was, those Moose guys could make it up and down the court like a bunch of kids, but they couldn't shoot to save their lives.

Alan Ray didn't play as much as he wanted to, and I felt sorry for him about that. He took about ten shots, and three went in, one of them was when he caught a rebound by reaching higher than anyone else. That was fun to watch, but then, right after the second half started, he chased a flying ball down the court, and threw himself backward as he flipped it back inbounds. He almost looked like a pro for a second there. Too bad when he tried to save the ball from going out of bounds, he tossed the ball to the wrong team. That was the moment when he pulled something in his leg, and he had to hop out to the bench and sit out the rest of the game.

His pride was hurt, sure, but also his leg really was hurt. "Fuck, fuck, fuckit," was all he'd say. His face was bright red, him hopping around on one foot, off balance. The whole crowd heard him, kids calling out, "Swear jar, swear jar, that's three dollars!" "Oh Chrissakes," he said. "Catch me if you can," he said, and he limped off toward the bar. I knew enough to keep my mouth shut. He finally came back to sit on the bench, a beer in each hand, and a little blonde-headed barmaid holding him upright as he limped to the stands, easing him into his seat. "I'll take it from here," I said to her, sliding over to sit next to him for the final shots of the game.

Hal the barber, one of the guards for the Gunners, stepped out of the doorway to the kitchen, wiping his hands on his apron. "Hey, Alan Ray, tell Billie why they hang a moose head on the wall of every lodge," he said.

"Why do they?" Alan Ray shouted over the noise of the running water. "Yeah, why?" yelled Gribble, another Gunner I hadn't met, a vet who was just back from a tour in Southeast Asia; even though he cracked a thin smile, he looked pretty grim.

"Because that moose head makes all the women in the bar look good," Hal yelled back at me. Ha ha ha. Hal went on talking, loud enough for the whole world to hear. Next he wanted to know why Coach Campbell had number 5 on his jersey. Coach spoke up and said that it was because he was not just a coach, he's a player too. Coach

Campbell seemed to be about fifty; he was tall and skinny, a backhoe operator. He had a great outside shot during the game, but didn't get around on the court much. He was old and slow, was the truth. He planted himself downcourt, near the sidelines, and looped one into the basket at least one out of every two times. Then Hal asked, in a voice somewhat louder than I expected, if the numbers on their backs have anything to do with the length of their dicks. Alan Ray yelled back, "Hell no, it's how many barmaids they've had." Hal shook his head. He was skeptical. Alan Ray was wearing a number 4.

If I had a number on my back, it would be 2, I thought. Times like this I think back over my life. How did I know I chose right when I chose Alan Ray? Maybe falling for Jackson Childs was the work of the devil, and maybe the devil has dogged me since. Look where it has got me to. Miles away from my boys, making more work for Dessie at a time when she could use a break herself. Who were all these people who lived their lives behind bottles of beer, their kids running into the street without coats on while they have another round? What was I doing here, this crowd of strangers, this strange place? This moose head with its big eyes seeing everything, as if it could keep all the unholy secrets and ease all of the doubt, guilt, and pain in the human heart?

On the bench during the first half of the game I sat next to Jaynelle, a couple of years ahead of me in high school. She talked up a storm, bouncing her little blond baby Freddie on her lap, a washcloth on his forehead because he felt feverish. She was engaged to Fred, number 6, for over a year now, and was waiting to set a date. I wondered whether she'd ever get a ring out of that guy. He was forty-two, six foot six, well built and handsome. I never saw that guy without a cigarette in his hand, even on the court. He only had one shot, standing two feet in front of the hoop. If someone threw him the ball, he could pop it in since he was taller than everyone else. He truly was the worst foul shooter on the team. I kept wondering if he needed eyeglasses. He swore to beat the band and cursed the refs, like they all do, but truly, the refs seemed like the only ones who knew what they were doing.

During halftime the whole Gunners team was back upstairs at the bar, smoking cigarettes with the Moose boys while the refs took turns passing, dribbling, taking layups, and shooting from the foul line, and those guys put on a real show. On the drive over, Alan Ray told me Fred's got five daughters from five different women, and a son from Jaynelle. I knew this was true, since Jaynelle told me that she's twenty-six, had little Freddie, five stepdaughters, and two grandchildren. "Sometimes it gets to be too much," she said.

THE GUYS from the Moose were great sports after all. None of them seemed to have a bit of a problem with us kicking their asses and then paying up on the side bets. We raised about a hundred for the AmVets club from the food, and we each came away with about twenty dollars, not counting what we put into the TIPS and SWEARS jars. We had beer and shots, and Billie had her dinner too. I began to think I might be able to put down a layaway on a pair of high-tops, something to look forward to when my leg quit hurting.

Me and Billie were the last of the Gunners to leave the Moose, not sure where they all got themselves to, but I guess I was in the mood to celebrate. I bought a six-pack of Iron City for the road, threw it under the seat, headed out of town, and glad I had that beer since a good buzz can take the edge off. My left leg was pounding from my knee down to my ankle, but at least it was my clutch pedal foot, not my gas pedal foot. I wasn't going to let that ruin a great night. Being on the team was more fun than I'd had since I left the Guard. If it wasn't for that piece of shit rubber surface floor, instead of a real basketball court made of wood, I'd have never got hurt.

The driveway was plowed around the New Martinsville Moose Lodge, and most of the streets were clear, though more snow fell while we were playing. Out of town, I was glad to see that the roads were empty. Probably the cold kept everyone drinking indoors.

Seemed like the town police had stayed home too, which was pretty surprising on a Saturday night. Now all I had to worry about were the Staties, but there wasn't any barracks between New Martinsville and Fairchance, and Staties didn't usually give me a second look, a working man in a pickup, not the kind of guy who is going to be drag racing down an empty stretch of road at 110 miles an hour. Not on a night like this, especially; well maybe if I had a V-8 instead of the straight 6.

There was no need to go back through Fairchance, and I knew a back way home on county roads that could save some time. The township roads were pretty clear almost to Jacksonville, or at least in some places they were clear, but the further east I went, the harder it got to see the blacktop through the snow cover. I could tell there was ice, but I couldn't tell much or how deep it was since the snowdrifts had covered any tracks. That one wiper on the passenger side kept getting stuck, and that made it harder to see the edge of the road. The hill rose up steep off my right-hand side, and the wind came in from the north, blowing with such a force that the gusts howled in the cracks of the fly window. Sometimes blowing snow drifted off the hillside in a ridge like a small mountain range down the middle of the road.

Finally, just before Reader, I saw some lights on and pulled over into an Amoco station under a streetlight, to fill 'er up with some of my winnings, scrape the windshield, and free that damn wiper blade. I about yanked the rubber from the blade off; the no-account wiper was coated in ice and frozen in place. I knew I would have to wait until it thawed to get it working again. I took about the longest leak of my life out back, paid for a Little Debbie and the gas, asked the guy if the roads was clear, and he said no one's been out to tell him otherwise, so I climbed back into the warm cab of the Ford and settled in to see what the last part of the drive had in store.

The roads were plowed to the edge of town, and after that I knew enough to hug the midline, since there was only the faintest hint of tire tracks through the gusts of snow. I opened a cold one for the last part of the drive, just to keep the buzz going. The radio was mostly static, with some weird AM station that seemed to have the news and weather from Chicago, and not a bit of anything else. I was starting to hope for a human voice to keep me company, Billie being asleep against the passenger door with her head on the armrest. Once or twice I got her up so that she could see how hard the snow was pounding down, great polka-dot clumps hitting the windshield and sliding down into slush. "Oh my," she'd say, then settle back down, her feet curled under her butt.

Heading over the ridgetop at the county line in Pricetown, I took her easy around the first few S curves. You don't want to give it too much gas and you don't want to give it too little gas. Too much gas and the Ford might fishtail, too little gas, it might not make it up the hill, especially if there's ice under the snow. I've seen trucks slide backward on a steep road, and ass-end-up in a ditch was not the way this little Ford was going to wind up, not on a perfect night like this.

About halfway up the hill there was this one steep curve. We called it Kiss My Ass, because that was just how narrow the curve was, switching back and forth as it climbed. Year-round, you'd hear about kids wiping out there. I slid through that one, just barely swinging the ass end toward the next switchback, and gunned it. A blur of snow came at us, full tilt, and I could feel the rear wheels slide around and grip, slide, and grip, like a giant hand had come out of the snow and grabbed hold of the bottom of the truck, and all I could do was hope for the best. The Ford headed over the top of the hill, God love it, but suddenly not a track to be seen or even the edge of the road in front of me, just white on white, snow on the ground and the snow in the air, tires spinning but not grabbing, us sliding sideways into a drift of snow halfway up to the door handle. The tires spun, but the snow was deeper than the tires, no way to tell how deep. As the man says, we was a-goin' nowhere, fast. I did the only thing I could do. I turned up the heat, kept her idling, took a long swig of Iron City, and settled back into the seat to wait it out and puzzle out some next steps, our small red pickup on the wide white hillside, gusts of snow blasting across the hood, the wind roaring out across the ridge like a runaway locomotive, trying its best to suck the heat out of the cab.

I WASN'T sleeping so much as thinking, or at least I thought I was thinking, but I might have been sleeping a little too. It was my brain, skipping around, as if I was watching a play or reruns on a little TV screen, starring those girls whose husbands and boyfriends were on the team. I was picturing us, together at the Moose, the stories they told me, their lives so heavy that I could only listen and nod. My tongue felt stuck in my mouth, I never knew what to say in return. There was Jaynelle, tiny as a peanut, that bristle-haired baby on her knee, so fevered and so big for his age she could hardly lift him, five more to care for at home. There was Brenda, Coach's wife, who told me she'd had a breast removed last year, and every bit of her hair fell out, week by week, from the chemo. I didn't realize she wore a blond wig, tight curls, under her wide scarf. Over her green eyes, her eyelashes were glued on, her eyebrows drawn with a colored pencil. The only one she trusted to cut her hair as it was coming out in clumps was Hal the barber, she said, and only because he'd understand, since he'd troubles of his own. Hal's son had up and left his wife and their children and run off with Gribble's seventeen-year-old daughter while Gribble was stationed in Hanoi. I didn't know what to do with these stories, these sorrowful lives. I saw Hal, trying hard to smile, his face pinched, drinking doubles. I saw Gribble, slouched into the bar at the end of the game, head in his hands, his eyes darting back and forth, looking like he wanted to find a place to hide.

It was bright in my head, brighter than the real Moose Lodge, where the bar had been kind of dark and by the end of the night, kind of quiet. I wondered if I was dreaming these women, these men, and dreaming their stories. Then, for some crazy reason, I saw clear as day a snapping turtle that Alan Ray'd caught last summer. He'd kept it alive locked in a big white cooler, feeding it worms and stew meat; he'd wanted me to cook it for him. Its head, when we opened the cooler, bigger than Alan Ray's clenched fist, raised up in reflex, its terrible open mouth raked at the air. But I must have been dreaming this. I kept thinking that I could feel every bit of what they all were feeling, that it wasn't too late for me to tell them all I loved them.

And then I saw bright spots, shining spots, headlights, two sets of them, coming from somewhere, seemed like maybe from across a field, and then from far off, Pap's voice, breaking through, saying, "Wake up, wake up in there," and Lux's voice, yanking open the truck doors, saying, "Get them some air," him shaking me and shaking Alan Ray, the glare of headlights against a wall of snow, hauling my whole self back from who knows where. "Get them chains out of the truck bed," said Lux's voice. Then someone who sounded a lot like Pap saying, "It's the fumes, it's from the tailpipe, there's gas trapped in the cab, quick, get them some air now. You, Lux, just get out of the way, let me over there. Wake up, baby, wake up. Oh, dear God, give me back my baby girl."

EIGHT

GUN SEASON (1979)

ON A BLUSTERY DARK NIGHT IN MID-NOVEMBER, LUX and Dessie sat in the parking lot of the Reader School in the cab of their black Ford pickup truck, deciding whether to keep their truck-load of government surplus food. Two streetlights barely lit the parking lot, and Lux observed that if they cut the headlights and drove around the back of the school, they could unload the unopened boxes of powdered food right into the school's dumpster.

Dessie shifted their two-year-old Tommy onto her other knee, toward the middle of the truck. Tommy kept wiggling around, first trying to pop up the door locks, then trying to roll down the window.

"Let's get going, Lux," Dessie said. Cars were pulling out of the parking lot around them, and parents and teachers stood in the lit doorway of the schoolhouse, chatting and smoking. Dessie covered Tommy's shoulders with her sweater. The air was damp, and Tommy could get a chill. "Can't we just keep the food?" She sat the baby down firmly between her legs on the floor of the truck and held onto his pudgy hands so he could not reach any of the levers and buttons on the inside of the truck door. "I wouldn't want us to get caught throwing it out. What would they think of us?"

"That stuff ain't real food. It's just somebody's idea of food. Someday I'd like to tell them where they can put them commodities," Lux said. He started up the truck, but left it in neutral to warm up. He cracked open the driver's door and spit. Dessie didn't say anything. She hoped Lux would quit thinking about the boxes of food in the back of the truck. There was bound to be something there that she could use to stretch the remaining food stamps. She was more focused on the night's parent-teacher conferences and how her kids were doing in school. The school building was brand-new. The county had just consolidated and blended the K–8 schools, and it meant getting to know a whole new crop of teachers. Lissy's sixth-grade homeroom teacher, Miss Crowe, a surprisingly young woman with a feathered hairdo and red fingernails that clicked on the desk as she opened her grade book, told her, "Elisabeth is not working up to her potential. She does her work, but nothing more, just enough to get by. School seems to frighten her. She's too quiet."

Too quiet? When Lissy's at home, Dessie thought, she's so chatty she follows me around the house. All she talks about is school. Dessie couldn't stop staring at those fingernails. They were the most useless-looking things she'd ever seen. Dessie thanked Miss Crowe for her time. She wished she'd had the time to check this information with all of Lissy's teachers. But Lux was waiting out in the truck with Tommy, and Dessie had to visit two other sets of teachers.

Little Lux's first-grade teacher also didn't seem to have any idea what he was really like. Dessie had wondered during their conversation if Mr. Catalano had him confused with someone else's son. He had no problems settling down at home. If she did say something, perhaps ask more questions, would Mr. Catalano think it was disrespectful? Would he hold it against her son? *Are you sure you have the right Luther Cranfield Jr., the one who builds army forts for hours out of Lincoln Logs, setting up and strategizing battles on the kitchen floor?* The more

Dessie settled herself down into the student-sized desks and looked up at teachers whose desks and chairs dwarfed her own, the more her stomach began to hurt, and her heartburn began to act up.

Worst of all was what Dessie heard from all four teachers about Ron, their fifth grader. By the end of the night, after she'd made the rounds, she felt like she was the one who had failing grades. "Lux," Dessie began, "what are we going to do about Ron? He doesn't do his work, his teachers say he won't give them any answers at all, and he sneaks out of class to go God only knows where when their backs are turned. We need to talk to that boy and find out what he's doing all day."

"Jesus, Dess. What the hell do they expect?" Lux revved the Ford's engine and put it into gear. "Ron's smart. He knows the score. He's got sense enough to know when he's being spoon-fed a cart full of horseshit. He's just too polite to tell 'em all what he really thinks." Lux switched on the headlights and pointed the truck out of the parking lot toward home, ignoring the dumpster. "I'll tell you what," Lux said, "they may be an educated bunch, but ain't a one of them could teach me anything useful." Dessie flashed back to Miss Crowe's fingernails. *What would Lux think of those?* She wondered if Billie had noticed them too. AJ was in the same class.

"Well, maybe you can talk to Ronnie about getting better grades, Lux." Dessie said, smoothing little Tommy's hair, but then she stopped. She could tell that the night had put Lux into a mood. She did not want to get him started. The entire town of Fairchance had been up in arms about the school consolidation. Lux would say that the problems were not his kids at all, that if the kids had teachers who knew them, knew the family, there would be no issue at all. That was very likely where this conversation was heading, and Dessie did not have the strength to hear it all again.

Tommy stood up straight when the truck began to move. He started bouncing up and down on Dessie's lap, reaching for the steering wheel. "Hey, buster," she said to Tommy, "you stay put and let

Daddy drive." She tried to wrap the seatbelt around them both. But she hadn't lost all her pregnancy weight from Tommy yet, and the belt barely clicked.

Dessie could see Lux's point; there was something about the way the teachers in this new school talked to the parents. The teachers were all strangers from New Martinsville or somewhere to the west, and the whole lot of them talked like they thought they were better than the kids they taught. Before the teacher conferences, the principal, Mr. Stillwell, practically forced them to take all that commodity food. The way he put it, with the gymnasium light shining off his bald little head and his extremely precise pronunciation, "I am confident you people came for the good of your children's education, and just remember, good nutrition makes good students." Dessie looked down at his shoes, for a moment thinking that the fussy leather wing-tip shoes on his feet might cost more than Lux made in a week at the mill. It was hard to look back at his face. What kind of a simpleton was he to think that her children didn't eat well, Dessie thought. Her kids' grades did not come from her kitchen.

Lux switched on the radio, and soon Tommy fell asleep. The truck turned toward the narrower local roads. With each pothole, Dessie heard the rattle of the food boxes over the voice of Merle Haggard. Of course, they could use surplus food. This time of year, work was on again off again. But who could get a man like Lux that was raised on fresh milk, scratch-made cornbread, and fresh-dug potatoes to eat that government surplus? Two huge boxes of powdered milk, four of powdered potato buds, twenty-five pounds of rice, honey and square rubbery blocks of orange cheese, even powdered biscuit mix.

Dessie's mouth felt dry after the long wait in hallways of the heated building for the teacher conferences. She rummaged around in her purse and found a hot cinnamon jawbreaker. The kids liked fried-cheese sandwiches, so she knew that if she bought a loaf of bread, at least the government cheese wouldn't go to waste. Come gun season, starting the Monday of Thanksgiving week, Lux could shoot a deer, she thought. Thanksgiving they could eat stewed venison with the last of this year's turnips. Maybe the First Apostolic would take the commodities if she couldn't figure out a way to sneak them onto their dinner table.

SINCE HE was failing in math, social studies, and English, and since Lux did not weigh in on the matter, Dessie told Ron that he had to go to school on the first day of gun season. After Lux left for work early the next morning, she sat Ron down in the kitchen and broke the news to him, just loud enough for Lissy and Little Lux to hear, to put some fear into them, too. Ron, a lanky, blond eleven-year-old, fidgeted silently at the table, and then finally spoke up. "I'll make you a deal, Ma," he said. "If I bring home an A on something, anything at all, will you let me go out with Dad to get my buck?"

Dessie stopped mixing up the powdered milk and dried her hands on a dish towel. Tommy sat up in his high chair when she put another handful of Cheerios for him on the tray. Then she came up behind Ron and began smoothing his wavy hair. "You bring me home one A, honey, in any subject at all," she said, "and I'll find some money to buy you a whole extra box of shells."

But that afternoon, when Lux arrived home early from the mill, he said Ron had to help him hunt regardless of that bargain. Work had slowed way down at the mill due to the weather, Lux had taken the following week off for gun season, and he wouldn't be getting paid. "We spent thirty dollars on a vest for the boy and a hunting license with the buck stamp. And come winter, there ain't enough lumber coming into the mill. They can't drag nothing out of the woods when it's so slick out there." Lux was at the kitchen sink, scrubbing at his fingernails.

"What am I supposed to do, Lux?" Dessie asked. "When's that boy going to think about his future? He's got to go through school if he wants to get anywhere. Do you want him kept back?" She stood at the stove, adding diced-up bacon from last year's hog to the government rice, trying to cook up something interesting. She blew on the rice, tasted it, shook her head, and reached for the lemon pepper seasoning.

Lux shrugged. "Let him take his licks if he won't do his work. I ain't going to be there to hold Ron's hand his whole life."

Dessie looked up at Lux to gauge how far to press this. She was trying to get it right. She told Lux that she'd been giving it some thought, and that Ron had Thanksgiving, and even the Wednesday before, which was also a school holiday, to go out deer hunting. The more she talked, the more he shook his head from side to side.

"Aw, shit," Lux said, hanging on to his eyepatch while he took off the A-1 Lumber cap. He ran his wet hands through his thick black hair. "You know we gotta get out there on the first day. All them out of state boys come in from Ohio and Michigan, they drive up here and run off our deer. The deer get wind of all that activity in the woods, and they get scarce in a hurry. I'm taking Ron first thing next Monday morning. We're getting out ahead of the sunrise, and we'll find those bucks before anyone else gets to 'em. First day's the best, but hell, we'll have to be pretty lucky to get one anytime. It ain't like we live up the hollow where they used to walk right past our front door."

Dessie held her tongue. There was no way she could answer that point. Sometimes it seemed like he carried the world on his shoulders, she thought. It felt like yesterday they'd moved back down the hollow, but it had been two years. She stirred at the rice, trying to keep it from sticking.

Lux strolled across the living room and stretched out his arm like a rifle. He took aim out the window, pointing his index finger in an arc at an imaginary target. Then he frowned. "You know what I heard? I heard that over in Monongalia and Harrison County they close the schools all week during gun season. Now there's a bunch of folks that have some thought about putting food on the tables of the kids they teach." He walked back to the bedroom to find a flannel shirt before starting the evening chores.

Dessie chewed on her lower lip and looked up from the rice, out the steamy window to where the kids would soon get off the school bus. Ron still had a couple of days before the weekend. Maybe he would bring home an A, she thought. Otherwise she was going to have to let him go with his dad anyway, and then what in God's name would keep that boy in class?

But as the bus stopped and the kids got out, Dessie could see Ron trudging up the driveway carrying something huge. Little Lux had Ron's coat draped over his arm, hanging almost to the ground, and Lissy had his bulging bookbag. When he finally made it up to the house Ron poked his head in the door with a grin on his face, and he threw his cap up into the air toward the gun rack. "Hey, Ma. Come on outside and see what I brung you!"

Dessie smiled and turned off the burners on the stove. Then she picked up Tommy and hurried down the front steps of the porch, over to Lissy, Little Lux, and Ron. There, halfway across the yard, under their old apple tree, as big as life, was a large plywood cutout of a bear, painted dark brown with red gums, white circles around its eyes, white teeth, lips pulled back in a snarl, and a red tongue. From the front, with the sun creating a low shadow behind it, the bear looked oddly realistic, just like a small, shaggy, bristling black bear was standing under their tree, near the edge of their field, getting ready to snack on the last few apples that had fallen to the ground. "Take a good look, Ma," said Ron, and he pointed to some writing on the back of the bear, where the plywood had been left unpainted. "I been saving this for a surprise," he said. Dessie knelt down to read what the shop teacher had written. "Nice Job!" it said in red magic marker, up the inside of one forepaw, and then, on a hind leg, the letter A.

Dessie looked up at Ron. "Hang in there, Ronnie," she said. "I knew you could show them. Just look what you can do when you put your mind to it."

Lux walked across the yard, looked at Ron's bear, and started to laugh. "Hey Ron, what'd you bring home now, a new dog?" Ron looked up at his dad, not sure whether to be mad or to laugh. "That's no dog, you blind old man, that's a bear." Tommy echoed his brother. "Dat bear, bear, Daddy, dat bear."

"Come out in the woods with me on Monday, I'll find you a real one to paint," Lux said, and under his short black beard a smile curled the corners of his mouth.

OVER THE weekend, all Ron could talk about was buck hunting. In fact, all Lux and Alan Ray could talk about was hunting, too. There was an apple orchard way back at the head of the Goshen Road, with the last few apples dangling off the branches. Lux had been up there on Dakota and seen buck scrapes on saplings and deer tracks along the creek. The two men had also built a tree stand a few years earlier above a natural mineral lick beside the creek. They decided that before sunrise on Monday, Alan Ray and Ron would walk from opposite sides of the hill and try to drive any deer over toward the salt lick, while Lux waited, ready to shoot, above the trail in the tree stand.

When Monday came, the weather was crisp and clear. The men got out into the woods long before sunrise and took the pickup up the Goshen Road, leaving it at the old house site. Then they spread out in the woods. Leaves on the forest floor crunched loudly underfoot, and the wind whipped around behind Ron and Alan Ray. Lux realized that it was going to be hard to walk without being noticed, but he found his way to the tree stand and climbed a good fifteen feet above the trail to wait. But except for the raucous and continual warning calls of crows, it was as if all the wildlife in the woods had disappeared, not a grouse or even a squirrel.

That afternoon, Ron, Lux, and Alan Ray came home empty-handed and late, almost as late as the younger children came off the bus. As soon as he got in the door, Ron begged and cried to take another day off school. "You know they don't do anything in school on the day before a holiday," he told Dessie, but she put her foot down. "You need to do all your work," she said, making room at the table for him to have a snack, and for Lissy and Little Lux to start on their homework. "More good marks next year, and then ask me about it."

"Next year?" Ron said. "Goddamnit," he cursed softly under his breath, but before Dessie could threaten to wash out his mouth with soap, he raced outside to ask his father.

But on Tuesday, when Lux got Dessie up at 4 a.m. to pack Lux's lunch, Lux didn't bother to wake Ron. It was sleeting outside, and the temperature had dropped. Dessie was relieved that by the time Ron got up and realized that his dad was gone, it was too late for him to do anything but get ready to go to school. Late that afternoon, when Alan Ray and Lux came home from hunting, Ron's bear was covered with a thick glaze of ice, and the sky was as dark as the men's mood.

Dessie and the boys sat at the kitchen table while Lissy heated up water for the dishes. Tommy pushed away his bottle full of powdered milk; only when she mixed half powder and half real milk could Dessie sneak a bottle by him. The Velveeta cheese was still a hit with the kids, and they ate cheese sandwiches and baked beans that night for supper. Rose had stopped by earlier, and she'd brought Dessie a ham to fix for Thanksgiving dinner from the Prices' freezer. She and Bertram were headed to spend the holiday with Aunt Nelda, who was getting around better after a second hip replacement. Also, Bertram had wanted to give the children some spending money for pop and candy.

Just as Rose was heading out, Alan Ray came back up to help plan out the next day's hunting. He still wore his camouflage, but his usually ruddy complexion was pale, his voice low. Lux wouldn't say much, but when Ron found out that his uncle had been to town, he couldn't help but ask Alan Ray for the news. Alan Ray told everyone that the largest buck checked in was a fourteen-point, and a bunch of young four-point bucks and six-points were tagged; yearlings and does had been spotted everywhere.

WEDNESDAY WARMED up a little, but was still cool and very foggy. Ice dripped off the porch stairs. By the time the children got up, Ron and Lux were out in the woods, and the fog was lifting. The kids were happy to get a break from school. Between looking after the little ones and getting the house cleaned up for the Thanksgiving dinner, Dessie did not know where the day went. Throughout the day, Dessie and Lissy heard gunshots, though it was hard to place their exact direction. At first, each rifle crack and shotgun echo made Dessie hopeful, but when several hours passed and Ron and Lux hadn't come down off the Goshen Road, the pit of her stomach filled with dread. She tried to push the thought from her mind, but even worse than the idea of them coming back empty-handed was the idea of an accident way back in the woods.

When Ron and Lux finally returned Wednesday evening, their vests, pants, and boots were covered with mud and briars. They had seen a couple of deer, and Ron had fired off a couple rounds, but he couldn't get a decent shot at anything. Ron looked completely worn out as he came into the kitchen after hanging his hunting clothes outside. "I almost shot a doe," he said. "I was going to sneak it home through the woods and not check it in. That way you could have something for Thanksgiving tomorrow, Ma."

"That's all right, Ronnie," said Dessie as she set him out a cup of hot cocoa. "We've got the ham from Papaw's hog, and we'll get our buck sooner or later."

"Not if them hunters from Ohio already got it," Lux said from the living room. Dessie hadn't seen any out-of-state license plates, but she kept that information to herself, glancing back at Lissy as if to say, hush now. Lissy took the hint, setting aside her schoolwork, helping draw bathwater and put the younger kids to bed early, so they wouldn't get on Lux's nerves.

Dessie quietly cleaned up the kitchen and started making pie crusts for the next day. "No old ornery buck is going to ruin my Thanksgiving dinner," she said to Lissy, and they both got so involved in the routines of measuring ingredients and rolling out lard pie crusts that they didn't notice that Lux and Ronnie had fallen asleep in their long johns and woolen socks, sprawled out on the living room floor in front of the heater.

WHEN LUX, Ronnie, and Alan Ray returned from the woods Thanksgiving morning, Alan Ray said they'd seen some deer, but all the animals in the woods were moving like they had been spooked. They hadn't even gotten off a shot; they still had all the shells they took up into the woods that morning. Lux wasn't talking about it, and neither was Ron. Sullenly and silently they sat on the porch, cleaned the guns, and went into the house to get changed. Only Alan Ray was as cheerful as usual; it seemed to Dessie that any time Alan Ray was away from work he was as happy as a boy. He said his good-byes and yelled up to Dessie on the porch that he'd "be taking any last-minute orders for her sister," and that he'd be back before long with Billie and their two boys to eat an early Thanksgiving dinner.

Right after that, Lux left for town. He wanted to wash the truck and go to Cleve's Grocery for the news, since Cleve's was the nearest check-in station, open even on Thanksgiving, and because Cleve would trade food stamps for cigarettes and beer. Lux took the youngest boys with him as a special treat, and to get them out of Dessie's hair. Little Lux bounced down the porch stairs into the truck, talking about how he could buy caps for his cap gun with the money from Papaw.

Ronnie was sweeping off the front porch as Lux came back up the drive. Ron said nothing as his father walked by, just hung his head down and worked at a stubborn spot of mud. Dessie was glazing the ham, and, with the help of Lissy and the little ones, she had made two big trays of biscuits from the powdered mix and a skillet full of gravy. Lux walked into the house, set two six-packs down on the table, and took a couple of cans for himself.

The house had been cleaned up and the kitchen table pulled out into the living room. A folding table had been set up too, and two gingham tablecloths overlapped both tables. Since Rose and Bertram had taken off the day before, the long, combined table was only set for ten. In the center stood a construction-paper cutout of a pilgrim man and woman that Lissy had colored at school several years earlier.

Lux scanned the room, then pulled the two tables apart and pushed one against the wall. The clatter of plates and silverware brought Dessie out from the kitchen. "Lux, what's going on in there?"

"Where the hell is a man supposed to sit if he wants to watch football?" Lux said, propping up his long legs on one of the folding chairs.

"You know dinner's almost ready," Dessie said, but just then Tommy came out of the bedroom, toy trucks in hand, and settled onto his dad's arms. "Look after your daddy," she told Tommy, trying not to stare at the disarray, but then she turned back to helping Lissy slowly stir the gravy.

As soon as Alan Ray and Billie and the boys came over, Lux cracked open two more beers, but when Alan Ray refused his, Lux kept both. Alan Ray stood up and paced between the kitchen and living room. He was chatty, saying they still had until Sunday to hunt, and mentioning a few other places in the woods that they could use as a blind. Lux seemed to be lost in thought. Ronnie and Billie set the table back together, and Lux didn't seem to notice as Billie lifted his legs out of the way. Dessie brought out some corn chips and then returned to the kitchen to take the rice casserole and the ham out of the oven.

Dessie's home-canned green beans and pan gravy were on the stovetop; in the oven keeping warm were whipped-up instant potatoes and biscuits from the government surplus. Two golden sweet potato pies cooled on the counter. Billie brought brown sugar baked beans, Mountain Dew, and also Cool Whip with two Jell-O rings for an extra dessert. Lissy got the boys cleaned up and settled in at the table. Dessie set out as many platters of food as the table would hold and took her place next to Billie, where they could easily move from table to sink to stove top and back again. She popped Tommy down in the high chair next to her. Across the table, AJ and Bertie were already reaching for biscuits. Lux turned down the TV, but he sat at the end of the table beside Alan Ray, so they could keep an eye on the game.

"Lead us in grace, Alan Ray," said Dessie, with a little smile in Billie's direction. Alan Ray rose. He stared in all directions until the group became silent, raised up a can of Coke, and in his deepest voice said, "OK, y'all, hush. A moment of silence." He winked at Ron, "Rub-a-dub, dub, thanks for the grub, yaaay, God."

Everyone echoed the final cheer. Billie's family dug in. But Dessie's family picked at their food. The kids whispered back and forth, the game droned on, and Dessie scanned the table to see if the food was disappearing. Lissy was doing her best, and so was Billie. Lux's plate was full; he'd eaten maybe a few forkfuls of Billie's beans. And Ron hadn't put anything on his plate. Dessie finally spoke up. "Ronnie," she said, "take something."

"I can't eat, Ma," said Ron. He swallowed and nodded at the platters.

Lux turned to Ron. "What the hell are you doing? Settin' here feeling sorry for yourself? You could have got one yesterday, if you could shoot straight. You should've been practicing all along, like I told you." Lux leaned forward. "Eat some of this, will you?" He took up an overflowing spoonful of Billie's beans from the bowl, and reached down the table to put them on Ron's plate. The closer the spoon came to Ron, the more Lux's outstretched arm began to shake. A brown mound of beans landed at the fluted edge of Ron's empty plate. Dessie tried not to look as it slid down slowly into the center.

Ron kept his eyes down his plate. "Me? I can shoot straight," he said under his breath. He struggled to keep his cracking voice steady. Then he surprised everyone by staring straight at Lux. "That goes for you, Pa. You're the one who can't shoot straight. Don't you think I can shoot straight, Uncle Alan?"

"Whoa." Alan Ray finished chewing and gulped. His face suddenly became as red as his hair. "Keep me out of this!"

"Watch this," said Ron. "Just you watch." Ron took a spoonful of the rice casserole and launched it across the table at his dad. He was aiming for Lux's plate, but a solid chunk fell onto Lux's lap. A few flecks of rice stuck to Lux's sleeve. Tommy laughed out loud from the high chair, and before Dessie could hush up the baby, Alan Ray called out, "Good shot!"

"Yeah, great shot!" said Little Lux. Dessie covered her mouth with her hand. All she could think of was how glad she was that Rose and Bertram were absent. Those boys ought to have more sense than to make a game out of this. They were raised better than that. The cousins started to giggle, and Tommy banged his spoon against the high-chair tray. Lux slapped his hands down hard on the table.

"Now, Lux . . ." Dessie began. Everyone stared at him.

"Why, you little shit," Lux said, glaring at Ron. Everyone watched as Lux pushed himself up from the table, slid his uneaten dinner aside, and brushed the flecks of rice onto the floor. Every glass of water on the table shook, and the silverware clattered while Lux held onto one of the table's corners to steady himself. "OK, boy, we'll see who can shoot straight," he said, adjusting his eyepatch and grabbing up his beer. He walked over, and his fingers took hold of Ron's shoulder. Ron's chair spun around. Then Lux pulled Ron up out of his seat by the collar of his flannel shirt. "Come on, Ron. We'll just take this up outside."

Dessie stared across the table at Lux's swaying form as he walked across the living room floor, reached up to the gun rack on the wall for Ron's Winchester Model 94, took a box of shells from the drawer, stopped near the door for a second to slip on some mud boots, and stepped outside. Ron slid out of Lux's path, then he took up his boots and headed for the porch. Alan Ray stood up and shrugged at the women before he ambled out. The younger boys raced out of their seats after them. "You young kids better stay on that porch!" said Dessie, and she and Billie went to the storm door to see what was going on.

Outside, Lux stooped over, wrestled a medium-sized rock from the flowerbed next to the driveway, and walked across the yard to the plywood bear under the apple tree. With the edge of the rock, he scratched a big X on its chest, scraping off the paint, and then he walked back about thirty yards across the front yard. Just then, Ron raced over. "You just wait," he yelled. "Just you watch this! Watch me shoot, you blind old man!"

Lux handed the gun to Ron. "OK. Y'want first shot? It's your gun, go ahead and show everyone how good you shoot it."

Ron loaded all seven shells into the tube, cocked the gun and shot, then cocked and shot again. Each time the gun fired, Dessie could see the boy stagger back almost before she could hear the crack. But she could see it was no use. Ron's aim was off, or the bear was too far away. He missed every time. Ron cocked the gun a final time and shot again at the brown shape far across the yard. "That damn thing's always been off," he said, and threw the Winchester into the dirt.

Quickly, Alan Ray bent to pick it up. "Give me that," said Lux, and he took the rifle. "You just stay right here, Ron," Lux told his son. "Let me show you how to get your deer."

Ron stopped and stood behind Alan Ray, looking like he didn't care anymore and he would rather watch the other boys on the porch. Lux ignored him. He checked the barrel to see if there was any mud in it, and then pulled his flannel shirt out of his pants and wiped the stock down. He backed up about another ten yards and then adjusted his eyepatch, reloaded the gun, squinted and aimed with his right eye. His first shot flew just over the head of the bear, but Lux cocked, aimed, and shot, and cocked, aimed, and shot until the bear lay flat on the ground with three holes in its chest, one in the center of the X.

"Get down there and set that back up, Ron," said Lux. Alan Ray took up the gun next, while Ron ran around to the bear to set it up again. The kids on the porch called out to see if they could come closer to watch. When Lux gestured for Little Lux and the cousins to come into the yard, Billie and Lissy went out there, too. Dessie could not watch. She turned away from the door and looked back toward the cluttered dinner table.

Tommy squirmed in his highchair. "Boom, boom!" he said, then put his hands over his ears. "Never you mind about that noisy old gun," Dessie said, turning off the sound on the TV before she eased herself down next to Tommy. She surveyed the all the food that was left on the table. "Nobody likes this stuff but us," she said to him. "You like my cooking, don't you? Look what your mama's got for you."

Tommy's eyes widened as Dessie pulled all the plates of uneaten food over and began to pick out pieces of meat and beans and untouched servings of commodity rice and biscuits. Dessie sat with Tommy, cutting up his food and feeding him small portions. Outside she could hear repeated rifle shots, but she was done watching. And no one seemed to need her; no one had called her name. "Look here, baby," she said to Tommy, taking the colored construction-paper pilgrims from the centerpiece. "Here's the pilgrims. They came from far far away, to try to live in the new world full of rivers and forests. Let's feed the pilgrims." She held out a spoonful of instant mashed potatoes to the pilgrim man. He was dressed all in black, with a stiff formal hat, and he carried a musket. "Mum, mum, mumm," she said. Then she held it to Tommy. But neither he nor Mr. Pilgrim wanted any, so she ate some herself. The shapeless blob of instant potato hung in her mouth, salty and smooth, but nothing like a homegrown new potato. "You're right, honey," she said. "This ain't food. This stuff's awful." Pointing at the musket, Tommy said, "Boom." Dessie nodded.

Dessie held up her hands and started clapping, one and two, buckle my shoe. Tommy settled down in his chair, so Dessie kept on going, telling Tommy about building log cabins and growing corn in the New World, about the Indians and Pocahontas and Captain John Smith, whatever she could remember from her school days, making up rhymes, hogs and logs, corn and born. She talked on, about the arrowhead that Lux had found many years earlier and given her, about her childhood memories of Thanksgiving, the hams in her smokehouse, chasing turkeys around her yard with handmade bows and arrows, the rows of canned homegrown food in the root cellar, as if it wasn't really her life, like she was just another character in the Captain John Smith story. Tommy smacked his lips and opened wide for ham dipped in gravy and sweet baked beans, but clamped his mouth shut for rice or potatoes. Anytime that the baby wouldn't eat, Dessie helped him out. When their plates were both clean, she stopped talking.

Dessie lifted up Tommy from his high chair and walked him over to the window. Outside it seemed strangely calm. Lux and Alan Ray had set the Winchester into the gun rack at the back of the cab in Lux's pickup, and it looked like they were getting ready to drive back into the woods to catch an hour or two of daylight. Billie was smoking; she and Lissy stood out on the porch, squinting at the afternoon sun as it began to head behind the tree line of the blue-gray Barker Mountain ridge in the distance. Over at the apple tree, Ronnie had taken out his Daisy BB gun, and he'd organized the younger kids into a game. What was left of the plywood bear was propped against the tree, and the kids were taking turns, shooting it with the BB gun, and then, when they were out of pellets, heaving rocks at it. Little Lux had managed to lift a rock almost as big as his head.

"See that bear, honey?" Dessie asked.

"Dat bear? Dat Ronnie bear?" said Tommy. He squinted out the window to where the children were lined up. He pointed out his thumb and his index finger and made a fist with the other fingers, as if his hand was a tiny gun, Tommy stretched out his chubby arm and said, "Boom, boom!"

Dessie set the toddler down near the storm door where he could watch the children outside as she headed for the kitchen. She covered the two golden sweet potato pies and set them up on top of the refrigerator. The kitchen was a mess. Bowls and plates were stacked everywhere, but Billie and Lissy would help clean up. She scraped everything that was half-eaten onto a single plate. Then, she looked at all those cartons of food, still taking up useful floor space in the pantry behind the kitchen.

Dessie rummaged through the pots and pans in the pantry and found the largest cast-aluminum canner, the one Rose had given her when she and Lux were first married. She picked a carving knife out of the sink and sawed open each cardboard box of commodity food. Into the canner she poured out all that was left of the government rice and covered it with the white powdered potato flakes and floury biscuit mix. She blinked the dust out of her eyes, brushed her hair off her forehead with the back of her hand, and then added the leftovers from the table. Then, she balanced little Tommy on her hip, took hold of the pot by the handle, and together they headed outside into the chilly dusk air, down the lane, across the field, and toward her mom and dad's farmhouse. It felt good to get outside, get a chance to feel the cool breeze on her face. What was she thinking when she took all that crap? she wondered.

"What do you think, Tommy?" she said to the toddler. "Let's go see Bonnie and Clyde." There, behind the farmhouse, was a path she'd walked hundreds of times as a girl with leftovers from dinner. Leaves crunched under her feet, and though the air was cool, she could smell the warm muck of the mud and pigshit as she got closer to the pen. Just like the good old days, she thought, the sow nosing out the boar, the silky dust spilling out of the full canner, landing in the mud and on the wiry coats of the two hogs that jostled back and forth, happy for the attention, and shoving each other to be first in line.

NINE

SUNDAY RUN (1982)

THE LAST HILL ON TOP OF PECKINPAW RIDGE BEFORE Fairchance was a dump. It wasn't a privately owned, charge-if-the-owner's-around dump like the one before Sheep Run on Northfork. It was a wide spot about one hundred yards off the road, at the top of a steep, barely paved county road with no houses in sight, where folks pulled off, checked downhill to the north and downhill to the south for the game warden or county sheriff, and their household and yard trash was out of their truck beds, into the wide gully, and out of sight.

On a crisp, bright Sunday morning in August, Lux pulled up to Peckinpaw Ridge in his black Ford pickup, got out, and spit into the mud. He aimed carefully to miss his boots. He was in his midthirties, tall, wiry, a pale-skinned man whose wavy black hair was flecked with gray. His thick black beard almost hid the collar of his flannel shirt.

Three boys, ages five, ten, and fourteen, slid out of the passenger door and jumped to the ground. "Tommy, don't you climb on that trash there," he told his youngest son, and then to the oldest, he said, "Well, git, Ron, quit your poking. Take that stuff and heave it." He pointed from the used siding and roofing and household trash in the bed of the truck to the vast cluttered gully below the road.

The dead one lay between a pile of old clothes and rusted car parts as if it was just another home appliance that quit working. Its skin was the color of two-year-old Copenhagen cans, and its hair was gritty with thick clotted axle grease.

"Hey, Daddy, lookit me," said black-haired Little Lux as he drew a bead with his pellet gun on a large brown wood rat that was scurrying along the edge of a grimy washing machine without a motor. "Here, take that, sucker." Keh-pop, keh-pop, keh-pew said the gun, and the rat hit the ground with a dull thud, shook itself, and ran into the tailpipe of a rusted muffler. Tommy and Little Lux took off after it, Little Lux with his gun, Tommy waving a long stick and shouting. High in the trees, crows cawed, always a bunch of raucous hecklers.

The dead one had pools of tawny silt under its arms and soft green moss between its legs. Long-legged red spiders hid under rust flakes between its fingers, and slender inky-cap toad-stools colonized its groin.

Lux looked at Ron, who was hauling the last of the dead batteries out of the truck bed. "You got those?" Ron, who never said much to his dad, nodded. "Uh huh." "Come on, boys," Lux yelled, "you get up outta there. Time to get your sister and Ma up at the church." Sunday was the best morning to make a trash run. The law was in church too, he figured, or tired out from chasing down drunks on Route 20 the night before. Then he scowled and added, "If we leave them there too long, them old biddies will start in a gossiping, and I'll never be able to get her home." He did not want to spend any longer than he had to in his hot pickup, waiting for the First Apostolic to dismiss. Ron scowled too, under the brim of his cap, at this jab at his mother, but kept his mouth shut and headed for the truck.

Lux scanned over the bank, past the trash, trying to see whether the creek bed was dry. The boys were banging on a pile of rusty sheet metal, trying to get the rat to emerge. He climbed into the cab and hollered out the window, "Tommy, you get up outta there or I'll wallop you. Daddy's got his belt on, you know I will use it if I have to. Look out for snakes there, Little Lux. Ron, you done yet?"

The dead one lay face downward. Its eyes were like coal and its teeth were like amber. Small opalescent snails tunneled into its hair, red-spotted newts found its mouth. Fine golden strands of mycelia made a forest for nematodes; blind naked baby mice sought out its ears.

"Hey, Dad, looky here, an ol' scooter. Can I have it?" shouted Tommy, the youngest and the one who paid the least mind to his dad's threats. He pointed into a pile of old clothes and broken chairs, not twenty feet off the road. "Yeah, sure" said Lux, "Ronald, fetch it up on the truck here, and watch you don't scratch the tailgate." Lux squinted down over the hill. "Will you look at that? It probably just needs a little paint."

"Hey," said Little Lux, running over to the truck. "I found it first."

"Never did," said Tommy. "It's mine."

Ron walked over toward the pile of rubble, curious about what kind of shape the scooter would be in, but stepping slowly because he knew that copperheads and rat snakes nested nearby. Whew, but something smelled bad. He was just about to reach down and grab the rusted chrome handle of the scooter when he saw it. He turned and scrambled up the hill, his eyes wide and his face white.

Some of the dead one swelled and sweated, pungent and over-ripe in the summer heat. Some of it shriveled and dried like a desiccated lily. Reptiles and small rodents swarmed to it like bees to the fresh-cut stump of a sugar maple.

"Whatsa matter, Ron? A-scared of snakes?" Little Lux asked. Ron shook his head and ran up to his father.

"Ron ain't a-scared of no snakes," said Tommy. "You remember the time he found us a big old black snake under the woodpile?"

Little Lux looked strangely at his brother. "Hush you, hit ain't no snake down there."

The boys turned and squinted from the scooter to Ron, and then to big Lux. Ron was watching quietly and nodding at his father. His thin face was the color of chalk, his eyelids blinked rapidly in the glare of the sun. He slid into the passenger seat and pulled the brim of his cap down over his eyes.

Lux called Little Lux and Tommy into the empty bed of his pickup truck. He told them to forget about that scooter, that it was all rusty and banged up, and next payday he'd take them into town and buy them one to share if their ma could part with some of the bread-and-butter money. Ron added that there was some old rotten skunk down there; a coon hound must have crippled it and left it to crawl off and die. "Phew, but it was rank," he said as they scrambled into the truck for the drive back to town. Little Lux and Tommy shouted from the truck bed that a new scooter would to be way better than an old one, that they could hardly wait to tell their cousins that they were getting a new scooter.

Ron sat in the passenger seat with his window rolled down and listened to his young brothers shout back and forth to each other.

"Pa?" Ron said, his voice trailed off.

"Let me tell you something my pa used to tell me," Lux said, rolling the truck out of the short pull-off, making sure the road was empty on both sides of the hill before he eased onto the blacktop. "Don't go looking for trouble, son, and tread careful when trouble finds you."

Ron was not exactly sure what his dad meant, but he set those words into the category *things my pa repeats every so often, that his pa used to repeat to him.* In general, that meant that it was best to keep his mouth shut. He sat beside his father, watching the twitch of his father's right eye, the left one hidden behind the eyepatch as always, the hollow of his father's cheekbone above the wiry dark hairs of his beard. Ron wondered how long it would be before he was allowed to take the truck on these back roads, and he wondered if his dad would let him try target practice with his high-powered deer rifle instead of the Winchester, and he wondered, for a brief minute, just why that person would have climbed up in among all that junk to hide, and just how long it took before that person died.

The dead one blew gas out of orifices. The dead one sent up smoke bombs of putrefaction. Dogs came and rolled in it, bringing home corpse news to their owners. The dead one was king over the pollinators and the foragers, it judged the implements, and it absolved the mufflers and the siding. The dead one was covered with leaves in the fall and snow in the winter. And come next spring, on top of Peckinpaw Ridge, the barbed hawthorn bush blazed brighter and redder, and the mountain dogwood cloaked the shambling hillside in ivory, each dark black branch decked out like a new bride, each separate flower, so pale and delicate, four white petals ticked with blood.

TEN

GARY BREWSTER (1984)

IT IS GETTING ON TOWARD THE END OF AUGUST AND school is coming up fast. *Stand up straight, Ron. Pick your head up, Ron.* Here it all goes and goes and goes again. The leaves on the trees all have that washed-out late summer color, not really turning, not really sharp. Under the cover of the night, under the slim stifling moon, nothing moves except the endless crunch of crickets' legs, scraping their rough bodies back and forth. The noise makes me think of chewing, forever chewing and sawing.

We picked your uncle's peaches in the drizzle. When your uncle was off at work we fought over the pizza rolls—you wanted the cheese inside to run out sloppy all over the cookie sheets until it fried crisp in the oven. We fed each other warm bacon with our fingers dripping grease. You threw me over. What are you so afraid of?

Under the slim stifling moon somewhere, Gary Brewster, you fearing, fearful, afraid of nothing, you left; you threw me over, until I dig into my cold chest, until my bare hands catch the crumbs of downy corners in the empty pockets of my jeans.

In late June when the flush of green life turned me, you came here, Gary Brewster. I met you at your grandfather's sawmill, the last cask worried by redheaded woodpeckers, the dry slabs stacked in shapeless vast walls, we sat in the shadows under long steel rails. The giant saw blades are black from lack of use. For forty years they shone and spun their way through oak and chestnut, splitting off slabs, flinging chips, screaming. You came here and split me apart, Gary Brewster.

UNDER THE night summer sky, at the rushing stream, we jump from rock to rock with dim flashlights you got from the glovebox of your uncle's Blazer. You are shouting above the flood. The creek is high. There is a racket of water, I remember. We pull our shirts off; we roll up our pants and throw 'em onto the far shore. I almost slip on the rocks. I hear a shout and turn around and you are gone, the shapeless water glinting in the lingering light. And they say it's always lighter around moving water. The darker shore patches of shadows overlapping and where are you, Gary Brewster? Are you somewhere on the shore or did you just step off one of those rocks into the creek like the way they say that little Clemons girl died; the flood rose up of a sudden and grabbed her from her yard. They didn't yet find her body. It gave me a case of shudders—

then you grab me from behind and call me a whore and in an instant I feel like one, too, though I had never had it before, and I start to split apart from how big you are. And how it feels, so good in me, until all of a sudden I hear a scream and it is me and I am in pain and don't even know my own voice or my own hurt.

And afterwards we stand on the bank of the stream and soak up water with our T-shirts and wash ourselves until the goddamn mosquitoes drive us back to our own houses.

NEXT DAY in the fresh morning light I come looking for you. You are sopping up the yolks of eggs with Bisquick fritters; Yerks lets you eat breakfast with your grandpappy's Farm Boss cap on. It is pulled low on your head. You look like a criminal. You look like an angel. "Pull up a squat, Ron," your uncle Yerks says, and I shake my head.

"No thanks," I say, not because I don't want to, but because I hurt still, too sore to sit down, and flushed, not from the walk over the hill. "I come to see if Gary Brewster wants to make some money," I say. "Pappy's busy and he needs someone to drive his truck to the Ford garage and wait for it to be fixed and bring it back."

"Hungry?" you ask me. You sure are. Just watching your lips took me back to the night and I shake my head to clear my eyes. You take that as a "No," just as I was about to reach for a fritter, so I hold my hand.

"Gary can't come" is all your uncle says, so I say, "Well I'm still on my driving permit and Pap is offering to pay five dollars, and I thought I'd split it with him for the company."

"Noope," Yerks says, shaking his big jowly head back and forth. "He's a-goin' to help me get that sawmill off the ground, that's why I took him on for the summer. The flywheel's seized up and them tracks is all pitted. Come back when you can and I'll put you to work too, Ron."

You nod your head, not looking like you care one way or another about nothing.

ALL SUMMER long you kill snakes in those woodpiles, and I haul rotten planks out of the mill and burn them. Every night after work in the smoldering burnlight when we open sandwiches together you tell me the killing stories over and over. Long fat slow-moving black snakes sunning like a piece of rubber tubing on the top of gray boards you chop into chunks with a hoe; garter snakes under rocks, slim and stripy, you outrun and stomp in your steel-toe shit-kickers; and at the bottom of the woodpile, poison copperheads flecked in gold with heads as wide as a fists you take a thick hickory switch to, then you beat them into the ground, their lifeless bodies twiching until dark.

"WHY DON'T ya work at a real sawmill?" my pap asks me, must have been the end of July, a Saturday, him being home and all. "I'll take you to A-1 with me. Why're you always up there hanging around with those Brewsters? They ain't nothing but a bunch of drunks and buggerboys."

"They ain't neither," I answer. "B'sides, Yerks pays me good enough money." I hang my head so low he can't get past the brim of my hat to fix my eyes.

"Oh yeah, what's good money?" my pap says. But I gulp down my Kool-Aid and head outside quick like I am going somewhere.

"Will you eat something, Ron?" Mama calls from the kitchen. "I'll fix a fried cheese sandwich. Y'ain't eating like you should, Ronnie."

But I pretend like I don't hear, and I take off for the woods, though I really don't know where I am going. I am hoping to head up onto the trails, I guess. I am hoping that you would be on the old logging trail at the top of the hill, scouting out some cherry for Yerks to cut, since wild cherry means big money, I head for the path at the edge of Pap's cornfield. I want to get right out of that house. I don't care where, I think. I just want to go.

Over the hilltop, behind the last stand of spruce trees and crab apples the land flattens out for a bit, and once some old deer hunters set up a shanty. Now the roof is overrun with vines, and a poplar tree is growing out where a window used to be. Scattered in the scrubby brush are tin cans the color of clay, the glinting litter of broken window glass, busted quart jars, even some good enamel pans hardly even cracked; there are smooth spots in the grass where the deer bed down and fat does and bucks leave deep two-toe tracks.

My pap once said it's an old snake pit, but I didn't see any old snakes. Just two rusty flathead shovels leaning against the door, propping it shut, four plank steps rickety and curled, and then I am inside, in the cool sooty dark, a big hole in the floor, a set of metal shelves and a busted-out window where the metal sink was, the countertop made of pine planks, a bunch of steel butter knives fanned out and a hole in one of them planks—maybe a hand pump for water had set there. No chair to sit down in, so I sit down on a solid spot on the floor and I think about you, Gary Brewster. Again.

And I want you to find me here, I want you to come walking in that door, your milk-white face and your long skinny arms and gold curls on your shoulders, and I am as hard as I ever could be. And I hold myself and think I am a cornholing buggerboy and I am bad, I need a whipping and I am hot for Gary Brewster, and maybe all the world knows it. And why don't you come on up here, now, Gary Brewster? Soon it will be fall, and then time for you to go. And I rock myself in my own empty arms.

AND ONE night, behind Yerk's sawmill in the dark, you say, "Hear that, Ron?"

"What's that?" I say, thinking you hear some old snake in the piles of dry slabs, or a she rat making a nest.

"The trees, up high on the ridge, blowing back and forth like that," you say. "It sounds just like the ocean, like they're waves, saying, 'Wish, wish.'"

I listen and it is true. I wonder why I never heard it before. I mean I heard those trees, but not in that way, ever. And the wind picks up and the trees begin to creak like the legs of old tables and chairs when you sit down to dinner. And I wonder what the other seasons would bring, what Gary Brewster would call the wind in the winter.

You pull a coal from the fire to light a cigarette you stole from Yerks. Your fingers glow red in the light and you cough. "One, two more days and I'm going back to North Carolina."

"How far north is that?" I say, and you start in laughing.

"You dumbass," you say, "it ain't north, it's south of here, God, you're one dumb hick."

"Fuck you," I say.

"Fuck you back," you say back, and the light glows red on your dark lips.

Then, two days later, you leave.

At the fairgrounds of the county fair I wander the midway, wanting. The weather is so hot—burning hot and dry. The grass is shriveled, the creek beds are bare puddles. Fall is coming on. All the jocks have their heads shaved for football, standing at the food booths shirtless and hardheaded, slapping at their girls. I wish you hadn't left, Gary Brewster, so you could be here to say, "God, will you look at all them dumbass hicks," but hey, it's just the guys from here and there, like always at the fair.

I keep passing the food tent and swinging around to get another look at what's there. I'm not even hungry but I want to taste every-thing—the sweet cherry-red cotton candy, fresh-squeezed lemons dipped in sugar for lemonade, cool kraut and warm hot dogs with ketchup. I want to run my tongue over the hot dogs and lick out the ketchup. My little brothers won't eat nothing, and they are scared to go on any of the good rides except the bumper cars and the carousel. I set them on the horses, and I stand and I stare.

Under the slim stifling moon somewhere, Gary Brewster, you fearing, fearful, afraid of nothing, you left me, threw me over, until I am so alone, until I dig into my cold chest, until my bare hands catch the crumbs of downy corners in the empty pockets of my jeans.

And I listen to the loud rock-and-roll guitars playing "Stairway to Heaven," playing "Born to be Wild." And I follow the shining rides with my eyes, how the lights on them all move forward and don't stop, all except the giant Ferris wheel, a sissy ride, but one that goes up high and takes you back down, forward and then backward. And I want to ride them all, especially the ones that don't turn back. The wooden roller coaster called the Cyclone, the roundhouse ma-chine that spins in strung-out circles called the Scrambler, the Tilt-A-Whirl that sets you in a little cage and turns you upside down, head over heels. And I wonder which one would be best, then I know, the

Cyclone, with its rails and wooden ties snaking over itself like a shiny sawmill, and its car of boards and splinters; and I want to get into the rickety little Cyclone car and ride up those clappety oak planks to the very top. And when it comes speeding down I will stand up and step out into the air and cry out your burning name, Gary Brewster Gary Brewster, until those words catch in the clacking racket of the ride and follow along, follow me up and then race me down, until the words burn and turn to tears and stream from my eyes, until the brakes squeal, and all of it comes crashing to a stop, and I will be lost, lost again, but this time, no one will find me.

ELEVEN

CANNING PEACHES (1985)

"DAMN, THAT show always gets me crying," Dessie said. She was leaning against the doorway of her narrow kitchen, keeping one eye on *Search for Tomorrow* in the living room and the other on Billie at the stove.

"What are you sniffling about now? That little tramp got just what she deserved. How long did she think she could go on cheating like that, flaunting it in front of the whole world?" said Billie, smiling, shaking her head. "Shame, shame, shame, bad, bad nursie."

"Oh, I know, I know. It's not about her. That one's trash. She's on a fast train to the federal pen, and she ain't a-comin' back. Sometimes, well, it's just too much, day in, day out. Somebody sick, blink your eyes, then they're gone," Dessie answered, her face flushed. Another tear trailed down her ruddy cheek. With a nearby washcloth she wiped it and drew off beads of sweat from her forehead and upper lip.

"I swear, you'll tear up about almost anything. You always did." Billie's long black hair was tied back loosely over her neck, and she

165

shook her bangs out of her eyes as she stirred the warm syrup in front of her. "Like the first time Dad got the gallstones. You thought we lost him, you remember? You were sobbing so hard on the phone I couldn't tell what was going on. I took off running across the field, and by the time I got to the house, he was sitting at the table drinking his Nescafé like nothing happened."

"Turn up that flame a little, would you?" Dessie said. "Don't quit stirring when I add the sugar. Once the syrup starts boiling, if no one stirs it, it'll scorch the pot." She hiccupped and drew in her breath. That memory was hard to shake. She had dropped in with the mail a few weeks after Mom had passed away, and found Dad on the kitchen floor, moaning and grabbing at his chest. He might have been having a heart attack. Dr. Madison even said so. Instead, Dessie said, "Well, he had five good months after that, didn't he?"

Billie nodded. "He sure enough did," she said softly. Dessie wiped her eyes with the back of her hand and turned to the cluttered kitchen sink, still full of mason jars that had a faint scent of mildew from being stored in the spring house. They needed to be scrubbed with the hottest water possible, and then set into boiling water in the canner to sterilize.

These past few weeks, time had gotten away from Dessie. There was Dad's funeral, with the suddenness of his death, all the nonstop details. His service seemed a repeat of Mom's, but even more so, since the memory of Mom's passing stabbed at her with each ritual and prayer. The whole family once again in the graveyard beside the First Apostolic, the turf still turned over and clumped up on her mom's side of the plot. Aunts and cousins from Pennsylvania taking over the farmhouse, digging through closets and cupboards for clothes or keepsakes she wasn't ready to part with, all of it overwhelming, until Lux told them that they had to go back home. Then, the rush of getting the kids ready for school, scraping together money to pay off layaways on school supplies and new clothes. All the while, the garden growing and producing, pole beans on wooden tripods getting less tender with each passing day, and all these ripening peaches. They had to be put by; it would dishonor her parents' memory to let them go.

A second batch of quart-sized clean mason jars were lined up, wet from their last rinse. So far, so good. None of the glass jars from the first batch had burst when she set them into the boiling water to sterilize in the deep, cast-aluminum canner. Dessie glanced over at the TV in the living room. In an obviously staged commercial, a fussy baby boy in a wet and saggy plastic diaper pouted, then a happy baby boy cooed in a cozy and tight plastic diaper. It was hokey, but Dessie couldn't help but smile. "Hey, mister, we made it through four kids, and never bought a single one of them plastic diapers!" she yelled through the doorway at the voice of the TV announcer. Then, turning to Billie, Dessie added, "Every day I praise the good Lord that I'm done with the diaper pail." Billie laughed. "That same goes for me, too. The whole house filled up with the smell, and those fumes from the bleach," she said, wrinkling up her nose, as if the smell of simmering peaches was driven right out of the air.

Dessie slid past Billie's side of the stove, set the clean canning jars carefully to warm on the stovetop near the gas flame, and reached for the wooden spoon out of Billie's hand, so she could take over stirring the syrup. It was the trickiest part, thickening the syrup, and she knew she'd better tend to that herself.

"Thanks. I didn't figure it would heat up that fast," Billie said. She used the back of her hand to brush dark wisps of ungathered hair off her face, then went to work on the remaining peaches at the kitchen table. A ceramic crock brimmed over with pale-fleshed peaches, already skinned, ready to be halved, pitted, and checked for bruises and rust spots. Dessie had given her the sharpest paring knife in the drawer.

Until this year, Billie was just as happy to let Rose and Dessie handle the peaches. Sharp knives had always made her nervous. Ever since she'd sliced into her tendon a few years back while helping Alan

Ray to skin a deer, her left pinky finger stuck out straight and got in the way. Billie dug the traces of rust off the surface, then sliced each peach in half and placed the large pit into a separate bowl. Each peach was more slippery than the next; juice dripped down her fingers and onto the surface of the kitchen table. Her hands were shaking, but it was too late to stop and get a dish towel. Dessie might be watching, glancing back over her shoulder, or was she looking at the TV? Her sister might have something to say if the peaches did not come out looking like they were on a magazine cover or headed for judging at the fair.

"When's the kids coming home?" Billie asked over the sound of the television. "I can't get used to them being back at school. I keep wanting to check to see what they have got themselves into."

"Four, maybe, or later this year with the new bus route. When the bus comes around the corner those redbone pups will start in." Dessie stared out the window, took a breath, and glanced at her sister. "Hey, Billie, what time's Alan Ray coming home?"

Billie frowned. "Who's asking? He never tells me," she said. "Uh-oh! Stop right there! It's time!" Billie said, smiling. She set the knife into the sink, rinsed off her hands, wiped them on her shorts, and turned to the living room. Dessie and Billie looked at each other. On cue both sang out, "Lights . . . Camera . . . Action!" Billie deepened her voice, drama building with each tick of the clock on the TV set, "'Like sands through the hourglass, so are the days of our lives.'" Billie conducted the flourish of theme music with an imaginary baton. "Pap liked that show," said Billie. "Mom got him hooked. He never wanted anyone to know, but after he retired, he worked out his day so he could be home to watch it."

Dessie looked at her sister and nodded. She always saw Bertram's brown eyes in Billie's, lighting up when they laughed, almost hazel. Dessie turned away, searching for something that needed to be done next, wiped down the tabletop, inspecting Billie's unfinished crock of peaches. Some were still whole; they held onto their stones like small white fists. "It's time to add these," she said. "I'll get the rest of this batch."

Billie leaned against the doorway. "I got into those scenes from last week, and I almost forgot what we were doing. Like Alan Ray says, seems like lately 'All the lights are on, but nobody's home.'" She fumbled with a cigarette pack in her pocket. "First we get that syrup boiling, right? Then put the peaches in? Do we bring it back up to a boil?"

Billie needs a break, Dessie thought. "Yes. Get off your feet. Holler at me if something happens on the show." Dessie said. She wondered whether she should've mentioned Alan Ray. After their Dad died, Alan Ray'd gone on a two-week bender, missing work, closing the bars at night, sleeping it off during the day. He had Billie call in sick for him each morning. Today was his first day back on the job.

Dessie set the next batch of heated jars into the covered canner to sterilize, stirred the almost simmering syrup in the speckled blue enamel pot. She turned to the table, to Billie's crock of peaches, finding the last of the brown spots, scraping them off, slicing the rest of them in halves. Every action recalled their mother's attention to detail, it was reflected in her joy when she served the fruit to the family. If Rose was there, she would not approve of the state of the kitchen, Dessie thought. Her bare feet stuck to the linoleum; it got worse with each step. Juice from the peaches must've somehow dripped onto the floor, but there was no time to worry about that now.

Steam began to rise in great billows above the enamel pot. The syrup turned rosy as Dessie added spices her mom used, cinnamon, mace, and nutmeg. Billie glanced over to the kitchen as Dessie scooped the peach halves and syrup into the jars, cleaned and tightened the lids, and used canning tongs to set the first batch into the canner. "This heat has got me wore out," Billie said, lighting up a cigarette and breathing out with a heavy sigh. It was only slightly cooler in the living room beside the rotary fan.

"Me too. Now that school's started, I keep awake worrying about Ronnie," Dessie said from the sink. "I'm afraid he'll be home for good before the month's out." Dessie poured the remaining peach halves into the steaming syrup, adjusted the flame, and kept watch over the newest batch, wooden spoon in hand. She blinked back the steam; beads of sweat gathered on her temples and around the bridge of her nose and slid down into her eyes.

Billie looked over at Dessie. "Ron'll drop out? Why?" she asked. Billie knew Ronnie did not want to start eleventh grade, but after the pipeline job had fallen through, Dessie had talked him into it.

"Ron told me he'd be better off at home looking for a job, that there's no sense going since he has Miss Springer again. This time it's for West Virginia history," Dessie answered. "He's sure she'll flunk him."

Billie paused. She wanted to catch the start of what she knew would become a love scene. "Well, Lissy got through Miss Springer last year. What's Lux say?"

"Lux says Ronnie don't stand up for himself. Lissy says Ron's right, Springer only likes the town kids. Ron's gonna have to hunt for a job, but he hasn't any car." Dessie waited for Billie to respond, but all she heard was the rising volume of violins set off against whispers of the lovers on the TV screen. Dessie glanced at the back of Billie's head, then beyond, to the TV set. On the grainy screen, the camera, like a passionate suitor, moved closer toward a woman's full ruby lips, moved to the string of pearls around her neck, then a hint of cleavage. Then, seamlessly, the camera angle rose up so the viewers could see what the woman was seeing: a man's dark, almond-shaped eyes; his clean-shaven chin; a tailored collar; a hand with a huge gold ring reaching for her cheek; then, more violins.

From behind, Dessie heard the hiss of steam rising and escaping through the top vent of the canner. She placed the steam gauge onto the vent, lowered the flame, and set the egg timer for ten minutes. She knew she would have to wait for a commercial before the conversation with her sister could continue. Dessie stared out the kitchen window over the sink. On the front porch clothesline hung the clean jeans, colored tees, and flannel shirts for the boys' back-to-school clothes.

Lissy was married last year at the end of eleventh grade, though she promised she would stay in school and graduate. She and Glenn lived in an apartment in town close enough to walk to the high school. Across the meadow, to the west, was Billie and Alan Ray's yellow trailer and garden, mostly tilled under now. Alan Ray's rusted red Ford pickup truck sat beside their trailer on cement blocks, both front tires off the rims. Back against the hillside beside the two peach trees were apple and pear trees, planted before she was born, heavy with autumn fruit. Her boys and Billie's boys had picked peaches last night until sundown, filling two five-gallon buckets and filling their bellies. From her kitchen window, if she looked toward the east, Dessie could keep an eye on her mom and dad's empty, white clapboard farmhouse and the large cornfield and family garden.

Thinking about her parents, Dessie's eyes started welling up. Dad had just begun to adjust to living on his own, getting out and socializing with cronies at the AmVets, stopping in to her place or Billie's for supper or to pass the afternoon watching the shows with Dessie, spending time playing catch or fishing with his grandchildren, no longer coaching, but helping umpire baseball all spring. He left Dessie's after supper, settled into his La-Z-Boy on the porch, and passed away with the game on and a beer in his hand. Lux went down to check on Bertram when he saw the lights on after midnight and found him. It was too much, too soon for Dessie and for Billie too.

At the sink, Dessie frowned out the window at the empty driveway next to the farmhouse. Until this morning, her Dad's dark green Lincoln had been parked there. Until Alan Ray took the car to work. To make matters worse, and Dessie knew no one wanted to face it, there were going to be some hard conversations: the farmhouse and barn, the fields, the car, all of it was in Dad's name, and he hadn't made up a will.

The sink was still full of water. Dessie looked around for the last few canning jars to soap and rinse. She and Billie had been down to the farmhouse and the springhouse the night before to retrieve the quart jars. Dessie had sorted the jars until she'd found the best, no nicks or scrapes on the rims, classic Atlas and Ball glass canning jars. Her mom had used clear quarts and pints to put up beans and pale blue quart jars for peaches, so light wouldn't brown the pale fruit. It felt strange to rummage through her mother's pantry for the spices, to bring all the canning supplies back to her place, but with Billie beside her she didn't feel like she was taking anything behind her sister's back. Dessie looked past the empty farmhouse driveway toward the creek and the old footbridge Dad had built, and then to the school bus stop at the paved road. Across the road, the green wooded hillside was beginning to show hints of autumn color. A red-tailed hawk circled just above the hazy skyline.

"Chicken hawk's back," Dessie called to Billie. And then, thinking about Ronnie again, she added, "What's the use."

Billie, in the living room, said, "Huh?"

The next batch of syrup boiled up in rhythmic eruptions. Dessie scooped out hot peach halves and sweet syrup and carefully filled the sterilized jars within a fingernail of the top. Mom used to say, "A babe's kiss from the lid." *Where did that come from*, she suddenly wondered. *Why didn't I ask her when I had the chance?* Dessie wiped the rims and sealing lids, closed the rings, then used the wooden-handled tongs to carefully place each filled jar into the canner. She stepped back away from the heat and leaned against the doorway, waiting for the water to return to a boil.

"Cleve's out of lids again. Lux bought the last batch. And the price of sugar's up again," she said. She exhaled, then took a breath. "It's steamy in here."

"What do you expect? It's canning time," Billie called back. "Come on in and set in front of this fan and watch the end of this scene with me. I'll show you steamy!"

"I'm watching the pot, and anyways I can see perfectly well from here." The whole kitchen smelled like sugary syrup and ripe fruit;

water beaded up and dripped down the metal cabinets and the front of the fridge. The afternoon sun streamed into the screened-in window, and the temperature in the kitchen had gone from tolerably warm to too damn hot.

Dessie put the steam gauge back on the hissing canner lid and set the timer on the stove for ten more minutes. She filled two tall glasses from the drainboard with ice and lemonade, then headed toward her sister. "I want to talk to Alan Ray, Billie," Dessie said. "I'm going to need a car, and Ronnie is too. I'm planning to get my license."

"You aren't," said Billie. Her mouth opened and closed again without a sound. She reached out her hand for the lemonade, her eyes fixed on Dessie's.

"You watch and see if I don't." Dessie shifted her tired weight from left foot to right. "Now that Dad's gone, how're we supposed to get to the grocery or get the kids if the school calls?" Billie looked away from the set. "Umm, yeah." Billie nodded. *Just one more reason to grieve her father's loss*, Dessie thought. *These many ways that he kept the world turning for them all.*

"Well, uh, Alan Ray's home most of the winter, and almost always on rainy days when they don't cut timber," Billie said. She paused. "What'd Lux say about you driving?"

"Lux said I could drive all right, if I can get a license and get legal." She looked over at Billie. She knew Billie was testing to see how far the plan had gotten.

Billie stubbed out her Marlboro. "Well, I do declare, if he lets you do that, what's going to be next?" she said, exhaling smoke rings, her mouth making big O's. The smoke rings lingered like spectral presences, and, as the fan rotated around, they slid away in the breeze. In mock surprise, Billie began fanning herself with the *TV Guide*. "How much does it cost to take the test?" Billie asked, and added, "Have you got that rule book yet?"

"I do, remember? From when Ron got his learner's permit." Dessie reached up to a shelf in the hall closet among the cookbooks.

"It don't cost a dime to take the test, but if you pass you hand over four dollars for a permit. I thought I could get Ronnie to study with me since he passed on his first try." Dessie placed the West Virginia Highway Safety booklet on the arm of the recliner for Billie. It had a bright yellow cover with a photograph of a station wagon stopped across from a school bus. The driver at the steering wheel waved as children crossed in front of him. But Billie's eyes were directed at the TV. Dessie walked back to the kitchen to check the stove timer. The second batch of peach halves in the canner was nearly done, and the pot with the last of the halved fruit would have to come back up to a boil. *What did Billie really think about her driving?* Dessie wondered. Sometimes Billie could be hard to pin down, harder to second-guess.

Billie should take a look at the permit book too, Dessie thought, and together they should both get licenses. Hard to know if Alan Ray would agree to that plan. It isn't hard to learn to drive, clutch, break, gas, forward and reverse. Just takes practice. Lux gave her the keys to the old farm Bronco when they lived up at the head of the Goshen Road. But the Bronco would not work as a road car, or for the driver's test, since it would never pass the state inspection. The logical choice was the Lincoln, and it even had an automatic transmission. She'd have to master parking that big boat against a curb, steering it around cones, memorize the laws, but if she could manage to get the Bronco up and down the Goshen Road, she felt pretty sure the Lincoln's power steering and brakes would be easy to figure out.

Dessie set the last of the jars on the stove top to warm near the remaining peaches in syrup and set the flame for everything to heat up slowly, then walked into the living room and stood beside Billie's chair. "I just don't see why Alan Ray had to take the Lincoln," Dessie started. "You all have a perfectly good pickup setting out there, and he can't drive more than one at a time."

Billie's head jerked up. "Hey, that pickup's got a busted brake line and you know it, and anyway—and he just does what he does, that's all," she said, her dark eyes shifting rapidly between her sister and the show. Billie rose out of the recliner, walked over to the set, changed the channel to ABC for *One Life to Live*. Then she added, "You know Alan Ray."

"He hasn't got the money to keep up the insurance on two vehicles," Dessie said. The words came rushing out of her mouth. "What's he going to do? Leave that truck sitting there? A-1 won't pay him to keep a Lincoln and a pickup on the road," Dessie continued. It wasn't what she wanted to say, but she couldn't seem to stop herself. Somebody had to take the lead here, Dessie thought, or nothing is going to get said. Was that what she wanted? She didn't know. The timer interrupted with a loud buzz. Billie stood in front of the TV set, her arms crossed over her chest. She looked like she did not know whether to sit or to stand, whether to help out or to return to the recliner.

Dessie turned back to the kitchen and started taking the processed jars out of the canner with wooden-handled steel tongs, placing them to cool on a couple of folded towels on the kitchen table. She set out a long row, eight steaming glass jars packed with fruit and syrup, then rearranged them into two rows of four quarts each. She could feel the room start to shrink around her, her sister in the living room getting further away, smaller. Billie had sunk down into the recliner, the ashtray balanced on her knees. She didn't turn around.

Dessie frowned at the TV, at the permit test book on the arm of the recliner, and at the clouds of cigarette smoke blowing away from the back of Billie's head. Dessie almost stopped herself, but then she said, "You all don't even have the money to fix the truck you got sitting out there now. How are you going to keep up the insurance on a second one? Y'uns don't even have the money to share in the sugar and the lids for these peaches."

"Hold on a minute, just hold it right there," Billie said, shaking her head from side to side. Dessie waited, to see if she would say anything else.

Billie leaned forward in the chair, turned down the TV's volume, and reached for a cigarette, turning her back to Dessie. She tapped the pack into her palm, then Dessie could hear Billie draw in her breath. She coughed and coughed again. From behind, Billie's shoulder blades bounced up and down like the wings of a fledgling bird. Billie caught her breath and turned toward her sister, a weary look in her eyes. "What do you want, Dessie? You want the farmhouse? You want the Lincoln? Just go on then, but it don't feel right, you two getting it all."

Heaven protect me, can't a person have a conversation, Dessie wondered, feeling heat rise in her cheeks, tears welling up. Now what? "Oh, that ain't it at all," she answered, almost under her breath. Dessie wiped her eyes with the back of her forearm. Billie's head faced the TV set. Over the drone of the fan and the music's pauses on the TV, Dessie heard the "ping" of the lids as they sealed themselves onto the cooling mason jars. Then, silence, as if all the sounds in the room had been switched off, even the whispers on the TV were barely audible.

Dessie headed back into the kitchen to check whether all of the jars of fruit had sealed. It was almost time to take the second set of jars out of the canner. She began to gather up the dirty bowls and the last of the utensils. With each footstep the floorboards creaked. She felt like she'd tracked sweet sticky syrup all over the floor. She hated how the plates and glassware rattled in the cupboards as she moved from the sink to the stove, how large and clumsy she felt, knocking into things as she walked, or like she was clattering things around loudly on purpose to get Billie's attention. It reminded her of when they were teenagers, when they argued and couldn't figure out how to make up.

The low rays of the sun landed on Dessie's form like a spotlight; as she moved, her own shadowed figure followed her back and forth on the kitchen wall. Billie reached over and turned the volume back up on the TV set. On *One Life to Live*, a young girl had found out she needed an ovary removed but decided to go through with her wedding anyway, without telling her wealthy husband-to-be about the operation or its possible side effects. Dessie and Billie had always liked that girl. She dressed nicely but not suggestively, never looked or acted like a slut, and they could tell that she came from humble people. Together they had wondered whether she would ever get up the nerve to tell her future husband that she might be unable to bear his child. Now the two had set a date to be married, and that girl held onto that terrible secret, her grief and shame tightening like a noose around her slim, pretty neck.

Dessie couldn't help it; she felt sorry for them both. Usually Billie, and Bertram too, could be counted on to make some sarcastic comment at these kind of overly dramatic, tragic points in the story. But Billie just smoked, stared at everything that flickered across the TV screen, including the commercials for baby food, plastic diapers, and laundry detergent, and occasionally whacked at the fly on the window sill. The timer rang again, and Dessie returned to lift eight more jars out of the canner. As the last bit of the show ended and the sign-off music came on, Billie stood up to leave. "I'm going to start supper," Billie said. "It's already three o'clock. The kids will be here soon, and you never know when that man of mine will show up, but you can bet he'll be hungry as a bear." She gathered up the lemonade glasses and brought them back to the kitchen, handing them to her sister at the sink.

Dessie blinked her eyes and swallowed hard. "Well, I'll finish up the last of these. Lux said he'll be home around five today." She looked past her sister at bits of coming attractions flashing across the screen. "Nothing worth watching tonight, anyway, still reruns," she mumbled. Nodding agreement, Billie opened the screen door to the porch. Dessie noticed a dirty fingerprint next to the door handle. She tried to think of something to say. "Hey, Billie, wait," she started, then she said, "You taking down any of these jars?"

Billie paused, looking out across the yard toward home. "You just keep 'em all."

"Now look here," said Dessie. It was the best she could manage. Her soapy hand gestured at the table, where the double line of canned peach halves cooled in the sunlight, two dozen cornflower-blue quart jars, two dozen shiny brass lids, the bright shimmer rising above the shadowed pattern on the kitchen wall.

Without turning, Billie stepped out onto the porch, and her thin face disappeared under the clothesline. "Nah," she said, heading across the porch, and then added, "Oh, the boys will probably come up for some later."

From the sink, Dessie stared across the yard while her hands scrubbed away at the shreds of fruit that were burned onto the edge of the deep enamel pot. With each step Billie's slender form became smaller and slighter; her long black hair almost disappeared in the glare of the sun as she set out across the hayfield. Taking hold of the tongs, Dessie placed the final batch of filled quart jars into the rapidly boiling canner and set the lid. She leaned against the counter, eased herself down onto all fours, bunched up a towel under her knees, and, working her way backward from the stove, past the sink, to the doorway, she scrubbed at the floor of the kitchen, working the sticky spots off the linoleum and then drying the floor with a towel. The canner began to hiss once more. She set the valve on the lid, reset the egg timer; one last time, ten minutes. She headed to the bathroom next, and washed her bare feet.

In the living room, she picked up the Highway Safety book, glanced at a couple of random pages, then put it back on the shelf in the closet. Some man on the TV set was yelling about Super Value Days at the Ford garage, shiny rows of cars and trucks lined up behind him. His face was distorted, pushed hard up against the screen. His unblinking eyes popped out of his face. "Who the hell are you staring at, mister?" Dessie asked the announcer, smacking her palm into the switch on the set and shutting him off. Then, pressing her moist cheek against the sleeve of her blouse, Dessie closed her eyes and sat down on the recliner in front of the clattering fan to wait.

TWELVE

NOT TO TOUCH THE EARTH (1990)

I'M A DEER. MY LEGS ARE LONG, LEAN, POWERFUL. I take great leaps and bounds, I can fly over the earth. Over the road, Lissy races. Up near the top of the ridge. Sky spreads out before her, wind streams against her upturned face. *I can leap I can fly I can run.*

Her body stretches, her heart races—her deer's heart thumps faster and faster in her chest. *I can run. I can run.* Her legs pump and her arms pump too, they're like second legs, propelling her through space. Her body bounding, perfectly fleet and nimble, leaping effortlessly.

The sun is setting. It is late for her run. Not too many people live on this strip of road; no one is around. *Freedom to be alone. To not be seen. Complete freedom. Finally. To run alone.*

To feel her feet fly in spurts of strength; in high school she had been a sprinter, not a miler, but tonight she wants to run her animal heart into the ground. *How would it feel to be a deer? How would it feel?* Her deer hooves are light. They barely touch the ground. *Down the hill. Keep going. Not done. Don't turn back. Do not go home.*

Home. Her husband is home. Their little girl. Home—their house—or is it? Her car is at home, and it's broken. Useless. Who needs it? She can run over road, over field, over hillside. She leaps off the blacktop, over the ditch, down onto the path along the corn. Into the field. She is fleet. She is free.

Well, maybe not fleet. Maybe not free, either. The day's events charge at her. How her Jeanie, in a fit of anger, locked herself into the car. They were all in town. At the supermarket. It was a crowded Saturday afternoon. Jeanie was mad, pouting; she couldn't get her way. She is only five. She acted, well, childish, in the store. Jeanie was pouting. *So I could see—see what? see what I did to her? I had to get a job. No one's buying timber these days. When will they call Glenn back to work?*

Lissy's legs begin to throb from the rough ground. She looks back to the road. Briars and burrs grab at her shins. She looks for a way to get back onto the blacktop. At the end of this endless field maybe. She urges her legs on.

Glenn sent Jeanie to the car. He gave her the keys. She went there to sulk. Glenn took her car keys and gave them to Jeanie. Jeanie sat there. *This is the weekend*, Lissy wanted to say. *Time to shop. We all need to help choose food for the week. We don't live on grass and bark.*

She limps a bit as she runs. The ruts and rocks are hard to jump. The sun has set. Up ahead a streetlight flickers on at the intersection of Route 20. It is getting cooler. Cool damp pockets of air brush against her cheeks. Her animal eyes narrow. A slender shape along the road. *Is it a mailbox? a hitchhiker?* It is getting too dark to tell.

She knows she is out late. Time to go back. To the child. To him. To hell with Glenn. To the car. To the broken-out window. *To my new car that I drive to my new job. My job. To my only car with my window smashed in. What a joke. Driving to work with the window rolled down. But there is no window. It shattered in a million pieces. Not even one large chunk. Just a spray of glass all over the inside. All over the dashboard. The shifter. The seat. Jeanie.*

She locked herself in. "No," said Jeanie. "You can't come in here." She had Barbie in her hand. She made a face. A slightly satisfied, slightly unsure face. She is such a child.

"Give me the keys, honey. Please, Jeanie. Don't get Daddy mad. Pass it through the window, doll." The shopping cart behind the car was filled up with groceries. Frozen peas getting warmer. Ice cream melting. Jeanie looking at her Barbie doll. Cars pulling out of spots all around them. New cars pulling in.

Lissy's heart pounds in her chest. The memory weighs her down. Her knees buckle. Her deer arms grab at the air. *He kicked in the window. Glenn kicked in the passenger window to get at a little girl. He dragged Jeanie out and his arm was cut and bleeding. Served him right that his arm got cut.* The whole car shook sideways once, toward her, and then his foot crashed through the window. Glass was everywhere. The keys were on the seat. Then the door was open wide. Jeanie was crying and out of the car and Lissy was loading groceries into the trunk. In the parking lot on a sunny afternoon on the chunks of glass. While a small girl in pink suspenders was crying and a tall man's bare arm was bleeding. And Lissy's stomach cramped hard enough to knock her down. And cars of all sizes were waiting for parking spots.

Lissy's chest heaves. The soft ground gives under her feet. *Jeanie was bad all day. She shouldn't have done it.* Words pile up like stones. *He's been off work a lot lately. She's just a child. I can't take it anymore. I'll take her. I can't go to work anyway. What can I tell them? I have no window. I have pieces of window. Pockets full of rocks. I can't tell a soul. Shiny bits of glass and pockets full of rocks. At least I can run. Like a sleek and silent deer. I can run.*

She rounds the field. She reaches the intersection. She jumps the ditch and climbs up over the embankment. Time to turn back. Her legs are burning. She's panting and grasping at the air—the dark air. The edges of the road are very dark now. A new shape's coming up the road. It's a long shape, a man, on the road. A motorbike. She hears it before she sees it. *Why isn't its lights on?* Her senses prick up, her deer ears. She hears a noise. *Where is it?* Her blood pounds. Her thighs ache. Coming toward her. She rounds the turn and feels her bad knee begin to give out. Not now. She stiffens her leg. She won't limp. She won't look tired.

She starts back up the hill. She stretches to full height. There were rapes. Not on this spot, but closer to town on roads much like this one. Girls have gone missing. She seeks out the brightest spot in the road. *A woman needs to be in the light. Or does she?* The brightest spot is not very bright. And soon it will be gone. She can't run any more. Her legs are drained. Her deer heart has pumped out its blood. She knows she is jogging slowly and she knows she is prey for someone. A stranger. A hunter. Anyone. She rounds the hill toward the cutoff to her house. No one follows.

It is pitch-black on the gravel lane. She can barely see her own hand. She has to walk carefully. She could trip. She looks for the trees that hug the sides of the lane. Their branches point toward the distant sky like long slender fingers. Long limbs arch and intertwine, like a steeple over the road, like her mother's fingertips pressing against hers a long time ago. *Open the doors and see all the people.*

The road is mostly rock now, and it is steep, and it is pitch-black. Her feet make crunching noises. The woods make familiar noises. Hoot owls call, "Hoo-hoo-hooo, hoot-hoooo." Crickets sing, "I know too, I know too, I know too, I know too." Lissy's pounding heart races inside her chest, but her body is only inching. So slowly through the dark space; her legs tremble onward.

The closer she gets to her house, the less it seems she moves. Some lights are on around back. Glenn would be out in the garage. Jeanie would be alone upstairs in her room. It's time to put her to bed. A deer could browse around, could take her young daughter and go graze someplace new. She is not a deer. She has a family, a house, a new job at the Whispering Pines, a car loan, and a shameful busted-out car window. She can't move, can't even speak. Each leg feels so heavy that it barely moves at all. They don't even bend; they just barely sway. Her shoulders stiffen. She takes a deep breath. She is almost there, almost back home.

Then Lissy knows how to be. She is young, and she is still strong. She can stand tall. She can become a tree—*a tree*. Trees must bend, yes, but not break. She will be strong. Be still. Be silent. She will shelter her daughter under her boughs. She will stand unmoved and hold her head high. She will shake off his sharp words like leaves in the wind. *I am a tree.*

She is not a deer. She stands at the front door of her silent dark house. She raises her arms high above her head, presses the steeple of her fingertips hard against each other, and closes the massive wooden doors of each chamber of her pounding heart. Lissy takes some long, steady breaths, and soon she is able to breathe so calmly, so steadily, it is as if she isn't even breathing at all.

THIRTEEN

THE WHITE SHAWL (1992)

ON THE DAY OF MY DAD'S FUNERAL, MY MOTHER Dessie wore her white shawl. Great-Great-Grandma Elisabeth made it by hand, her mother's grandmother, handed down from Ireland. It was a beautiful shawl, long white tassels hanging down, tightly woven in fine silken thread. If you look closely, you can see that the weave makes a pattern of little squares where the fine threads cross each other. Mom kept it in a soft cloth pouch on the top shelf of the closet. I used to beg to wear it when I was little. I wondered what kind of message she was trying to send, a white shawl wrapped over the shoulders of her plain black dress. Mom shook her head from side to side, crossed the edges of the shawl around her shoulders and arms, and said, "Lissy, honey, I haven't even got a black shawl, and besides, they can say what they will, but I just can't bring myself to sit there like an old crow in the front row of the First Apostolic in solid black."

The morticians from Jarvis Brothers did their best. Dad had a split coffin, so no one could see what those logs that slid off that flat-bed truck did to his body. I was glad his face was spared. No one understood me or paid me any mind when I said this, but I wished I could have seen him, his body, what he really looked like, before they put him in that poplar box. I don't know why, but something made me want proof, to see what actually happened to him, maybe to say my good-byes to the real him before the funeral home got to work.

After I saw Dad laid out in front of the altar at the church, the whole accident was almost too hard to believe. But it was him all right, his gold wedding band that never left his finger, his fingernails impossible to get completely clean, hands crossed over his heart, clean blue-jean shirt with the pearl buttons, bristly black curly beard, jet black hair gone to gray at the temples. No eyepatch, though, just both his closed eyes, the left eye bearing the traces of scars that no mortician's box of makeup or even a magic wand could ever erase. There were Dad's crow's-feet around his eyes, and Dad's grooves along his brow. That part felt like they got it right. But Daddy's lips looked too puffy and were too pink, that part was off, wrong, someone else's mouth found its way onto Dad's somber countenance. Glenn couldn't see it, but my brothers and I noticed that right away.

Aunt Billie took one look at Dad and burst out blubbering into Mom's shoulder, dabbing at her eyes with the hem of her sleeve. Ronnie wouldn't come up to look at him, and neither would Alan Ray. They settled into the family pew with their caps pulled down low on their heads. Reverend Shorter told Mom that he thought they made it look like Lux Cranfield was asleep with the angels, but who ever knows about that? I know he is supposed to say those sort of things, but maybe it is the other way around, maybe the angels come to earth and sleep with us? Mom answered Reverend back, that she thought Dad might've had one or more guardian angels looking out for him all these years, for him to make it on this earth this long. I've wondered about that, too. Maybe we walk with them always, during these few short days we are given, though we do not know how to listen for signs of their counsel. Where are they then, when we need them? I wish I knew. A person's mind can go to those sort of places, sitting in church waiting for her father's funeral to be over. All I can say is Daddy looked almost calm, the strain of his worries gone. For once his soul at peace, outwardly at least.

I had an ankle-length black dress, borrowed from Glenn's mother, high-necked and stiff, the way you're supposed to feel at your own father's funeral. At the end of the service, Uncle Alan Ray took his A-1 cap off for the first time since I can remember. Funny that his red hair is almost all white, and he's getting bald and heavyset now too. He and his boys didn't wear anything black, though, and neither did Glenn, nor did my brothers. To me, that felt wrong, disrespectful almost, to Dad. Even back here where no one is watching, I believe that these old ways have meaning. Mother said it was fine, though. She said Daddy don't care what his boys wear, it don't trouble him now, not a bit.

The First Apostolic wasn't even half-filled, though people had filtered in. Some folks knew Dad from the firehall, some old-timers knew Alan Ray and my Granddad Bertram from the AmVets, some men from A-1 Lumber, Dad's age, Glenn's age, and a few of their wives. Glenn's mother and father sent flowers. None of Dad's people were there; most of the Cranfields haven't come around Mom and Dad since their wedding. As Dad used to tell it, his dad Everett never wanted Daddy to marry Mom, and most of his people took up for him. The morning of Mom and Dad's wedding, Everett drove up to the churchyard with a shotgun and fired off a couple shells to get everyone's attention, and then declared to all that there would be no wedding on that day. Dad and Dad's Uncle Ron stood guard, like human shields in front of Mom and Granny Rose. Granddad Bertram tore out of the church, right up to Everett, and told him that if he did not want to stay and celebrate this union, his presence was not required. Dad said that Granddad reached out his hand to take the gun, but Everett told him to go to hell and watch his back, that he'd be coming for him before the day was out, and then he left out of the churchyard. All through the ceremony, Granddad Bertram and Dad's

Uncle Ron guarded the front door of the First Apostolic in case Everett thought about coming back around.

Dad said that he and Mom didn't even stay for the reception. Mom tossed the bouquet behind her as she ran past the choir room. They slid out of the back of the church after their vows, hopped into Dad's Jeep, and took off down the main road with a gang of lumberjacks in pickup trucks running defense like the famous Steel Curtain. After the wedding was over, the sheriff found Grandad Everett and locked him up for thirty days.

We kids never met the man, although once at the gas station Dad turned the pickup around and told us his old man was at the pump, and that we would stop for gas later. Then, at one point, we heard the mortgage and loan took over Grandad's property and boarded up the house, and word was that he was headed to Florida. Dad used to say that being raised up by a father like that was the best thing that happened to him and the worst thing that happened to him. Now it is too late to ask what he meant. I know he had a special fondness for his uncle Ron. A couple of times we met him and his boys before they sold their farm and moved south. Not many Cranfields live hereabouts anymore. Dad had that one cousin in Shinnston, his uncle Ron's granddaughter Clairey, who called him on the phone for Christmas, but she never came to visit while he was alive, so it didn't surprise us that she didn't come to see him be put to rest.

MY DAUGHTER Jeanie cried herself back to sleep the morning she heard about her Papaw Lux. She favors Dad, too, with her black curly hair and big dark eyes. She's so tall these days. And she was good for the whole service in the church, sitting on my lap, eyes brimming with tears, a little black purse stuffed with tissues. She went up to see her Papaw in his box and put her first-grade school picture in there to keep him company, then she came back and buried her little face in my chest. Mom said the last thing he said to her was that she should be careful when she went out to feed the dogs, since it was slick out there. Then he walked out the door in the pitch-black of the morning on his way to work.

Next to Mom sat Ron, skin as pale as a sheet of paper, looking down at the tips of his shoes like Dad used to do in church. We're just a year apart, and I know him well enough to read his thoughts from the look in his eyes. I know he's worried about having to look after Mom. "For God's sake, Ron," I told him, "Daddy's not even cold yet. Don't you think Mom could use a little looking after now?" He works on the pipelines and never comes home. Half the time we don't know where he stays or what he gets himself into.

At church, all three of my brothers acted like they were in jail or the school detention room: Ron, Little Lux, who had a week's furlough from Parris Island, and Tommy, who's just sixteen but as tall as the rest of them. He's going to start pitching for Varsity this spring, and Dad was so proud, that was all he talked about. They fidgeted and whispered to Billie's boys through the entire funeral service. I thought Mom might say a few words, but she kept her eyes closed, her hands folded in her lap, and her head bowed down. When Reverend Shorter was through and everyone stood to leave, my brothers just sat there in the pew together. You'd think they were old enough to know better. Mom had to tell them to get downstairs to help Uncle Alan Ray get Dad's coffin out to the truck in the rain.

No one from the First Apostolic could understand this, but we declined to put Dad to rest in the churchyard, though Granddad Bertram and Grandma Rose are buried there. Daddy had always said he wanted to be buried up on the Goshen Road. There's a small country cemetery above the old orchard, mostly for Smiths who used to own land on the ridgetop. Dad said he'd promised Grandad Bertram he'd never sell that land, and now it'll be forever his, I guess. "Your dad never was one to stay in town any longer than he had to, so I reckon we should grant this one small wish of his," Mom said to us right off. "Just so long as there ain't any Barkers buried up there," Mom said. "Your Daddy couldn't abide waiting for Kingdom Come next to any Barkers."

I STAYED back with Mom while she thanked the folks who came to the church service. Ron, Little Lux, and Tommy got Dad's coffin onto Uncle Alan's pickup, and then they came and got us. I looked around, half hoping I'd see a line of cars, like when the mayor died, a hearse, little flags on each car, but that vision vanished when I set foot outdoors and only saw the Reverend's Ranger pickup and vehicles we came to the church in, not another car or truck, not even the men from A-1. Folks said their good-byes, promised they would stop by the house to look in on Mom, and then left to go on with their lives. Ron drove with my brothers in Dad's Ford F150, Alan Ray took his pickup, and his boys had their Chevy Luv, and Aunt Billie came with Jeanie and me in the old farm Bronco. Glenn went off to work. "It would pain me too much to see Lux Cranfield laid in the ground," Glenn said, which surprised me, but there was no way to know if he really meant it.

THE COLDEST rain started coming down, harder and faster as we headed up the Goshen Road. That hollow was muddy as ever, but no one much has driven up there lately, except for Dad, or Alan Ray and the boys when they're coon hunting, so the ruts were not too deep. I led the way in Dad's trusty maroon-and-white farm Bronco with the lugs turned in for four-wheel drive, with Billie holding Jeanie in the back and Mom beside me. Mom turned up the heat full blast as soon as we got out of town. She kept saying how cold she was.

It was one of those rainy spring days, just slightly warmer than a couple of days ago when Dad died. If it hadn't been so cold and icy, the log truck mightn't've slid like that, the logs tumbling out. Dad was in the wrong place at the wrong time. He always said that when his number's up, it's up, and he hoped it'd come fast when it came. Glenn says the same damn thing. I sat in the church and prayed to our dear Lord that Daddy didn't even know what hit him.

"I've been up this road one too many times. Too many times," Mom said, shaking her weary gray head from the passenger seat. "Look at this place."

I looked around to see what she was talking about. The road itself was soaken wet, slick and muddy, but just firm enough for the Bronco's tires to still have traction. Below, out the window, past my mother's pale, drawn face, across the narrow valley, the grass was starting to green up. At the wood's edge was a row of sarvisberry trees without leaves, the first pale flowers sprayed out along the black branches. Out the driver's window, on my left, on the sharp edge of the shale cliff face, winter was not ready to give way. Water dripped from every hanging dagger of an icicle, every icy crack between every layer of rock, filling the ditch and running over into the tire tracks, and icicles hung white as bones against the shadows. The bones and the branches, I thought, remembering long walks along the creek in the early spring, the collection of small animal skulls I started as a girl. The signs of creatures that did not make it through this hard winter, right before the full green blast of spring hides all the evidence.

The scrawny wild blueberry bushes were stunted and leafless, scruffy red stems so thin I could hardly see them against the wet shale. We four kids followed Dad up this road for years, me and Ronnie in the lead, the little ones behind us, and we pulled the blueberries and blackberries from the stalks as they hung off the bank of the road. Dad and Alan Ray set out rabbit boxes and worked on their tree stands. The ground underfoot felt different every day, depending on the weather, the time of day, the season of the year. That might have been yesterday, but it's really going on ten years ago. I don't know what it is about seeing the bare thorny whips of multiflora rose overtaking a pasture that used to be all timothy grass that can make a person so sad.

I sighed. "Oh, Mama," I said. "I'm so sorry about Daddy. He was a good man. He didn't deserve to go like this."

She looked at me. Her hair had almost completely gone to gray. She began wearing it shoulder-length and wavy lately, like some old mother of the hills. Now the color was gone from her round cheeks. She was trying so hard not to cry that she had to bite her bottom lip.

We passed the shambles of the old Barker place and started to climb the steep rise to their old house site.

"Your Daddy wasn't a real good man. Some days he was a good man, but some days he could be a real son of a bitch," she said, almost whispered. Oh Lord, I thought. Not now, Mom, I thought again. Aunt Billie and Jeanie were in the backseat. I doubt they heard us, between the noise of the wipers, the splash of rain against the fenders and on the roof of the Bronco, the rattle of the muffler, and the grinding of the engine.

"Oh, Mama," I said. "He loved us the best he could."

I stopped talking. I could see how upset she was. Her lips quivered, tears rolled down her cheek, and her whole face seemed like it was going to come undone. In the passenger seat her left hand came out from under her white shawl and covered her mouth. I don't believe she's ever taken off that gold wedding band from the day he gave it to her. She hiccupped a few times and caught her breath.

I stopped the Bronco to wait at the top of the rise near their old house site. The land leveled out to a narrow stretch of field edged by clumps of willows and sumac above the creek. In the center of the field where they once used to live were the only remains of the foundation stones from the old Smith house. A line of jonquils poked out of the ground, ragged and yellow. Why do country people have ragged jonquils, while in town all they have are perfect, tidy daffodils? I wanted to talk to my mother, to tell her something. Daddy was no son of a bitch. I knew something about being married to a son of a bitch. *There are men out there that can take you away from life itself, Mother.*

While we parked there, Alan Ray drove past, slowly, his truck in low gear. Dad's casket box was mostly under the camper top of his truck, and the rest on the tailgate, strapped on and covered in a blue tarp. Mom's eyes were brimming over. She took her hands away from her mouth. "Alan Ray's a son of a bitch, too," she said a little bit louder.

"Mom, don't get Billie started," I said.

Why was she comparing her life with Aunt Billie's, I wondered. Uncle Alan Ray hadn't worked steady in five years now. He started drinking soon after Granddad Price died; he'd go off to work and end up in the bar. His back hurt too much to cut any more timber, he said. Now he got a disability check once a month, handed it over to Billie, but seemed like he didn't care where he slept or who brought him home. My dad worked until the day he died.

Aunt Billie's two boys came up behind us in their Chevy Luv pickup. The engine ran so rough I could hear the motor stop and then start itself back up again. In their headlights the rain looked like little silver straight pins. Cousin Bertie waved us on from the driver's seat, and then he and AJ shrugged their hands as if to ask what we were waiting for. I put the Bronco in gear and drove with my lights on, slowly up the dirt lane toward the graveyard.

Mom went on, like she did not care who heard this. "Your dad punched the hell out of me when we were first married. Ronnie got it, too. You didn't get it the way Ron got it. Neither did the other boys. You remember his temper."

I remembered. But I didn't know what to think. Ronnie needled him more than the others, that was some of it. Dad got mad, yes, blew up, tried in stupid ways to make up for it. I stared up the hill beyond their old house site. Rows of wide red rhubarb had pushed their thick, tightly curled leaves out of the ground. It marked where the garden used to be. A well-made post-and-rail fence, the horse corral, and a lean-to shed stood as if waiting for another unlucky couple of homesteaders to take their chances. Glenn and I used to drive up here the summer we started going together. In those days we lay together in the bed of his old Ford with the doors wide open and the truck radio turned way up, nothing but the wide, star-filled sky and shooting stars above us. I didn't even worry a bit once I got pregnant, and I was proud as ever when we got married. Who was that girl? It seemed like a hundred years ago.

"I was too young then," I said to my mom, shaking my head. I wanted to clear these memories out of my head. I wanted to pay attention to my mother. She was the widow now. She was the one who needed looking after. I didn't want to speak ill of the dead, and I did not want to think about Glenn.

Jeanie was squirming around in the back on Aunt Billie's lap. I didn't know how Aunt Billie could look Alan Ray in the eyes after all these years of his drinking and catting around. Once I realized how things were, I used to wonder why she kept letting him roll back in as if he was never gone. But these days he didn't seem to pound the beer as much as he used to. Alan Ray looked more like sixty-seven years than forty-seven. His face was blotchy, and his eyes were ringed with pouchy circles. He complained about everything. He had the chest pains, had the sugar diabetes, but he wouldn't see a doctor. We knew he was afraid that a doctor would tell him to quit smoking and drinking, and that would never fly with a man like Alan Ray.

I slowed down and eased the Bronco over the some of the largest ruts in the road. Up ahead, Alan Ray's truck was pulled off to the side. I drove up alongside of him and let the Bronco idle. I hoped that Billie's boys didn't come sliding up behind me. They might get that Chevy hung up in the mud if they had to stop too quickly.

"The road's too wet. We're going to carry Lux from here," Alan Ray said out loud. He motioned to my brothers, and they hefted the box out of the truck. Alan Ray shook the water off the tarp and draped it back over Dad's coffin. I could tell from his voice that he was sober.

Aunt Billie got out of the backseat of the Bronco and walked over to Alan Ray, said something to him, and lit up a cigarette. She shouted for me to keep on driving while she walked, showing me where to put the tires for the best grip. I rolled the window back up to keep from getting soaked before I even got out of the car. I didn't want Jeanie getting out yet. She was still wearing her patent leather shoes. She could get a bad chill if the rain kept up. Somewhere in the back I had packed a bag for her, galoshes and a little rain slicker. I would see how close I could get the Bronco. I drove through the grove of poplars and pulled over onto the berm, just enough room to turn the Bronco around. Through the edge of the woods ahead was the cemetery, marked by some scraggly tall evergreens and cedars.

"About like I remember it. Not much of a graveyard," Mom said, looking out the window. A split-rail fence that had marked the edge of the plots was dragged down as if a herd of deer had run through it. There was one extremely tall cedar tree in the center, bushy and thick, and about ten or so big stones, with some small slab markers for all the buried children, lying flat. I'd been out here once or twice before and read the markers. There's a Casper J. Smith, who fought in the Civil War and died in the 1880s. There has not been a Smith buried up here since we owned the land, and likely this small plot has been long forgotten. Today in church, Dad's boss Bobby Burns said he'd help Mom out with buying a stone. I figure we'll have to go to town and pick one after we see how much he'll give. Mom says don't expect much; Bobby Burns never gave Dad more than a quarter an hour raise twice in twenty-five years of work, and they carried the cheapest life insurance policy they could get.

"I see Aunt Billie's boys," I called out to Mom and Jeanie. Mom nodded. In the rearview mirror I could see headlights bouncing all over the field. Bertie and Junior had all five of the shovels rattling around in the bed of their truck. Bertie was just sixteen, but he drove fast like Alan Ray. They slid over next to us.

The rain began to let up, though the air was heavy and gray. I forgot how dark that north-facing hollow could be some times of the year. My brothers set Dad's box down on the truck bed and Alan Ray showed them all where to dig. He staggered a bit and he kept his head down. I knew he had cried like a baby when he heard the news. He always had worn his heart on his sleeve.

I wondered if Mom would get out now, but she showed no sign of moving. So I kept the Bronco running for the heat. Mom had wrapped the shawl tighter over her like she was chilled down to the bone. She kept her face veiled. I hoped she wasn't going to be sick to her stomach.

Jeanie slid out to be with Billie, who picked her up and held her to keep her out of the mud. They stood on a knoll beside the cedar tree and watched. Then, as the sky began to clear, all the boys cleared back the scruffy brush and got to work with the mattocks, picks, and shovels.

"What a day," I said to Mom.

"What a day? What a life, you mean." She stared into my eyes as if I was supposed to know what to say next. I shook my head. My tongue would not move, my throat felt blocked.

I looked over at her and lowered down the blower on the car. That heater made a racket. I thought about Dad, and how he got Glenn a job, and Ronnie, too. And I thought about Uncle Alan Ray, working in the woods, cutting timber all those years. A woman never could know whether the man she said good-bye to in the morning would come home in a box in the evening.

Mom's blue-gray eyes stared straight into mine. "Once me and your Dad had a row in Grandma's root cellar. I was pregnant with you, and he said he didn't want a male doctor looking at me." She nodded down, below her waist. "He slapped me so hard I cracked my head against the block wall. I never told you this, but as I blacked out I heard the voice of the Lord."

"You what?" I asked. I gave up trying to figure her out.

"I just heard this holy voice," she said. "It said, 'Go back, it's not your time.' Even though my body was not attached to my spirit, I heard those words, and then I saw a shining white finger pointing down at me. Then whoosh, I was back in that root cellar with your daddy standing over me, and Lord, my head ringing so bad that I couldn't even talk. He lifted me in his arms and carried me to bed. That was when we was living in the trailer down from your Grandma and Grandpa. I told everyone I fell. I don't know what your Grandpa would've done if he would have found out. I didn't want anyone to know." Mom looked like she was waiting for me to say something. "Where was I going to find me a female doctor?" She shrugged, pulled the shawl tighter.

Did she really say that? I thought. Should I make some excuses? Play my Dad's part? But he hurt her. Oh, my sad, poor mother. Oh, my sad, poor dad, who cannot be here to see this hurt. I wanted to plug my ears. I wanted to cry for the both of them then, to tell her that this crazy jealousy was because he was scared, because he lost his mother, because he cared about her. Mom had lived with him, loved him, had given it her best shot, even though she was angry that he lashed out and hurt her. Somehow, I knew, she was just as angry that he went and died, that he left her. After all these years, I thought, keeping the anger and the love twisted around each other like two tangled vines, honeysuckle and greenbrier, clinging to each other. They probably spent their time figuring out how to make things better for every one of us and not better for themselves.

I wanted some breathing room. I wanted to get out of the car. I wondered what Grandad Bertram would have done to Dad if he knew. I thought about what I'd wished Dad could do to Glenn if Dad was still alive. Now I'd let that chance slip through my fingers, it was too late. I sat in the driver's seat, window rolled up, staring at this scene as if it was some kind of movie. There was Dad's box, covered in a tarp in the back of Alan Ray's pickup. There were my brothers, almost men, all of them carrying some of Dad, their faces, their hair, their arms and shoulders. Half the hole was dug now; the boys stood in it shin deep. Wet reddish-brown clay was piled up all around the hole. It didn't look like all that much dirt had been moved yet. The earth was dark on top, but underneath it was the kind of clay that stuck to their picks, mattocks, and shovels. While Mom was talking, Lux Jr. found a glass aggie marble in the clay. I saw him clean off the shovel, pick out the marble, give it to Jeanie, and then return to digging. Though the rain had stopped, the fog hung low on the ridge at the tree line.

I turned toward my mother. "Did Dad hit you again?"

"Oh, a few more times." I almost broke in to ask something, but there is a time to speak and a time to listen, and today, it seemed right to listen. "The last time was Christmas, about five years ago. I packed him Christmas cookies in his lunch pail. He was late getting home, and he came roaring in the door, drunk and swearing, because some new guy at work had prettier cookies. My cookies were sugar cookies, but that other wife done hers up with colored icing. Your dad slapped me hard across the face. But by then I bet I outweighed him by a good thirty pounds. I told him that if he ever again lifted his hand against me, I would hit him back harder, and I meant it, too." She gazed at me, her jaw set, her pale eyes blinking hard, and she shook her head. "The days when he was late getting home, when I never knew if he was going to come home pissed off or just plain pissed." Then she stopped. She got this look on her face. It was like she said it, that was it. She gave it all she could. Like she deflated in front of my eyes. "But he came on home to me every night of my life, now didn't he?" she whispered.

I knew what she meant, and I bowed my head low, in sympathy and confusion, and then brushed her cheek with my hand, wondering at how I could have been so blind to all of this. Did she hide this from me, for all these years? I wanted to reach out, to apologize for my own blindness, but I held my tongue, hoping now that somehow, God in His heaven could heal my mother's rage and comfort her in her sorrow.

"He never raised his hand after that," she said. "He didn't have to. It was other things. Every time we had two nickels to rub together your dad spent 'em on some new gun, or some pedigreed coonhound. Look where that got me. I can't shoot the damn gun, and now I got to feed those yapping hounds."

I began to remember things now. My mom's pinched mouth brought them back. The boys' bedrooms with their unfinished floors and walls, the mice that gnawed their way into the house each winter and nested in drawers, chewing holes into our scarves and gloves. My mom heating water on the stove for baths and dishes, or my mom flushing the commode once or twice a day with a five-gallon bucket full of water that she drew from the kitchen sink. How I couldn't wait to have my own house, to get away from those chores. But I used to think that's what everyone's mother did.

There was a knock on the side window of the Bronco. I looked over to see Glenn standing with the Reverend Shorter. I lowered the window. "Where'd you come from?" I asked him. "The Reverend's Ranger got stuck in the mud by Barker's old place," he said loudly. "They sent me home from work on account it was so wet in the woods," Glenn said. I looked around, trying to read that scowl on his face. Glenn's new black boots were already getting muddy. He hated mud on his boots. It would put him into a mood. Right then I decided something. I wanted to go back home with Mom and take Jeanie with me. I would spend a few days, at least, maybe a week or two.

It was barely drizzling now. The Reverend Shorter took some time to walk around the small square graveyard and look at the slabs and stones while Glenn stood by and watched. Alan Ray took Tommy's shovel and helped the boys finish digging. I wondered if my mother was ready to get out into the cold.

Mom opened her door, and Jeanie ran over and stood with us. Aunt Billie helped her through the mud, up, under the cedar tree, facing Dad's coffin. When the boys put down their picks and shovels, Reverend Shorter came over to the graveside to lead us in prayer. The boys had placed the coffin on two thick oak planks above the hole, and I stared at the box, thinking about how Dad would have liked that coffin as a final resting place. It was a satin-finished, quarter-sawn poplar casket from the Mannington Casket Company. Maybe Dad milled those thick poplar boards, maybe Ronnie or Alan Ray or Glenn felled the trees. Did Dad ever wonder, in all that time at A-1, if his boards would get shipped to the Mannington Casket Company to be joined with wide dovetails and lined with black velvet, to carry his own body back to God up in heaven?

Reverend cleared his throat and began. He asked for God's forgiveness and grace, so that my dad would be returned unto Him in eternity, and said that he would be able to find a new body in Christ.

Reverend cast his gaze around us all, at the boys and me, at Billie and Alan Ray and their family, at Glenn, as if to say that it was not too late for all of us to live right in the sight of the Lord. Somehow, wherever his eternal spirit resided, I hoped Dad would be healed, that his body would be new, and that he would be watching down on all of us, Mom included, with two good eyes, and a newfound sense of peace that surpasses all understanding, and repent the pain he caused my poor, sad mother. Burning with devoutness, Reverend's voice became slower and more purposeful as began the last part of the service, ending with "Ashes to ashes, dust to dust." As he concluded, Alan Ray looked straight at the Dad's casket and said, "Lux, ain't it true what I told you? Them woods will always find a way to win." Then as if trying to catch his breath, he turned away and put his A-1 cap back on his head. Ronnie began to blow his nose, ducking his head down so no one could see his face, and Lux Jr. saluted and stood at stoic attention. Jeanie was in Billie's arms, clutching tissues in her small fist, her face pressed hard into Billie's neck, as Billie and Mom called out together, "Amen."

I stood quietly, too flooded with my own grief. For a brief moment, all was still on this silent hilltop, with only the rushing sound of the headwaters of the Goshen Creek in the background; then Mom began to cry, the sound of her like gasps for breath. She was drowning in sorrow and grief. I reached over awkwardly to hold Mom's hand, but she wouldn't let me. Instead, she took off her white shawl, gradually unwrapping it off her arms and from around her shoulders. She walked over toward the coffin, and Billie set Jeanie down and rushed over to help steady Mom. Together they walked out on one of the planks and spread the shawl over the box, so that a little point of the delicate hand-knotted fringe hung down from both sides. Mom stared down at the casket, then, and in a low voice, said, "Lux, I will be with you again soon, as God is my witness." Then she began to sing. *"Shall we gather at the river, the beautiful, the beautiful river . . ."* Bit by bit, we all joined in. Then, still holding on to Billie, Mom turned and walked back toward Jeanie and me.

I THOUGHT Mom would want to leave right away, but she said she wanted to stay until the boys were done, lowering the box into the ground, filling in the grave. Glenn left right away, saying he'd remembered things he needed to do. I told him that me and Jeanie would be staying with Mom for a few days, maybe even a week or so, and he shrugged. Actually, I took that as a good sign.

When the boys were done, they were the next ones to drive back down the hollow. They probably wanted to change out of their church clothes so they could head up into the woods again. Then Uncle Alan Ray and the Reverend Shorter came over to us and both told Mom how sad they were for her, offering their help in any way possible. Mom said thanks, that they'd both been so kind, that she was fine, and that she had a wonderful family that would help her through this.

It seemed to me that the whole family meant to do just that; Uncle Alan Ray and all the boys had been really kind about things so far, and Glenn hadn't touched a drop all day. And the Reverend had come all the way up the hollow to bury Daddy, instead of burying him in the church cemetery. As Aunt Billie said, it was just as well that Lux Cranfield wasn't buried in no churchyard; his own boys would never come to visit him that way.

Finally, the four of us, Mom, Aunt Billie, Jeanie, and I, walked back to the Bronco, trying not to step in too many puddles. Jeanie reached into her purse, took out a crumpled-up tissue, and unwrapped the marble. It was very old; the glass was pitted and etched with mud, but it was a sort of milky blue and white with gold streaks through it. "Little Lux said Papaw would want me to have this," she said to me.

"That's right, honey, he would," I told her. "Like a little bit of buried treasure to keep with you, maybe a good luck charm." I settled her into the backseat, and she climbed onto Billie's lap for the ride down the steep and rutted road, toward the main road where Mom and Tommy now lived, one less light in the window, one less voice to fill the rooms. I drove slowly out of the hollow. With no rain, we could keep the windows down. I thought about how, in a month or two, maybe me and Jeanie could plant a small tree beside Dad's grave site, maybe a holly or another cedar, something to stay green year-round. Maybe the boys would come up there too. No one spoke while the Bronco crawled out of the hollow. Trees rose up on both sides of the road. The hill got steeper, leveled off again. The wet mud splashed against our tires, and the fresh air smelled like clay combined with wild onions.

As we rounded the last steep bend, before we approached the main road, Mom began to sing. "Amazing grace, how sweet the sound . . ." Her voice echoed off the cliff beside the road. Though I wanted to join in, I held my tongue and let her and Billie sing. They held each word long and slow and clear; then, as Mom completed the fourth verse of the hymn, she reached over and took my hand firmly in hers. I turned onto the blacktop, took it slow, then pulled off again at her driveway. I marveled at the way it seemed like I felt something there in her hand, a strength that I did not sense before, and her touch felt suddenly warmer. I could feel it in her palm, out to her fingers, a small flame.

AND THOUGH I do not dare to tell anyone, I know how I really wanted this moment to end. Not down here along County Route 57, at the end of this gravel driveway, not with the Bronco pulling in beside this lonesome farmhouse, but up on the Goshen Road, on that wooded hilltop in that little cemetery, at the graveside where they laid my father to rest. In my mind's eye, I am still back there, standing in that chilly drizzle, looking around at all those unruly graves, some with markers and some without, clumps of uneven ground and broken slabs of stone. I cannot undo the sight of how there was a great haphazard here, long thorny brambles in unkempt clusters hiding overgrown paths and unknown graves, headstones off-kilter or the little sayings unreadable, worn-down grave markers partly covered in mud, family names blurred, or no name at all, just a couple of initials or a date. We are all so empty and hopeless here, I wanted to say, and I cannot erase this thought.

My mother had not yet reached for me, as she looked only at that box, that dark hole in the ground, this dark day's somber ritual. But something in me got frantic. I wanted to break through that moment, I wanted to push against the darkness of my mother's grief, and I wanted to pick up that white shawl and take it off the coffin, keep it out of the grave. I wanted that shawl at that moment more than I ever wanted anything in my life. What I also wanted to say, but what I didn't say, is that the satiny, milled boards of the poplar box would be just right for him, the damp clay of the cool earth was fitting enough for him, but that I needed that white shawl for me.

FOURTEEN

SAVING JASMINE (1992)

MY SISTER DESSIE STOOD IN MY KITCHEN ONE SUNDAY
in mid-September, not quite six months after Lux's passing, com-
plaining about her newest charge, a one-year-old baby named William Lee. She'd stopped in after church as I was about to set out
dinner, wearing a dark gray dress that used to be snug but now hung
on her shoulders. The high collar lined in black made her complexion
look pale and her face seem smaller. Her graying hair was gathered
back into a bun, and unruly strands framed her face with curls.

"This little guy's without a doubt the saddest, most pitiful baby
I've ever seen," she said, picking up a knife from the counter. Notic-
ing where I'd left off, she started slicing a knobby batch of my fresh-
picked carrots into tidy, quartered sticks. "He holds his little hands out
toward the door and cries, 'Mama, Mama,' all day long." She brushed
beads of sweat from her neck and under her chin with the back of her
hand, the knife waving around her face like a small dagger.

"Can't you get him down for a nap?" I asked, taking a tray of
rolls out of the oven and giving the stew a stir. Her eyes met mine

for a moment and darted away, like she did not talk to people enough or get enough fresh air. I cranked open the kitchen window over the sink, but the heat of the outside air mixed with the heat of the stove to make the kitchen even warmer.

"That's the worst of it. When I think he's worn himself out, I tiptoe him into the living room and set him into the crib. Soon as he settles down and starts to breathe steady, up pops his bald little head, and he starts in again, like he's afraid to give in to sleep. You wouldn't believe how worked up he gets. He's got a set of lungs on him. It's a wonder you haven't heard him over here. He'd try to flop himself backward over the crib rails if I didn't watch him." She found a plate in the cupboard for the carrots. "That little man is not happy unless I hold him. Then he falls asleep on my shoulder, and when I go to set him down, it starts all over again. I pray my back won't go out."

She nibbled on a carrot. Right before she took William, she'd mentioned that babysitting children under the age of two would be too much work. Dessie had gotten the ball rolling by watching Jeanie when she came off the school bus from half-day kindergarten. That was last spring, while Lissy was living with Dessie and working at the nursing home in town.

Jeanie was a perfect way for Dessie to start babysitting, easy-going, curious, helpful, and good company during the afternoons, and for whole days during the summer. Then school started back and suddenly Dessie had Jeanie after school and two little ones during the school day. Marcia Lee, the new second-grade teacher, arrived by Greyhound from Pittsburgh just in time for the school year with two towheaded kids and one suitcase: Theodore, four and still wearing a diaper; and one-year-old William, fussing from the time Marcia Lee dropped him off until she walked back in the door again.

"I can tell William's been through a rough go of it," Dessie said, rolling her wedding band around her finger as she spoke. "The way he clings, he was most likely taken off the breast too soon. And Mr.

Theodore Lee is going to need to lose those diapers before he hits kindergarten. He pitched a fit when I tried to set him on the commode. He's ornery, but he's a smart little guy. He can't wait to see Jeanie when she comes in after school. Last week Jeanie had him writing his ABCs at the kitchen table." As she spoke, I realized that even her fingers were thinner. Her ring used to be too tight.

Dessie picked up the plates I'd set out, put them aside, and wiped the table down with a dishrag, scrubbing until every spot was removed. Then she set the plates back out and looked up at me. "I just hope I can be a comfort to William Lee, God bless his sweet little soul. I pray the good Lord can guide me."

"Des," I said, "lately you think the whole world is racing toward ruination on a fast train." I held off saying what I really thought, though, that the way she was talking got me worried about her mental state. Certain words were sneaking their way back into her vocabulary and maybe her thinking, too. I worried she'd start back in scanning the very heavens and earth looking for heavenly signs. If there was a sign to be had, I hoped it wasn't a sign that she'd been watching those TV preachers again.

She stared at me, reading my thoughts, no doubt. "I know what I know," she said.

"Des," I asked, "are you staying for dinner? The guys won't eat much. They've been snacking all day."

"Oh, thanks," she said. "Not today, but I promise, sometime I will, sometime soon."

"At least take some rolls, then," I said. "I figured out a new recipe using that quick-rise yeast."

She smiled, eyeing the warm rolls, "OK, I'll take a couple. Look how nice the crust came out." She peeked out the window toward her driveway. "Thanks, Billie. I better run. I've a new mother coming over. I'll eat later when Tommy gets in from work."

"A new mother? I thought you didn't want to watch more than three?" I said.

"Oh, this one's for Saturdays," she said, her voice lowered. "I could use the money."

Who couldn't use the money? I thought, nodding back. Dessie was carrying a heavy load these days. Tommy helped with groceries, but she didn't feel right asking him to part with more of his salary. He was saving for an old Jeep with a blown head gasket that he wanted Alan Ray to help him rebuild. Dessie washed her hands at the kitchen sink, wrapped the roll in a napkin, and picked up one more sliced carrot. "You'uns have a good supper," she said. "God bless."

The screen door slammed and blew back a final whiff of her talc. "Don't forget to check your sugar after you eat," I said, not really sure if she could hear me, and not really sure if she would eat. I called to Alan Ray and the boys to wash up and come to dinner, then stood in the warmth of the kitchen window and watched the rear bumper of her tan Buick creep down the driveway, past our two gardens, and pull up into the turnaround spot in front of her house.

Alan Ray came out of the back bedroom as soon as she left. "How's Our Lady of Perpetual Prayer doing today?" he asked, only half-kidding.

"I don't know. She's lost more weight, and she was talking about taking another child," I said. "She wears herself out. William Lee is crying nonstop."

"He'll get over it. They always do," Alan Ray said. He winced as his back caught when he eased into his chair. My sister imagined the worst, but she had a way with children. She always took on too much, but I took it for granted that she would do that.

Bertie and AJ bounded in from the yard, and as they cleaned up I told them I wanted their help, and that we could all look in on Dessie later, to see if she and Tommy needed anything done around the house. "I just want to check on things. You know, take a look around and see what she has got herself into," I said.

Alan Ray looked up at me, one eyebrow raised, checking to see if I wanted him to come along. His eyelids seemed heavy, about halfway closed. It was the back medication. "You can't hardly sit up," I said to him. "Don't you worry, we're just dropping by for a minute." Dessie wouldn't ask Alan Ray to do anything most times, even if I offered to get him to help. No, she insisted, she would do it herself.

COME SUNDOWN, I rounded up the boys. We grabbed flashlights and headed across the hayfield on the footpath to the farmhouse. I rapped on the edge of the screen door and popped my head in. Under the yellow glow of the ceiling light, Dessie sat at the kitchen table in paint-splattered blue jeans and one of Lux's old plaid flannel shirts, pencil eraser in her mouth, scowling at her checkbook. Bills were stacked in piles, spread out like homework.

On the radio, the *Family Hour of Prayer* blasted in from New Martinsville, parishioners singing their hearts out, full of feeling, but off-key as ever. Lux would've had the ballgame on. For a moment, when I walked into that kitchen, I knew it was Dessie, but my mind flashed back to Mom, how she wore her hair back in a huge clip, how that same old show on that same old radio was her evening soundtrack as she fixed our supper. The boys raced upstairs to see Tommy. "How'd it go with the new mother?" I asked.

"Well, it's just strange," Dessie replied. "I only met the girl, her name's Jasmine, and the grandmother, Mrs. Wills. Jasmine's the cutest thing, long curly black hair, freckles and bangs, with eyes as big as saucers. She's in fifth grade, but she's already eleven. She might've been held back. She didn't say a word. I also never heard one bit about her mother and father. I don't even know who they are." She looked down, set the pencil on one of the envelopes in front of her, looked up at me. "Just watch. I feel like this one's going to be a real case."

"What's the grandmother do?" I asked, turning down the radio to catch Dessie's full attention.

"She's a weekend nurse at the VA," Dessie said. "Jasmine just started staying with her. Do you know she remembered taking care of Dad after his gallstones?" Dessie began to blink, her eyes watery.

I thought back. "Nurse Wills. She's got that short-cropped white hair. She barked orders at Dad like a drill sergeant. I was scared of her, but Dad gave her, uh, heck right back," I said. "Are you going to babysit Jasmine?" I asked.

"I guess. I mean, I said yes," Dessie said. "I promised. I'll start next Saturday. It will give me a chance to get caught up. I figure I can charge five dollars an hour, and that way I can keep four and give the fifth to the Lord."

Ahh, yes, I thought, wondering again why the collection plate did not seem to be enough for the Almighty, and what He needs with this extra from family and neighbors, all sweet and caring people whose ends ain't never gonna meet. The All-Powerful does not need to exist on food stamps and commodities like us mere mortals. I held my tongue, but only because I had already said my piece about that, and it did not go over all that well. "That sounds good, Des," I said, thinking that at least these days she was tithing to our family church. "It will give you a chance to return her kindness to Dad."

Dessie nodded. She looked worn out. She didn't offer me any tea or coffee, didn't seem to want the company. I started to ask if she needed a hand with anything, but she stopped me. "Thanks for stopping in, Billie. We're fine. Really. We made it through another week now, didn't we?"

AFTER LUX'S funeral, at first Dessie seemed to be trying to keep things as normal as possible for the sake of Tommy and Lissy, maybe even for the sake of keeping snoopy neighbors away, and that's one reason I did not notice right away that she kept to herself too much. Soon I saw that she kept to the house, she did not even go to church, she didn't want to put in a garden, she kept conversation short when I called or stopped by. I'd stop by, see Lissy tending the flowers. Give her time, I thought, give her time.

But after a few weeks, it was obvious something was not right. Dessie's body was there, but it was hard to talk to her, as if her mind was snatched up or her brain changed a channel. We used to watch the daytime soaps before the kids came home, keep company with Kelly and Mason, Sophia and CC on *Santa Barbara*. Suddenly, afternoons, there was a different kind of soap opera on Dessie's set, a cast of TV ministers every weekday and Sunday, too. Comb-over men with their big-hair wives, their clothes too shiny, their smiles and hands too big, crying themselves red in the face about damnation or salvation.

Soon Dessie started sounding too churchy. Something on the news would set her off, and she'd start in with a lecture about the "decline of family values," as if it was her new calling to make sure everyone around her, including my boys and Alan Ray, got right with the Savior. Everyone said that only Lux had kept her from being who she really was all along, but I did not agree. I was pretty sure I figured out where this was coming from. It was because of the way Lux went, so sudden. I think she was terrified that if a bolt of lightning came down from the heavens and struck us down, not a one of us would find eternal salvation.

It did get trying. She wouldn't let Glenn or Alan Ray drink a beer in her house, Tommy had a curfew, and she wouldn't tolerate cussing or taking the Lord's name in vain. It spooked us all to go over there and have some preacher droning on in the background, and Dessie saying "Amen" or "Praise the Lord" back to the television set, and "God bless" to us, no matter what we'd been talking about. Lissy stayed with her mom a month or so, to keep her mom's spirits up after Lux's funeral, but then off she went, moving back with Glenn.

MIDSPRING, DESSIE got the first insurance payment from the accidental death and dismemberment policy through A-1 Lumber, and she'd already had some money from Lux's boss for the burial. That week she ordered a polished, jet-black granite stone for Lux's grave, with his name, Luther "Lux" Cranfield, and his dates, 1949–1992. When the stone was ready, we all trucked up to the little graveyard at the head of the Goshen Road. The boys and Glenn cleared the weeds off the grave site. Then Tommy and Ron dug a trench, chopped away any tree roots, and set his headstone firmly into the ground, tamping the ground to set the stone. It stood out, solid, solemn, dark, and tall, among the other weathered, moss-covered stone markers from ages ago. We knew we would all find him that way, there in the woods.

Dessie, Lissy, and I transplanted some prickly pear plants of Mom's from her yard, to protect Lux's stone, and Dessie prayed over the grave, telling the Almighty that Lux was His now, to do with as He saw best, and asked for Lux's eternal peace by the Lord's side. We stood together, heads bowed, saying Amen at the right time. I wondered what Lux would make of it all. Finally, after Dessie walked back to the Bronco and she couldn't see him, Alan Ray poured an Iron City beer and sprinkled some Copenhagen tobacco over the grave, for good measure, and also to water all the new plants and make them grow handsome and strong, he said.

After that, we held our breath to see how she would spend the remainder of the first installment of Lux's life insurance. When I saw her set up a checking account and begin sending daily checks to those wrath o' God salesmen, I missed Lux more than ever. She blew through ten thousand dollars by tithing it out, mostly to her two favorites, Robert Tilton and Oral Roberts. No one, not me, not Alan Ray, not Lissy, not even Little Lux, could tell her that those fat cats did not need a raise from Dessie Cranfield.

Of course they were going to take as much of her money as she was willing to send. Why wouldn't they? All that nonsense about miracle prayer requests, and the money disappeared in less than forty days and forty nights, with never a sign about whether or not Lux's poor soul was taken into heaven, and no miraculous improvement in her diabetes, just "Thank you, and, by the way, can we have some more now?" cards. Glossy magazines showed up in the mailbox from the Word of Faith Family Church and the Abundant Life Prayer Group, and that was about all she had to show for it. I wanted to shake some sense into her, but all that would have accomplished is that she would have added me to her list of people she wanted those ministries to pray for.

Alan Ray said that my sister was the living proof that televange-lists preyed on the troubled and the weak-minded. One day, after a few beers, he said that when he's finally too beat up to run a chainsaw, he's going to buy himself a bright pink suit, march himself down to WBOY-TV in Clarksburg, and start the Blessed Coal TV Cathedral, since the miners in the eastern and southern part of the state might as well tithe their pensions in his direction. I told him in that case, I'd have to do my eyes up like Tammy Faye Bakker, and he and I had a good laugh about where a person could go to buy the longest and cheapest false eyelashes and the flashiest neon-pink suit.

ABOUT A month later, the second half of Lux's AD&D policy was due to arrive. After a couple of strong hints, Reverend Clayton Shorter of the First Apostolic asked Dessie to a sit-down with him after church service on Memorial Day weekend. He asked me and Lissy, too. We knew Dessie would not refuse Reverend Shorter, as he had deep roots in the community. Though he was only in his thirties, his father had been Reverend before him, and Clay took up as an assistant to his dad until, as they say, the cup passeth.

Reverend's small office behind the pulpit was lined with tall overstuffed bookcases, some books had shiny leather bindings and others had tattered cardboard and cloth bindings. There were at least twenty versions of the Holy Bible, and holy books from other religions, including the Jehovah's Witness, the Book of Mormon, and the Hebrew Old Testament. On the desk was an Unabridged Webster's New International Dictionary at least five inches wide, a dog-eared copy of *Unger's Bible Handbook*, and a soft amber stained-glass reading light with a pattern of the dove descending. Above his left and right shoulders hung a pair of matching leaded-glass transom windows with a ruby cross in the center, donated by the Paul Wissmach Glass Company in Paden City.

Dessie sat toward the front of an oversized brown leather chair facing the desk, her ankles crossed under her dark blue jumper. Lissy and I pulled up armchairs on either side of her. He was a slender man, dressed in a lightweight pale yellow button-down shirt, clean shaven, with bristles of sandy hair, long on the top. He had the softest hands I'd ever shaken in a man or a woman. A ceiling fan clattered overhead, spreading the rich smell of potato salad and fried chicken around the room, and I hoped my stomach would not start growling.

Reverend began by praising the mission of the ladies' auxiliary, and he mentioned the name of each woman who had given up her time to prepare food for the faithful and baskets for shut-ins and disabled veterans. We all nodded together, even me, heathen that I am.

Reverend's light green eyes were directed over his reading glasses toward Dessie with a mixture of concern and respect. "How are you getting along, Dessie?" he asked. I shook off the feeling that I was back in grade school in the principal's office. I focused on my sister.

A cluster of pink blotches broke out on Dessie's neck and cheeks, and she began scratching at the back of her left hand, like the whole situation had given her hives. Suddenly I thought about Mom. In a low voice, I said to Dessie that Mom would have been there with all the older women setting out dinner in the fellowship hall.

As soon as I said that, I felt like an idiot, like I might have added to her sorrows and losses by mentioning Mom. But Dessie nodded, and we all smiled at the thought. My sister became collected enough to answer his question. "Reverend Shorter," she said, "such a nice service today. Uhm, so good of you to take time out of your day for us. I know what we all are here for. I just don't know what to say. I feel like by now I should be fine. But, well, uhm, well . . ." Then she stopped. I looked at Lissy. Her dark eyes were brimming with tears. I wanted to get out of my seat and hug Lissy right then. Her loss of her father had been swept aside in all this. But I held off. I wanted to see what Reverend would say, if he had the kind of answers my sister needed.

Reverend got right to work. "It's not supposed to be easy, Dessie, and you too, Lissy. You both shouldn't take yourself to task if you don't feel like your old selves, like you can take on the world," he said.

"There is no magic spell, no one prayer, or special words anyone can say to take away the pain."

We sat there in the quiet of his office. Dessie and Lissy dabbed at their eyes. Dessie said, "I know that, Reverend. I know. Some days I can't figure out the right words to say. Then, when I talk, I can't stand the way my words bounce around the house and echo back at me." She looked into his young eyes, chewed at her lower lip. "I feel all useless and used up, like I'm an empty old vase without a drop of water left, set up on a shelf, all the flowers brown, all the stalks dried up." Dessie looked at us, and we nodded to show we knew what she meant. "Uhm, that's—well, when I turn on the TV, the preaching lifts my spirit. It helps me to think about the Lord. It feels so good to know that the whole flock, pastors, members, people all over the country are praying, praying for me," Dessie said, and then she looked around at all of us. "So I think that's the reason I want to give them something, to keep the shows on the air, so they can help me and help others in the same state as me."

Reverend looked directly at her. "Dessie," he said, "The people you watch on TV, the ones who you want to pray for you, they are not your loved ones, and they will not be the ones to heal your heart. Sometimes strangers on TV can seem like friends because they are in your house, but we know that they only just seem like that. Really, they are in some studio talking to a camera in a city halfway across the country." I hoped that got to Dessie. She sat stock-still, barely blinking. Lissy nodded. While he spoke, I sat there thinking about the difference between Clay Shorter's office and the corny, fake-looking Greek columns behind some of those TV ministers.

Reverend paused, as Dessie seemed lost in thought. "Dessie," he said. "If Lux was here, what do you think he would say to you?" he asked.

"That's just it, Reverend Shorter," Dessie answered. "Lux isn't here. It's crazy to say this, but there was always a plan, or a project, always something he had going, something we had to figure out together. Now I don't have anyone to keep me on my toes. Little Lux and Ronnie are gone off, Tommy is about grown, Billie is busy looking after Alan Ray and her boys, Lissy has Jeanie and Glenn and his whole family keeping her running circles. I don't want to be a busybody or push my way into their lives." She looked at all of us as if to say that this is how things stand, but it's OK, it's not anything that should change. She frowned. "Reverend, when you were talking about the ladies' auxiliary, I felt even worse, more useless, like I should have stepped up to help out, and also, ashamed for feeling sorry for myself. Does that make any sense?" she said.

Reverend looked at all of three of us, and then looked directly at my sister again. "Dessie, can I speak openly in front of everyone?"

My sister nodded. Reverend Shorter reached into his desk drawer and pulled out a magazine article about the legal troubles of the Bakker ministry. He also had a newspaper article with photographs of the million-dollar mansions, Oriental rugs, solid gold chandeliers, luxury limos, yachts, lavish possessions of TV ministers including Robert Tilton and Oral Roberts. Those kind of folks, he said, used people's money for their own enrichment. The cable company had graced them with a wide reach; they counted many millionaires in their flock. They would be well provided for without her donations, though they were going to act like they needed every last cent.

Dessie looked squarely at the Reverend. "Do you think I want that money?" she asked. "That money is just a bunch of paper, is all it is. That insurance money will not bring back Lux." Tears streamed down her cheeks. "I just thought I could send it to someone who could do some good with it," she said. I cast a quick look at Lissy. I wondered whether she was thinking the same thing I was thinking, that grief had taken hold of my poor sister's brain.

Reverend looked up at Dessie. "I get it. I do, Dessie," he said. "But please, don't confuse the message with the messenger." In the face of her recent loss, he said, those TV ministers could never provide her with the true sense of purpose, to enrich her life without Lux in a way that she so needed. She would not move on by sitting in front of the TV all day. That healing would come directly from the Holy Spirit to her through weekly worship and through service, doing the Lord's work.

The truth of his words was not lost on her. Reverend leaned forward, looking at all three of us, gently suggesting that so much was needed right here in Fairchance, where friends and neighbors cared for each other through the toughest times of their lives, where we all need each other, and that real charity begins at home. My sister reached into her purse for a handkerchief and nodded through her tears. Lissy patted her mom's left hand. Dessie reached out with her right for my hand, and I could feel her whole body trembling as the Reverend came to a close.

GLORY BE! Reverend Shorter's words began to sink in. When the final installment of the A-1 life insurance arrived, Dessie arranged with the First Apostolic treasurer to sponsor an outdoor spotlight in the parking lot in Lux's name, which was fitting since that was about as close as Lux would ever get to the indoors of the chapel. Then, come summer, when Tommy was done with tenth grade, she and Tommy made a plan to fix up her farmhouse. She said she did not yet know how, but it came to her that she would use it to do the Lord's work. One rainy afternoon in June I stopped in, and she showed me a sketch of her idea for a downstairs bathroom, all planned out on sheets of graph paper, all the angles and measurements to scale. It was worked out to the last detail, each wall and doorway.

With the help of some of the deacons from the church, she framed out a closet-sized bathroom by splitting off a section of the back bedroom. Tommy and my boys helped when they weren't at football practice. She broke out Lux's favorite toolbox, started remembering his carpentry tricks. Lux was by her side, telling her to measure twice and cut once, she said to me one afternoon, standing in the midst of her construction site, giant leather tool belt around her waist, pencil stuck behind her ear, Lux's A-1 cap on her head.

She even gave Jeanie her own tape measure, a pad, and a pencil case, and small jobs to teach her numbers and measuring. I sewed a small red-and-yellow shop apron for Jeanie, two big pockets in the front and a big letter J like the S in Supergirl on the chest, with a little red cape to match so Jeanie could keep her tools in the pockets. I was never good with tools, but when I could, I brought supper, fresh-picked garden vegetables, cornbread, and Jeanie's favorite, ice pops made from fruit juice.

Dessie found the sink, vanity, and commode on sale at the lumber-yard, and for the first time she called up to the house and asked Alan Ray to come help. Alan Ray, Tommy, and my boys did a whole bunch of head scratching, but after working on it all weekend, they figured it out. They would not take any money, but when she and Tommy offered Lux's coonhounds and the dog box, they did not turn that away.

By the time the A-1 insurance money ran out, just as school was ready to start around Labor Day, the outside of the old farmhouse was freshly painted, and that divided downstairs bedroom was done. Edgar Sutton came and set up a septic tank and drain field, so the house could meet the county codes. I told her that Mom and Dad and Lux would all be proud, and she replied that she wanted to do things right, so the Lord would see fit to put her to use. I don't know why or how these things happen, but that very week Marcia Lee showed up at her door with her two little boys in need of care.

Somehow that did not surprise me. What did surprise me was when a pickup truck pulled up the drive with a piano tuner sign on the side. It was old Mr. Mosier from the church, who had last tuned Mom's upright piano about twenty years earlier. After he left, I walked up the stairs to her porch with a bushel of pole beans that the boys picked. Not only was no preacher setting the fear o' God into the faithful on the tube, but as I stood at the door, I heard her picking out the slow and steady chords of "In the Sweet Bye and Bye." She kept at it, day by day, and sang when she played, mostly the older hymns, "The Old Rugged Cross," or "Just as I Am," or "All the Way My Savior Leads

Me." The words and tunes I hadn't heard in half a lifetime came fluttering back from some hidden pocket of my mind, as familiar as a nursery rhyme or the sound of the dinner bell.

Dessie took up reading too, and not just daily Bible devotional passages. Library books were stacked by twos and threes on the kitchen table. She found remodeling books when she and Tommy were working on the bathroom. Then she went after baby and child-care books, telling me things we should have known but didn't when we had our little ones, like how swaddling works, and how important it was to set babies on their backs to sleep.

Finally, she dug into Dr. Norman Vincent Peale's Power of Positive Thinking books, but for some reason, whenever she talked about living her life without a bit of worry, I started getting more worried. The televangelists were gone, as far as we could tell, but we still were not sure who Dessie would become. Tommy and Lissy said they wanted their old mother back, the one who watched soaps and wore her hair down, and cussed like a sailor when she thought no one was listening. They were afraid to tell her, but when they came to me, my only answer to them was to hold off and be patient. "Can you blame her?" I said, more to myself than to them, thinking about how some cracks might never get mended, not matter how much glue you try.

A FEW weeks after she began to watch Jasmine on Saturdays, Dessie stopped in one morning on her way to town, to see if I had any clothes I could spare. "She's a pretty girl, thin as a twig and tall for her age, like you were. She wears the same oversize T-shirt and torn-up blue jeans every Saturday."

"How's it going? How are you two getting along?" I asked.

"She's not that hard to get along with, but she must be going through a backward stage. I try everything to get her to talk. Last Saturday I asked if she wanted to bake cookies. She said she didn't, but then she hung around while I baked. Since she was right there, I gave her a little job, reading the recipe while I beat the shortening and the eggs. She stared at me the whole time, and I just knew she never baked cookies before. But you don't know the worst of it. She couldn't even read the recipe."

"Des, are you sure?" I said.

"Oh, I'm sure," Dessie said. "This girl could not get the word 'blend' or the word 'sugar' from the cookbook. She's got more than reading problems. She follows me around, saying, 'No. No, dammit, N. O.' to everything I ask her, but always touching, poking things. I don't know whether to hug her or to wash her mouth out with soap."

I didn't want to argue, but "sugar" might be a tough word to sound out for anyone who never saw it before. Also, being in a new place with new people could make everything more difficult for the girl. Dessie had a way with the young ones, but since Jasmine was older, she might be a tougher case to crack. And then, suddenly, I found myself wishing that Jasmine would actually be a good cause for my sister to take on, someone who could grow and learn under her watchful eye.

That afternoon I checked my closet for any clothes that a young girl would want. I found a bag of clothes that I had gotten at the church rummage sale, a couple of T-shirts and matching shorts, and a sweatshirt that had seemed fine at first, but later Minnie and Mickey seemed too silly for a grown woman to wear. "If they don't fit Jasmine, save them for Jeanie," I said when I brought the clothes over, holding them up for Dessie's approval. "By the way, have you found out anything more about Jasmine's parents?" I asked.

"Not a word," she said, "but something's going on there. I think Jasmine's mother abandoned her, and if her grandmother hadn't come to get her, the social services would have placed her into a home. I just can't figure out why she can't read. I mean, she's made it to fifth grade. She brings her Michael Jackson music and sings along. Y'ought to see her dance. It is something else again." Dessie got up from the kitchen table, stepped sideways, pushed her hips back and forth, then stopped, hopped forward, and grabbed at her privates, swirled around, and ended in an exaggerated and obscene thrust. If the menfolks were around, Alan Ray would have howled and Lux would have slammed out of the house. I didn't know whether to laugh or to pretend that I found it shocking. Then she frowned, so I held off. I called her to the porch with me, so I could light up a smoke.

"It's funny," she said, settling into the porch swing. "It's been more work than I thought, but every morning I look forward to Marcia dropping off those little Lee brothers. Lux was out a lot, always off at the mill, or helping folks, or in the woods, and it seemed like he was never around that much. But now he's gone, really gone," she said, walking back into the kitchen. "We all had to tiptoe around his temper sometimes, and he wasn't always easy. He was really hard on Ronnie, 'My way or the highway' with the all the boys, but this is much worse."

She kept talking, and I just listened. "Maybe I have too much time to think these days? I know I could have been different too. I think of the things I could have said, or what he would have said back. What if I failed him somehow? I want to do it all over again, do it better. I go to sleep praying to see him in a dream at night. Even the sound of his voice." She trailed off, and then she said, "If only I would have bought us an answering machine for the phone, or had us all make a cassette tape. I feel like I am losing the sound of him."

She looked up at me and blinked back her tears. I hoped she didn't cry. If she cried, I'd start in bawling too. Her blue eyes began to brim over, and I felt a shudder come up into my throat. She got up, held open the door, and I followed her into the kitchen so she could grab a napkin to wipe her eyes. "Oh, Billie," she said, looking around to see if Tommy was downstairs. "Oh, shit," she said. "That's the whole thing, and I just have to face it. It won't change. I can put the TV on, but I can't even look at those ministers anymore. I can play the piano, but as soon as I stop, it is just too damn quiet around here."

"You're right," I answered. There was no radio or TV show, also no preacher's voice rattling through some speaker in the house somewhere. Just then, a memory circled into the front of my mind. The night after Dad died, a screech owl started wailing at dusk in the valley below our houses. Just like that, it happened again when Lux died last spring. People say that screech owls haunted a homestead to let everyone know after a death. It hung around for about a week, wailing like someone calling from another world. It was such a sorrowful sound, I didn't want to go outside at sundown, but finally the little creature stopped as the summer came on. The crazy thing is that the silence was worse, like an emptiness that we could not shake.

"What can I do, Des?," I asked her.

"Do you want to come over and help out with Jasmine sometime?" she asked me.

"I'll try," I said. "What if I find some of my old makeup and a curling iron, bring it by for Jasmine and maybe for Jeanie? I have a giant baggie full of that stuff. I never use it. Where the heck would I go, all made up?" I said. "You remember? I used to love wearing Mom's makeup when we were little."

She looked a little surprised, then kind of smiled, but did not say anything. She never wore makeup any more. Neither of us did. Maybe these days she thought makeup sent the wrong message to a young girl.

I folded the clothes I'd brought over and set them on the piano bench. The kitchen and the living room were clean, no sawdust, no strewn-around tools or clutter, spotless floors with a green braided oval rag rug on the floor for babies to crawl on, a toy basket with little cars and trucks, children's Bible story books, but too damn quiet. High on the wall hung Lux's gun rack made of deer antlers, and then there were two barnwood shelves below. On the top one was Lux's baseball glove, his eyepatch, the arrowhead he gave her that he found on Chestnut Ridge as a boy. On the lower shelf, just below my eye level, a pair of his old steel-toe work boots, cleaner than they ever were in life. She must have set all this in place, somehow, and I did not stop to notice it.

On top of the piano, out of reach of the youngsters, was Mom's Redemption Hymnal and family photos: Baby photos of all the children, including my two boys. Little Lux in his Marine Corps uniform. Ronnie's middle school graduation with his shaggy blond hair hanging on his head like a sheepdog. Lux, just come down the hill from turkey hunting, still dressed in camouflage, all eyepatch and toothy grin, with a dead gobbler hanging upside down in each hand. Glenn hoisting Lissy in the air in her wedding dress. Mom and Dad smiling sweetly from the boardwalk in Ocean City. It struck me that Mom was as old in that photo as I was, at that moment, probably, midforties, but already settling into middle age. How can that be, I thought.

Dessie shook her head, running her hands through her hair. "Well, I wasn't really thinking about makeup. What would you say to this idea?" She looked over at the piano and then back to me. "Last night," Dessie said, "it came to me that I might start teaching Jasmine to read through the hymnal, maybe even give her singing lessons with the hymns."

Oh Lordy, please preserve us, I wanted to say. Mom would have tried that, and we girls would've hated it. I wanted to make some joke about what could happen if she took away Jasmine's Michael Jackson tapes and replaced "Beat It" with "Gimme That Old Time Religion." It was a bad idea. But she was my only sister.

I took a deep breath. "Des," I began, "no girl of eleven is going to want to set next to you on a piano bench while you try to convince her to sing the old hymns. She'll break out the power of negative thinking and add more 'damnits' to her 'no.' If I was eleven, I wouldn't do it, if even if you bribed me." I stopped. Something struck me at that moment. "Why don't you stop over to the library, see if they have a Michael Jackson piano book? If they don't have one, they might be able to tell you who to ask." I saw Dessie nodding. "She needs something like this, I bet." As best as I could, I hummed the first song that popped into my head, the opening to "Billie Jean," clapping my hand to the rhythm, so she could see my point.

"Don't you know, she plays that one all the time," Dessie said. "I wonder if I could play the chords for that on the piano? Maybe she could learn to pick out the words from a songbook? I'm sure she already knows them by heart. Or maybe I could listen to her tapes and practice reading and writing the lyrics with her?"

I nodded, wondering if maybe next Saturday I should try stop in to help out, but then I decided not to. This had best be left to them to find their own way, I thought. But I wasn't above volunteering Lissy. "Maybe Lissy could bring Jeanie over too, or you can pick Jeanie up?" I said instead. "They both can work on reading, and singing too."

Dessie brightened up, and thought I saw the younger Dessie, the one who sang at the top of her lungs if she loved a song on the radio, just for the pure joy of it. Then she became thoughtful. "I was wanting to ask what you thought about another little project. It would be something for the kids, and maybe you too. Lux used to say he wanted to do something to that ugly old storage room downstairs, behind the crawlspace. You know, we could paint the walls and the cement floor, even heat it." She was on a roll, and I let her keep talking. I knew where this was going to head. "It could be a playroom, maybe I could put in a little sink and a little table and shelves for art supplies? Then you could help out too, as many hours each week as you would want to. I know you could do art and even put on little plays and do makeup, too. We could take more kids that way, weekdays and after school."

I listened to this, trying to be open-minded, half-believing that it was possible. I nodded. Here's the thing I liked the most. As Alan Ray would say, she was starting to fire on all cylinders. I also liked that I was being recruited into Dessie's army.

"Wouldn't that be something! That's a plan and a half!" I said. "I can picture it all" I said, trying not to actually promise anything. I was hoping I didn't just climb out on a limb and start sawing it out from under me. Ideas can come and go, and there is no telling which ones will stick. On the other hand, I should try to keep some extra money coming in for winter. "I need a chance to run it by the committee, you know, and the chairman of the board," I said.

She smiled. "Just something to keep on the back burner," she said. "I will pray about it."

"Sounds good," I said, and walked over to give her a hug good-bye. We rarely did that, but it just sort of happened. Her arms, her shoulders, her whole frame seemed to freeze, like a mannequin in a clothing store. I stepped back. "Oh, sorry," I said, though I didn't know why I said that.

"Wait, wait, Billie," Dessie said. "Let's try again," she said. She exhaled, relaxed. She took a step forward and opened her arms, and we tried again. My cheek brushed her cheek. My arms wrapped loosely around her back. Her arms wrapped tightly around my back. All I could think about was how strong she was, my sister: hammer-slinger, wall-builder, piano player, Holy Roller, child fixer.

IT HAD been a dry September, the ground was firm beneath my gardening shoes, and the last few fireflies were rising over the hay-field. Mars, already bright, hung just above the ridgetop in the southern sky, a red ball set against pale lavender clouds. There was a glow in the west from the setting sun, and one in the east, as the moon was getting ready to rise. Though it wasn't full into fall yet, there was a chill in the air. Crows called back and forth as they settled into the pines behind the house. Soon it would be bow season, then youth hunting, then gun season. Maybe once Alan Ray and the boys were up the hollow, I could stop by Dessie's some Saturday afternoon, to see how things were going or lend a hand.

Midway back to the house through the hayfield, I stopped, amazed as always at how tall some volunteer sunflowers had grown. They reminded me of a ramshackle unit of sentries, defending the creek bank on the edge of the Goshen Road. The gray-green stalks were easily twice my height, broad leaves like Jack's beanstalks tapering up to round, bowed heads, wider than dinner plates. Tiny yellow finches chattered and darted around them in the dusk.

I began to think about Jasmine, the girl with the mystery past. She might already know how to read, she might be keeping her secrets to herself, but at least she was in good hands. She'd be looked after by my sister, the one who was just bumping her backside like a backup dancer for the King of Pop. I pictured a gawky, preteen version of me, saw her wearing my red Mickey and Minnie sweatshirt, sounding out the lyrics to "Billie Jean" while Dessie set the tempo on the keys of the Baldwin.

Off to the west, wisps of clouds glowed, lavender flowed into rose and peach. Random sounds of the night filled my ears. I waited to hear whether the screech owl had returned, but thankfully it was needed elsewhere. But there was something in every direction. The whole evening was alive. Katydids sawed away, grinding like a grain mill. Alan Ray had the Pirates game going on Dad's old radio at the workbench in the barn. Tommy, AJ, and Bertie were tossing a football out beside the garden, Tommy's husky voice snapping out the plays, Bertie cheering, AJ racing down the field with the ball. Where do these sounds go, I wondered. Could I call this September evening up in six months, in a year? Could I hold this moment, these sounds, each noise so perfectly blending into the next, but also, as clear as they can be in their own way? Could I lock it all into place in my brain, in case I need it someday to help me remember who I am?

The air had that glow, the one that settles on the ridge as the last rays of light slip away and the shapes of trees slowly begin to vanish. Just because it seemed like it couldn't hurt, I sent out a small prayer to whoever sets the tempo of the spheres up there. I did not want to ask for much, just that someday before too long, with a little grace and a little luck, this valley would echo out with one more joyful noise, the beat of the piano, a little R&B, joining with these sounds of life, all of it rising up from either side of this rough old road, to the tree line and the narrow strip of sky above. Holy sounds, all.